HACK

His job was to write the news.
Tricky, when you *are* the news.

HACK

SGM ASHCROFT

THE HACK PAPERS
ISSUE ONE

ISBN: 978-1-5272-7345-0
Felt Side Publishing

SGM Ashcroft
sgmashcroft.com
Cover design: designforwriters.com

For Naomi, with love and thanks

And in fond memory of
Malcolm Gray and Alan Barter

ONE

I SQUATTED OVER THE OPEN carrier bag and groaned with effort, dabbing at my watering eyes with toilet tissue. I needed a stool with ballast and attitude for what I had in mind, but I'd overdone the Imodium, almost to the point I could have used a midwife. I gave one last desperate push, straining myself dizzy, so that I had to place a steadying hand on the sink. When the thing did finally start to shift it just kept coming, until I had to climb off it, whereupon it toppled sideways like a felled tree, half in the bag, half out. Even in the context of a toilet, a stool like that has the power to shock, but in that bag it was truly horrifying. I took a half-step back, as if it were some swamp beast set to strike. How that same beast might look upon the church altar for which it was destined was beyond even my febrile newspaperman's imagination.

Elbows on knees, I perched on the edge of the bath long enough for my buttocks to grow numb. How had it come to this? Turds in Tesco bags wasn't what I'd envisaged all those years ago, when as a boy I fantasised about being a newspaper reporter. For as long as I could remember, I had believed journalism to be a vocation, a calling, something pure, like becoming a Buddhist monk.

The germ of this belief was sown way back, in my pre-school days, when a teacher told my folks I had the reading age of an eight-year-old. The only reason I know this is because Mum is still telling people about it, nineteen years on. She usually prefixes it with things like, 'Of course, it was written in the stars that Llew would become a journalist ...' In fairness, I've never given her or Dad much else to boast about in those nineteen years, which is why they are incongruously proud of me being a reporter. So proud, they have convinced themselves that journalism is a profession, much like medicine or the law.

'But I didn't even need A-levels to become a reporter, let alone a degree,' I remind them. 'There are plumbers better qualified than me.'

'Plumbers don't wear a shirt and tie to work,' Mum will say.

'Nor do I most days.'

'And they can't do shorthand or touch-type,' Dad will add.

'Nor can I.'

It was true. I hadn't even passed all of my journalism exams. But my folks will have none of it, and I've given up trying to convince them that journalism is a trade, not a profession. In truth, I think all parents are predisposed to be proud of their children, regardless of what they do for a living. If I were a cleaner of municipal toilets they would still find a way to work in a 'pride' angle somewhere:

'He was employee of the month for March.'

'You can see your face in those bowls.'

My best and oldest friend, Emdel Black, understands me far better than my parents. He knows and values me for what and who I am – a human being of modest abilities (compared to him, certainly) and one who shares his interest in science-fiction films and novels, German music, and drinking alcohol, roughly in that order. He also likes me because I make him laugh.

He is however dismissive of my claim that journalism was some kind of calling, like the priesthood. He says the only reason I became a hack is because my name is Llew. Indeed, he's proved as much.

See, Emdel doesn't do opinions and beliefs, only evidence and theories. That's because he's an über boffin, and always has been since I first met him in our primary school sandpit, where he had fashioned what I now know to have been a motte and bailey sandcastle. Like me he's an only child, which meant that in lieu of siblings we both had a highly developed imagination. Together we confected pretend worlds, kingdoms and galaxies of ludicrous complexity over which we reigned supreme. By the time we had progressed to secondary school in High Wycombe, Emdel's intellect was beacon bright. My core interests at that time were common-or-garden adolescent fare: ogling girls, football and toilet humour. By contrast Emdel's pastime of choice was theorising, and the jewel in his theoretical crown was his Theory of Names.

The Theory of Names posits that a person's name has either a neutral, positive or negative effect on the bearer's life, depending on circumstances, and that if those circumstances change, then so too does the influence exerted by that name. This was the theory Emdel deployed to disabuse me of the notion I was some kind of born-again journalist.

'That's rubbish,' the fourteen-year-old me had declared. 'My name's got nothing to do with me wanting to be a reporter.'

'Really?' Emdel had said. He had that look in his eye, the one he gets when he sees lesser brains heading exactly where he expects them to.

'Yeah. None at all.'

'Okay, answer me this then – what's your favourite TV show?'

'Lou Grant.'

'And why do you think that is?'

'Because I've always wanted to be a journalist, just like Lou.'

It was true. I'd wear Dad's braces over my school shirt, loosen my tie and pose in front of the mirror, pretending to conduct my newsroom as if it were an orchestra, just like grizzled LA newspaperman, Lou.

'Wrong,' Emdel countered. 'It's because the programme title contains your name. That's what drew you in. It was only after you started watching it that you wanted to become a journalist.'

'Rubbish. I mean the spelling of the names is totally different.'

'That's irrelevant. Names are verbal tags, and Llew and Lou are phonetically identical. If you end up being a reporter it'll be because of your name. Fact.'

'Okay, Einstein,' I shot back, 'what if Lou Grant had been about a kiddie fiddler instead of a newspaper editor? By your logic you're saying I'd have ended up being a nonce.'

Cue patient shake of the head from Emdel. 'Would you like to be a kiddie fiddler?'

'Er, no.'

'Then no amount of TV programming will turn you into one. But even if Lou Grant had been a nonce then you'd still have watched at least a bit of one programme because of the name-match.'

Emdel was probably right – he usually is, even now – but regardless, I still believe I was somehow metaphysically drawn to journalism because … well, I prefer that version of events, in the same way the folks prefer to believe I have a profession rather than a trade. I think most of us choose to believe the version of ourselves we like best, even if that means bending the truth to our will. In that sense we're all journalists at heart. Probably.

TWO

IT WAS EGGHEAD EMDEL WHO gave me my 'in' as a journalist, by achieving a clean sweep of A-star grades in his four A-levels, all in a single academic year, and at a crap school. They weren't rubbish A-levels either, like media studies. We're talking heavyweight: computer science, maths, further maths and physics.

While Emdel had been aiming for the stars, I was struggling even to make it to the launch pad. I was studying for my journalism qualifications by correspondence course but had failed miserably to land any work experience, without which I'd get nowhere.

High Wycombe's paid-for paper wouldn't touch me until I'd passed all my journalism exams, including one-hundred-words-per-minute shorthand – and I knew I'd be getting a telegram from the Queen before that happened. Meanwhile, the editor of Wycombe's freesheet, The Courier, had told me that eight young hopefuls were ahead of me in the queue for a work placement. But he'd added that if I were to bring him a great story then I might muscle my way to the front, and so I set about finding a 'great' local story. The trouble was, I didn't know what one looked like. All the yarns I enjoyed involved romps, celebrities, hookers and drugs, but I didn't know any local celebrities, and certainly none that did drugs or slept with prostitutes. But then Emdel got his exam results and, courtesy of me, ended up pictured on the front page of The Courier, flanked by his proud if puzzled parents, who didn't have a clue what A-levels were. My journalism career was underway. Sort of.

The Courier's editor, Harold Pole, was a crumpled septuagenarian whose signature scent was boiled brassicas and whose crowning journalistic glory was an interview he had conducted with turkey magnate Bernard Matthews for some trade publication. I know this because I commented on a cutting that was framed and hanging on the wall behind his desk. 'Bernard's fowl business is simply bootiful', ran the head.

'Whoever wrote that wants shooting,' I'd observed, eager to make conversation on my first day.

'I wrote it,' he'd replied, bristling.

After that, Harold never gave me anything interesting to do. I rewrote press releases and compiled an interminable digest of school and village fetes, and that was about it. At first, I badgered Harold for something else – anything else – to work on but each time I did, he presented me with the Wycombe-area telephone directory and declared, 'The plot is terrible, but the cast is amazing.' Was he seriously suggesting I call complete strangers to see if they had any news? I made only one such call, to a Mr R. Payne of Dawes Hill Lane, who said, 'Yeah, I've got some news: you're a nosy bastard, now fuck off.' After that it was fetes and press releases all the way, with no complaint from me.

Harold was an embittered old git who knew well enough that the entire point of my being there was to build a clippings file of by-lined stories so I could go on to impress at interview and land a salaried reporter role. Yet at the end of my two months on The Courier, the only byline I had to my name was atop a lame tale about an old codger who'd grown a pumpkin the size of a Mini Cooper.

With my shorthand still virtually non-existent and a cuttings portfolio leaner than an IRA hunger striker, it took me nine months and twenty-one job applications to secure my first interview. I suppose that in itself should have served as a warning.

It was for a reporter's position on the Southampton Clarion, another weekly freesheet. Its editor was Tony Davies, a bearded blob of a man with features saggy enough to make a bloodhound appear perky. He didn't seem at all bothered about my wafer-thin portfolio, with its preponderance of school and village fetes. Indeed, he offered me the job on the day, virtually keeping me hostage until I'd accepted. Ignoring the part of my brain that, cartoon-style, was sounding horns, klaxons and alarms, I told myself that while Tony was certainly no Lou Grant, he was sort of okay I suppose, and I took the job.

I was left pondering the gravity of that error less than a week later, when Tony invited me for after-work drinks to celebrate his thirty-fourth birthday. I almost toppled off my chair in surprise when he revealed his age; I'd taken him to be in his mid-fifties. It takes a concerted effort to age so catastrophically badly, and I discovered that Tony's not-so-secret ageing formula was stress and booze in vast quantities. The stress he created himself by being so pissed most of the time he could barely function. The full scale of his alcohol problem became clear one lunchtime when I was alone in the newsroom and a bite of sandwich went down the wrong way. Coughing my guts up, I swiped a bottle of water off Tony's desk and took a big gulp, only to discover it was pure vodka, which didn't much help the spluttering.

The booze meant Tony was disorganised and slipshod, not to mention intermittently unconscious, and it was a rare night I was home before nine-thirty. I didn't mind working late; I was learning fast, albeit out of panicked necessity. What I did mind though, a lot, was Tony's epic mood swings, which lurched from carefree sot brimming with bonhomie (late mornings to early afternoons) to benighted wretch with vile temper (late afternoons onwards). One evening he hurled a stapler at me, which whistled over my head and cracked the window. My crime? I'd accidentally deleted a story on my Apple Mac, an alien bit of kit I was still feeling my way around. I grabbed my coat and stormed out of the building. Tony spent half an hour leaning in through the passenger window of my shit-brown Austin Allegro, apologising – promising it would never happen again and, finally, begging. He said they'd sack him if another reporter walked and that he couldn't lose his job because he had a massive mortgage and a baby on the way. Then he started crying. He was so pitiable I returned to the office with him, even offering him a tissue.

Although he never threw anything at me again he did hurl plenty of bile my way, and ten months into the job I had come to despise the very notion of Tony. By that stage I had a host of job applications on the go, but in the end I didn't need to move jobs to escape him because in one of his more thoughtful moments, Tony went and died.

He thudded to the floor one evening when the two of us were alone, working late yet again. Cerebral aneurysm, I later learned. If he'd been nicer to me I might have attempted CPR although it didn't help that he had foam in his beard, like he was rabid.

Although not so great for him, Tony's death proved a lucky break for me. It turned out that The Clarion's publisher, Henry, was a twice-divorced high-ranking Fleet Street executive who had downsized his career when he realised he'd soon be thrice divorced if he didn't. As a result he knew a host of tabloid journalists, and he hired one of them on a freelance basis to edit the paper until someone could be found to permanently fill Tony's vodka-sodden boots.

So it was that two days after Tony's demise Alan Barrett sauntered into the newsroom and lit up my world. I felt him before I saw him. I was writing up a piece on the Apple Mac, minding my own business, when a pair of hands clapped down on my shoulders and shook me so hard my teeth rattled. Startled, I spun round, to be greeted by a toothy grin that was clamped about a glowing cigarette. I found myself looking into a pair of eyes that were back-lit by some form of joyous mania and that peered out from behind Michael Caine specs. He wore jeans, Chelsea boots and a dogtooth-check jacket from which a full-term gut poked proudly. His side-parted thick sandy hair had a helmet-like quality.

'You lovely, lovely boy,' he said, guffawing now and shaking me once more for good measure, sending cigarette ash tumbling into my lap.

I had grown up believing that all editors were clones of Lou Grant: rugged, dynamic and straight-talking. But Harold had been more like Compo from Last of the Summer Wine, while Tony had been a poor man's Oliver Reed at the height of his hell-raising lunacy. As The Clarion's new editor brushed ash from my upper thigh, his hand uncomfortably close to my tackle, I couldn't help but wonder if I had been liberated from Ollie Reed, only to be annexed by Keith Moon.

He lifted his hand from my thigh and offered it to me. 'Alan Barrett.'

'Llew Sabler.' I smiled uncertainly.

He made for Tony's desk and sat down. For want of an ashtray he dropped his fag butt into what he took to be a half-empty bottle of water. A blue flame spouted from its neck, sending him reeling backwards.

'What the fuck ...'

'Tony liked to take on board a lot of fluid,' I explained.

At that moment, Henry popped his head around the door. As usual, he was puffing on a pipe, filling the room with billowing smoke signals.

'I see you've met Big Al then,' he said in the clipped tones of one born into wealth.

I smiled no less uncertainly than before. The only things that were big about Big Al were his paunch and his personality, and I guessed it was the latter that explained his nickname. It sat well on him – better than his jacket, for sure.

Big Al pointed at Henry and, turning to me, said: 'Back in the day that posh bastard gave everyone a pay rise except for me.'

'You urinated in the art director's coffee cup,' answered Henry, grinning. 'I saved your job, Alan, and when we had that purge of staff who do you think it was that saved you again?' Battling to maintain a straight face, he wagged his finger. 'And you didn't even buy me flowers. Anyway, I'll leave you two get to know one another. Toodle pip.'

'Did you really piss in someone's cup?' I asked the moment Henry left.

'Right, Bandit,' he said, clapping his hands and rubbing them together with relish but studiously ignoring my question. 'Let's you and me do some hacking.'

'Who's Bandit?' I asked.

'You are.'

That was the first thing I learned about Big Al: he conjured nicknames for everyone. I have no idea how he arrived at Bandit for me; he simply divined it, or perhaps it was because he knew I'd survived ten months in journalism's equivalent of the lawless Wild West.

'You got anything for me that's got all the gear?' he asked, sparking another Marlboro. 'Something for the front page?'

That was the second thing I learned about Big Al: 'gear' was his term for the mystical element of a story, the part that makes a newshound's nose inexplicably twitch.

I shifted in my seat. 'Um, well, I did meet some bloke down the pub last Saturday who's changed his name by deed poll to John Mark Southampton Football Club O'Donnell. His girlfriend's a Portsmouth fan. She ditched him.'

'You lovely boy. You got his number?'

'Yeah, somewhere. Tony wasn't interested.'

'Well, Tony's dead. It's me and you now Bandit.' He broke off to light another Marlboro, ignoring the half-smoked one in the ashtray. 'And speaking of Portsmouth I'm in line for a gig down there in a couple of months, running a weekly paper. Fancy it? Proper city, Portsmouth. Naval port. Plenty of gear. You'll clean up, I know you will. You single?'

'Er, yeah.'

'You'll clean up on that front too, good-looking herbert like you. Pompey's crawling with talent in the summer.'

'Pompey?'

'It's what the locals call it. That's what you'll be calling it soon enough.'

Having only met him minutes earlier I was taken aback by the offer. I couldn't just accept without knowing about salary and stuff.

'Don't you worry about spondulicks, Bandit,' he said, as if reading my mind. 'You'll get half as much again as you do here, plus expenses. I'll need you in the pubs, clubs, bars, hangouts and dives, especially around the port. That's where it's all at. You can enjoy a few sherbets while you're getting me all that lovely gear but don't overdo it, like that tosser Tony.'

'Er, sure.'

It was possibly the shortest and weirdest job interview in history.

By the end of my first day sharing a newsroom with Big Al the air was so thick with smoke I could have spooned it out of the window. But my throat and eyes weren't the only things burning; my belly was ablaze too – with joy, excitement and surprise at discovering that sometimes reality can turn out to be better than dreams. You could stick Lou Grant. I had Big Al.

I remained with Big Al on The Southampton Clarion for a month, which is how long it took Henry to recruit a permanent replacement for Tony. The new guy was a mid-career journalist with a young family, and every bit as sober, businesslike and fair-minded as Tony had been sozzled, chaotic and volatile. Instead of staplers he threw sound advice and the occasional compliment my way, and had it not been for Big Al's job offer I would have stayed. Instead, I headed down the M27 in my wheezing Allegro, towards Portsmouth, Big Al ... and trouble.

THREE

JUST TWENTY MILES OF M27 separates the ports of Portsmouth and Southampton but it may as well have been twenty light-years, such was the difference between these naval and merchant cities and their people. POMPONIANS SEEMED TO HAVE FUSES shorter than the cannon that once lined the city's heavily fortified walls, and nowhere was this more evident than on its roads. In ten months' motoring in Southampton I'd had but one altercation with another motorist, yet within ten minutes of spluttering into Portsmouth I had 'cunt' bellowed at me no fewer than four times. And after one week I had seen more fights in and around the pubs and bars of Portsmouth than I had during my entire time in Southampton. Maybe this innate aggression is explained by Portsmouth being the only island-based British city, sitting as it does on Portsea Island – thus making Pomponians an island race within an island race. Little Englanders, squared.

Then there's the ethnic thing. Unlike Southampton, Portsmouth has so few black and brown people there may as well be none. This is a big city we're talking about and it's not as if it's so wealthy that less-affluent ethnic groups struggle to afford it, because tracts of it are extremely low-rent. I can only think that outsiders take one look at Pompey's endless warships, forts, battlements and military follies and conclude there are probably more welcoming places to settle, such as Southampton, Bournemouth ... or Beirut. Those émigrés who do brave the city's forbidding exterior probably last only as long as it takes for them to encounter its bellicose inhabitants.

Big Al had made significant changes to the paper by the time I arrived. The Portsmouth Times was now called The Pompey Probe, a name that he said was a better fit for the brand of news I'd be filling it with. He'd also 'managed' the incumbent reporter out of the door, by telling him he would be working under me, a tyro new to the job, prompting said reporter to turn freelance rather than suffer such indignity.

'I need lovely nippers like you, Bandit, feeding me proper gear, not some crusty old tosser with Tippex in his veins churning out shite,' was Big Al's explanation. 'D'you know how many photos of the mayor they published the week before I got here? Three. And guess how many cheque presentation snaps they ran? Four. Fucking four.'

Big Al believed that an overabundance of gurning mayors and outsized cheques was a sure sign of a paper on the ropes. But the Portsmouth Times wasn't the only title struggling in the spring of 1991. The country had been in full-blown recession for six months and ad revenue across regional and national papers had been plummeting. But while this was bad news for nearly everyone in newspapers, it was great news for Big Al, who was the Red Adair of print, with a proven track record of restoring the fortunes of ailing organs. The worse it got for everyone else the better it got for him.

'It's not rocket science,' he'd say. 'Give the buggers something to read and the money always follows.'

Under Big Al's tutelage I became a tabloid newsgathering machine. The ballast came from reworked press releases and stories buried in the minutes of Portsmouth City Council meetings but the bigger yarns, the *gear*, flowed freely from the watering holes of Old Southsea and the port, just as Big Al had said it would. I supped with everyone: port workers, students, tourists, the wives of sailors and submariners whose husbands were away at sea, as well as the assorted flotsam and jetsam that washed in from other naval ports the world over. It was intoxicating. Like a dangerous lover, Pompey made my head spin and my pulse race.

I sourced the raw ingredients and, with his Fleet Street pedigree, Big Al served up a weekly tabloid treat to the people of Portsmouth, a red-top town if ever there was one. The city was like a conveyor belt of scoops and exclusives. There was the agoraphobia self-help group who hadn't met for eighteen months because its members had been too scared to leave their homes. There was the polytechnic student who appealed his poor exam results by claiming he'd been traumatised by a UFO sighting. And then there was the arachnologist shopper, who was suing a supermarket because they'd 'murdered' the exotic spider that had emerged from his bananas at the till. 'I paid for those bananas by weight,' the miffed customer told me. 'That spider was mine.'

Although I was deliriously happy on The Probe, by the six-month mark I was also growing deliriously tired. It was a big job for just one reporter.

'Hang on in there, Bandit,' Big Al would say if he sensed I was wilting. 'We'll hire another herbert as soon as we can. I want a girl reporter. They go about things different to us, ask different questions. It's a chemistry thing. I just gotta get my feet a bit further under the table before I can get sign-off on it.'

In the event it took him a further five months to get his feet far enough under the table for the publisher to rubber-stamp the recruitment of a junior reporter.

We interviewed half-a-dozen young hopefuls, and while most of them seemed ideal to me none of them impressed Big Al.

'Too nice. She'd never ask the awkward question.'

'Too posh. They'd eat her alive down the docks.'

'Laminated cheque merchant.'

Applications from male reporters, meanwhile, were filed in the bin. I'd all but given up hope of Big Al ever finding the theoretically perfect female reporter when, one morning as he was opening the mail, he leapt from his high-backed swivel seat and waved a couple of sheets of paper above his head – triumphantly, like Neville Chamberlain with the Munich Agreement.

'We've got her, Bandit!' he announced, beaming. 'We've only gawn and got her!' The Marlboro glued to his lip nodded its agreement. 'Read this.'

He handed me a CV with a travel piece attached. The application was from a sociology graduate by the name of Thirza Kirkby, aged twenty-four, from Wiltshire. She had no journalism experience but had been travelling for a year, writing as she went. The piece she had submitted was about Cape Town. It was nicely written but it wasn't until I reached the final sentence that I saw what had got Big Al so excited: 'Sometimes, she wrote, 'a place is so colourful that only the most colourful language can do it justice. So I'll say this: Cape Town is un-fucking-believable.'

'Told you,' said Big Al, clocking my smile. 'She's our girl. I bloody know it.'

FOUR

I'M NOT SURE HOW MANY things you have to love about someone in order to fall for them – it's probably different for everyone – but for me I think it must be five because that's how many things I loved about Thirza right from the start.

The first thing I loved about her was her talent for profanity, something her submitted travel piece had strongly hinted at. Generally I find swearing an unattractive trait. Most people curse because their vocabulary lacks the firepower to give voice to strong feelings and emotions, or else they do it to fit in with their peers. But it wasn't like that with Thirza. She swore only when not to do so would diminish the point she was making. In her manicured hands expletives somehow became high art.

I discovered this on her second day at The Probe. I'd been giving her a lunchtime tour of Southsea when, wending our way back to the office, we'd passed a branch of Clinton Cards. With my mother's birthday looming, I shaped to go inside.

'Don't tell me you're going in there,' she'd said, pulling a vinegar face. 'Only knobheads and wankers shop at Clintons.'

'Really? So which am I?'

'Clintons is for lazy bastards,' she added, without providing the clarification I sought, 'and pricks who want a quick shag.'

'She's my mum,' I pointed out. 'I don't want to shag her.'

'No, you twat, you're the lazy bastard not the prick.'

'Okaaaay,' I said, holding my hands up in surrender, 'so I'm a twat, a lazy bastard, a knobhead and a wanker for wanting to buy my mum a card from Clintons?'

'Look, she's your mum,' she said, 'so just make a fucking effort. For her next birthday instead of buying the first piece of shite that comes to hand in Clintons get her a nice card ahead of time from a craft shop or a market – something that shows you've put some thought and time into it.' She pulled another sour face and pointed at the shop's interior. 'I mean for fuck's sake look at the place. It's pinker than my vulva.'

I laughed long and loud – louder and longer, even, than when Emdel caught his scrotum in his zipper and spent double history sitting next to me with a puce flap of it peeking out.

'Christ Thirza,' I said, wiping away a tear. 'What are you like when you actually get to know someone?'

She'd given me a quizzical look, as if that was a silly question, which it was because Thirza changes for no one, under any circumstances, ever, and that was the second thing I loved about her: she was out-in-the-open honest all of the time, occasionally hurtfully so but never mean-spiritedly. She was honest in the moral sense too, far more than I was. In WHSmith once she caught me slipping a paperback into my bag without paying and had growled: 'Put that back you twat or I'll fucking well shop you myself.' She would have too.

Things I loved about Thirza #3: she broadened my once-autistic musical horizons. All the other women we'd interviewed for the junior reporter job had turned up dressed for the occasion – typically in a blouse and skirt – but Thirza had worn jeans, work boots and a faded Stone Roses sweatshirt with frayed cuffs.

Having introduced herself, she wafted a contemptuous hand at my Gary Numan T-shirt and shook her head. 'Are you wearing that for a bet?'

Big Al had guffawed, nudging me in the ribs.

'What d'you mean?' I asked.

'Are you a Numan fan? Seriously?'

'Er, yeah. What's wrong with that?'

'Everything. For starters he sings like he's underwater and he also wears that stupid fuc … that stupid wig.'

'That's the beauty of music though isn't it – choice,' I pointed out.

'If that's typical of your choices then I won't be borrowing many of your sounds – if I get the job, obviously.'

And she was true to her word; she didn't borrow any of my sounds.

'For fuck's sake,' she'd grumbled when first thumbing through my record collection in my Southsea bedsit. 'You've got hundreds of albums here yet there's next to nothing I want to listen to. Hawkwind? Kraftwerk? Tangerine fucking Dream? And who's this bearded twat?' She held up an album by its corner as if it were unclean.

'That's Edgar Froese, co-founder of Tangerine Dream.'

'Ypsilon in Malaysian Pale? What kind of fucking title is that? Put it on. I've got to hear this.'

'Really?' I said excitedly, believing like a fool that I could make a Krautrock convert of her yet.

In the event she was able to bear no more than a couple of minutes of it.

'Holy shit on a stick,' she said, blowing hard and yanking the disc off the turntable. 'My kettle makes better music than that.'

'Oi, careful! That's a rare German import.'

'It's shite is what it is and you're lucky I don't stick it straight in the bin. I can see I've got a lot of work to do on you. I knew it the second I saw you in that Numan top. If it wasn't for you having a bit of Joy Division and New Order I'd say you were a hopeless case. Beyond help.'

'Okay Miss Aficionado,' I shot back, 'show me your collection and then we'll see who's hopeless.'

I feared it was a foolhardy challenge seconds after issuing it, but quite how foolhardy became clear when I first explored the thousand-odd albums that dominated her cramped Southsea flat. Her collection was everything mine wasn't: inclusive, broad, balanced and nuanced, with sounds for every occasion and mood, across multiple genres and eras – from Motown to Mozart via Madchester.

'So who's your favourite band?' I asked, gesturing at the library of discs hugging the walls.

'You know that already.'

'I do?'

'Think. What top was I wearing at my interview?'

'Er, hang on … oh yeah, Guns N' Roses.'

'Oh for fuck's sake.' She shouldered me playfully, knocking me off balance. 'Stone Roses, you twat.'

'That's what I meant. Put some on. I've not heard them before.'

She clamped her palms to the sides of her face, like the figure in Edvard Munch's The Scream. 'No no no no no. That's simply not possible. Jesus fuck, you've been buried in that German shite for waaaay too long. Here.'

She handed me an Old Holborn tobacco tin. 'Skin one up, lie back and let's listen to some proper music.'

She slipped on the Roses' eponymous first album, took the cushions off her two-man sofa, threw them on the floor and we lay back toking a spliff as we listened. Sometimes music feels like it's coming from within as well as without, and that's how it was that day, listening to the Roses with Thirza. From that moment on they became my favourite band.

And the fourth thing I loved about her? That's easy. She was beautiful, and yet this in no way defined her. She had long, shampoo-ad hair, raven and glossy, and the most searingly truthful hazel eyes I'd ever seen, peering from a blemish-free milky complexion that a hundred years ago would have seen her snapped up as a sitter for a Pre-Raphaelite master. But hers was no painted beauty. She wore no make-up aside from a beauty spot that she liked to pencil onto her cheek for special occasions, which killed me. And her smell ... boy. Women generally smell pretty good but Thirza? She filled her slipstream with something impossibly intoxicating – sweet, rich and spicy, a confection of perfume, hair conditioner and deodorant, perhaps. I drank it in whenever she walked past me. And then there were her breasts, her magnificent breasts, so magnificent that even the voluminous sweatshirts she so favoured failed to hide the voluptuousness that lay within. By underplaying her beauty Thirza somehow accentuated it, in my eyes at least.

The final thing I loved about her was that at work she and I functioned like a single organism. We shared the same journalistic sensibilities, both of us despising bullying in all its guises – domestic, civic, judicial, corporate and criminal. We were also natural-born suckers for a sob story. In her first year on The Probe pretty much everyone in Portsmouth who'd had a bad run of luck came through our office: the homeless; the maimed, lame, disabled and dying; the bereaved; crime victims; battered mums; wronged dads; vulnerable children; orphans; bankrupts; lonely/conned OAPs; reformed criminals shunned by employers; institutionalised servicemen struggling on Civvy Street.

We interviewed them all as a double act, Thirza softening them up with her beauty, honesty and empathy, and me moving in with the right questions at the right time. Our interviewees usually quite liked me but they always absolutely loved Thirza because they sensed, I think, that she was someone who would fight their corner, come what may.

Our shared love of the written language meant we were also forever subediting one other's conversation, as well as everyone else's. Once, after she had empowered a long-time victim of domestic violence to finally open up about her wretched home life, I told Thirza she was my hero.

'It's heroine actually,' she'd said, smiling.

And yet the most remarkable thing about Thirza was something I did not love about her at all: her propensity for violence against men, or to be more precise, her propensity for violence against creeps and idiots. She might have stood just five-foot-four tall but thanks to her upbringing on a pig farm in Wiltshire – where she'd spent her adolescence shovelling mountains of porcine dung from one place to another – she had the upper-body strength of an Olympic weightlifter. When drunk, her party piece was lifting the heaviest person in the room clean off their feet. I'm about eleven stone and she could hoik me off my toes like I was a suckling infant.

I first witnessed her violent streak when we were walking home one night along the seafront following a gig. A brace of kebab-munchers had come loping towards us, their swaying geezer gaits spelling trouble.

'Tossers alert,' Thirza said, bristling.

'Just ignore them.'

'I will, if they ignore me.'

But they hadn't.

'Lovely tits darling,' one of them said through a mouthful of doner. I think he actually meant it as a compliment, that in Tosserese it translated into something along the lines of, 'A fine evening, ma'am.'

But Thirza had stiffened. 'Come again, you little prick?'

'You fucking what?' Kebab Man barked.

He'd taken a stride towards us but that was as far as he got because a second later Thirza had him down with a flashing punch to the chest. He collapsed as if he had inflatable legs that had just been slashed with a blade. The other lad had the good sense to back well off.

On Thirza's orders we'd walked home in silence, which I'd found unsettling, and it wasn't until few days later – when we were taking a post-work stroll along the beach, eating ice creams – that I summoned the courage to ask her about it.

'Why did you hit that guy the other night?'

'Because I fucking hate pricks like him.'

'But what if he'd had a knife?'

'He was eating a kebab with both hands, Llew.'

'Well what if he'd banged his head on the pavement and died? That happened to a friend of a friend of my dad's and the bloke who lamped him got seven years.'

'So you're defending him then? It's alright for blokes to comment on my tits is it?'

'I'm not defending him, I'm just not a fan of violence. I can't see that it ever solves anything.'

'Okay then tell me this – will that prick or his mate ever demean me again?'

'I'd say probably not.'

'Then it's fucking well solved that hasn't it.'

I held my hands up in pacifying defeat. 'What was that move you pulled anyway?' I asked to plug the silence. 'Karate?'

'Krav Maga.'

'Krav what?'

'Maga. It's a mash-up of martial arts and street fighting. The Israeli Army use it. I did it for three years. I hit that guy in the solar plexus, where a load of nerves are bunched. That's why he went down like he did.'

'Why'd you do it, this Krav Maga? Fitness?'

She shook her head and cupped her hands about her heavy breasts, squishing them together. I tried not to stare and kept my thoughts to myself, in case my solar plexus might be next.

'Because of these,' she said. 'Once these arrived I had every fucker in Farmland buzzing around me. My dad's pigs are more civilized than most of the knobheads I grew up with.'

Farmland was how Thirza referred to the countryside, as if it were some sort of Orwellian dystopia. There could be little doubt she was now a happily adopted daughter of city living. Above her bed hung a framed watercolour of Portsmouth's Tricorn Shopping Centre, a Brutalist monstrosity that in 1980 was voted Britain's third ugliest building.

'So you did self-defence because farmhands were manhandling you?'

'No, I did it to stop them from even thinking about manhandling me. I floored some creep in a village pub because he had squeezed my arse, and after that, word soon got out that I wasn't for messing with.' She aimed a loaded index finger at me. 'That's another example of violence paying off. Men use it all the time to get what they want. Why shouldn't I?'

Kebab Man was later joined by REM Man, who Thirza encountered in the mosh pit at a gig at Portsmouth Guildhall. One minute I was watching the stage, singing along, and the next I was trying not to trample on a lanky denim-clad male in his twenties who was sprawled at my feet and clutching his crotch. Two beefy security men dressed in black had to drag him to safety.

'Was that your handiwork earlier?' I asked Thirza on the way home.

'Couldn't keep his hands to himself. He'll think twice next time, the little prick.'

Thirza was the most violent person I knew. Part of me respected her zero-tolerance stand against men who treated women like sexpots but I still believed her mouth was by far her deadliest weapon, and that she didn't need to hospitalise jerks in order to make an example of them.

Then again, I haven't got magnificent breasts the size of watermelons.

FIVE

In most cities the humble weekly freesheet is so far down the news food-chain that its big daily rival will barely know of its existence. But Portsmouth's daily paper, The Tribune, not only knew all about us but they also hated our guts. Correction: Tribune owner John Skinner hated *my* guts, because I had exposed him in The Probe as a one-time pornographer – a low-life chancer who had taken ownership of The Tribune because he'd been desperate to reinvent himself as a respectable businessman. In the wake of my exposé, Skinner had taken to phoning me at least once a month, to offer me a job on his paper.

'Come and join us at The Tribune, Mr Sabler,' he'd say, all breathy and reptilian. He always signed off with some thinly veiled threat, such as, 'I could make things quite uncomfortable for you if I wanted,' or, 'There are many people who have learned the hard way that it's easier to work for me than against me.'

If Skinner believed that I'd find his unsolicited overtures uncomfortable, then he was right, because the sound of his voice never failed to make me shudder, the way big hairy spiders make you shudder.

Big Al had coached me not to react. 'Skinner wants a rise from you,' he counselled, 'so don't give him the satisfaction.' And I didn't. Whenever he called I was unfailingly polite, almost to the point of obsequiousness.

'Thank you, Mr Skinner – that's a very generous offer, but I'm happy in my job.'

'I'm really very flattered you should think so highly of me, Mr Skinner.'

No one had taken greater pleasure in my Skinner story than Big Al; he despised the man. From my earliest days on the Probe I'd noted how he always mock-spat, theatrically and noisily, whenever Skinner's name was mentioned.

'Why d'you hate Skinner so much?' I asked him once, following another of his ghost gobbings.

'Because it's scumbags like him that give us journalists a bad name,' he'd said, going on to explain that as well as being Tribune owner, Skinner also had a burgeoning property development business.

'He uses that rag of his to smooth his property deals through,' he'd added. 'Anyone important who opposes him he'll undermine with skewed reporting, while his lackies enjoy a right royal arse-licking. He's a disgrace.'

'How d'you know all this?'

'It's my job to know, Bandit. And yours, by the way.'

The Skinner story had fallen into my lap. A shopfitter had been working on an empty unit in a parade of shops in Hilsea, to the north of the city, and had discovered a ledger wedged behind an old display rack. The ledger was full of columns of figures that were topped by lurid headers such as Gay Hard Core Magazines, Gang Bang Films, and Sex Toys. We'd learned about the ledger from one of our classified-ads girls, who was sister to the shopfitter.

'Follow it up, Bandit,' Big Al had said, gazing down at the open ledger.

'You wanna come, Thirza?' I'd asked. We tag-teamed on most stories and I'd assumed this one would be no different.

'No. I fucking hate porn,' she'd spat, hammering the keys of her typewriter with extra ferocity, to give her loathing its proper head. 'I might end up punching some prick or other.'

'Probably best you don't go then,' Big Al said, with a bewildered half-smile. He knew nothing of Thirza's capacity for violence, only that she had some very firm opinions that were very firmly held. 'Bandit, go grill some of the shopkeepers in that parade. One of them might remember something.'

*

'Oh *that* place,' one of the neighbouring shopkeepers had said. 'Yeah that was a private shop – you know, one of them what sells sex stuff. It was Skinner's,' he added in throwaway fashion, as if it were a piffling detail unlikely to be of much interest to a news-hungry reporter who happened to work for Skinner's rival paper.

'You don't mean John Skinner do you?' I'd asked, barely daring to dream.

'Yeah, that's him. The newspaper fella. Say, somewhere out the back I've got a picture of him outside his shop, taken the day it opened. I'll go dig it out.'

He disappeared through a doorway into a space that was rammed from floor to ceiling with teetering boxes of confectionery, crisps and cigarettes. One wrong move and it seemed he might bring the lot crashing down on him. Awaiting his return, I counselled myself not to get my hopes up, because no journalist ever gets *that* lucky.

'I've been taking photos of this parade for twenty-five years,' the shopkeeper said, returning with an album that was pregnant with pictures. He plonked it on the counter and leafed purposefully through its pages. 'Whenever a shop changes hands or has a face-lift I like to get a snap. Little hobby of mine. Now, let's see... I think it was around '73 he moved in. Yep, here we are.'

He turned the book so that it faced me, and tapped a photo. It showed a man of average height, sporting sideburns and shoulder-length hair, and who was wearing a flares-tanktop combo. He was stood in front of a shop window, across which was emblazoned the words Private Shop. The man was frowning into the camera. Also in frame was a young boy, propelling himself past the shop on a scooter. I studied the photo, looking hard into the man's face. I'd seen Skinner just once, across a room at some press function, but he didn't have the kind of features that stuck in your mind.

'Are you sure it's him?' I asked.

'Oh it's definitely him. Back in the day he had a dozen or so of them shops dotted about. I got a mate what went to school with Skinner and he says the shops is how he made his money.'

'Did you get to know him, Skinner?'

'Nah, you gotta be kidding. He gave me a right earful seconds after I took that picture, and I didn't see him again after that. Some other bloke ran the shop for him.'

'Can I borrow this photo?'

'Yeah take it – long as you bring it back.'

I could have sucked his feet in gratitude.

*

Big Al filled the entire front page with the photograph, overlaying it with the headline, 'Give it a few years, son' – a reference to the young lad on the scooter. The story ran to five pages and was the result of some good old-fashioned doorcraft. With the help of the shopkeeper's friend, the one who'd grown up with Skinner, I'd been able to pinpoint the location of each of Skinner's thirteen private shops. I'd then spent an entire week doorstepping people who lived around the old shop-sites. I must have knocked on two hundred doors. There was no shortage of people who recalled the shops, and none fondly.

'That shop was the bane of our lives,' one woman told me, pursing her lips at the bitterness of the memory. 'It attracted all sorts round here – queers, perverts, kiddie fiddlers, you name it.'

Her comments were echoed by many of the other people I spoke to, and by the time I was done I had enough dirt to bury Skinner's carefully crafted reputation three times over.

*

Heading home one night, shortly after my Skinner scoop had been published, a male cyclist mounted the pavement, and came barrelling towards me. I stopped, thinking that the safest option, but still he came at me. Just as I was about to dive for safety, he bumped down off the kerb and into the road. 'Watch your back, Sabler,' he called out, glancing over his shoulder. I didn't clock his face; he was wearing a coat with a snorkel hood.

I fought to put the incident out of mind, but whenever Skinner phoned me at work, that cyclist always hoved back into view.

SIX

FOR THE FIRST YEAR, THIRZA and I had a friendship so finely balanced it might have joined a circus. Outside of work we lived in one another's pockets, drinking and going to gigs. Thirza always sourced our live-music nights. I'd been banned from doing so after surprising her with a pair of tickets for us to see Gary Numan at Southampton's Mayflower Theatre.

'There's no fucking way I'm wasting a night on that adenoidal tosser,' she'd said.

'But I've bought the tickets,' I'd protested.

'Tough shit. I'm sure you can flog it on the night to some cyborg freak or other.'

Yet in the end Thirza had come with me, having lost a game of dare I'd talked her into. My forfeit would have been walking home from the pub in my underpants. Hers was accompanying me to Numan live.

'I'm begging you,' she'd said, having lost. 'Let me walk home in my bra instead of having to watch that wiggy fucking robot.'

While sorely tempted by her request, in the end I'd held firm and insisted she came with me. But Jesus Christ almighty, she bitched and moaned all the way to Southampton, throughout the entire gig, all the way back to Pompey *and* for most of the following day.

'I'm fucking traumatised,' she'd kept repeating. 'It was like being tortured by the Gestapo.' For good measure she'd scrawled 'wiggy shite' across her ticket stub, before sticking it to the wall behind my desk.

When we weren't gigging then the pair of us were invariably in our local boozer, The Barley Mow in Old Southsea. After just a month of drinking there, we had the place functioning like a newspaper district office staffed by specialist correspondents. The Mow's locals were newspaper gold – better than anything I'd come across when trawling the portside pubs for gear, pre-Thirza.

Naval Affairs Correspondent – no small thing in a city such as Pompey – was Lt Commander (retired) Alfred Ure, the only Mow regular whose surname we knew because he always introduced himself as 'Alfred Ure'. Alfred was an urbane yet regimented man who had found life on civvy street difficult, as many ex-servicemen do. Following his naval career he had spent eight months on the dole. He'd grown depressed, begun drinking heavily and then watched his eighteen-year marriage disintegrate around him. Alfred had gone on to spend fifteen unrewarding years as an office manager before retiring on his Navy pension to a life of radio-controlled boat sailing and recreational drinking. He ran all manner of organisations for retired mariners, and was an endless source of cracking Navy-related news.

But our most prolific source of stories from the Mow was Child Issues Correspondent, Bernie The Shirt, so called because in all weathers he always wore a shirt open to the navel, displaying an Axminster carpet of chest hair that was forever dusted with ash from his Silk Cut cigarettes. Given that Bernie had eight children and seemed to know Portsmouth's entire Irish community, and that everyone in that community had even more children than him, Bernie certainly had weight of numbers on his side. To cap it all his wife was also a dinner lady at a local secondary school. Bernie fed us stories about talented children, bereaved children, abandoned children, sick children, disabled children and once, even conjoined children.

The thing with Bernie, though, was his West Cork brogue was delivered at Gatling gun velocity, so we'd understand no more than one word in five. Luckily for us Bernie drank with someone who was able to translate for us. We dubbed him UN Mickey, after those headphone-wearing linguists you see at United Nations pow wows. It turned out that Mickey's dad happened to be from the same town as Bernie, meaning he was able to dissemble Bernie's barrage of distressed vowels.

We had other regulars who gave us tips about goings-on both at the city council and Portsmouth Football Club but Bernie and Alfred were our mainstays, and we paid them in Guinness (Bernie) and brandy (Alfred), all on expenses, naturally.

If the Barley Mow was our newsroom-at-large and its locals our correspondents then its desk editor was Blanche, the landlady. In her mid-thirties and handsome rather than pretty, Blanche's symmetrical features topped a short frame of pleasing curves that glided behind the bar as if on rails. Unlike Thirza, Blanche preferred to keep her iron fist in a velvet glove, and said fist was never more velvet, nor iron, than when pissed-up football fans swung into her pub. The moment any of them got out of line they'd find a five-foot-two idiot-seeking missile in their midst.

'No swearing, no singing,' Blanche would tell them, always addressing the chief trouble maker. If things kicked off then she would glide back behind the bar, produce a red phone from nowhere and make a big show of dialling 999.

'Police please,' she'd say. 'Yes, it's the Barley Mow, Southsea. We've got some troublemakers. They're kicking off. OK. Thanks. See you in a minute.'

She would then produce a Polaroid camera, snap the party, and pin the photo to a noticeboard that was full of similar pictures, before carrying on serving customers as if nothing had happened.

I saw this scenario play out half-a-dozen times and it always ended the same way: the oiks would trade uncertain glances and opt to scoot, but not before mouthing some choice obscenities as they went.

'Works every time,' Blanche would say, waving a disconnected phone line in one hand after they'd left. 'It's not the coppers turning up that scares them, it's the threat of them turning up.'

'But why the photo?' I once asked.

'Stops 'em doing my windows later.'

Blanche lived above the pub with her brother, David. He had feminine features, more so than Blanche, and he shared his sister's fluidity of movement; they'd've made great ballroom dancing partners. Occasionally, when the pub was quiet, David might appear downstairs to wash a few glasses or to sweep the floor, but other than that he was rarely seen. On the few occasions we had exchanged pleasantries, his words came floating on a breathy, camp whisper that was barely audible. There seemed to be something broken in him. Blanche didn't like to talk about David, and I hadn't pressed her on the subject – yet.

Thirza's connection with Blanche went beyond the landlady-drinker relationship the rest of us had with her. The two of them seemed made for one another, like adjoining pieces in a jigsaw. They would always greet one another with a hug and a kiss, as if they'd been apart for eighteen months rather than a mere eighteen hours, which is what it usually was. And Jesus, how those two talked. Also, one was always touching the other. When one of them made a point, invariably a hand would accompany it, placed softly on a shoulder, a forearm or a wrist. The only people I touched like that were girls I was sleeping with.

'How come you two are so close?' I once asked her.

'Why is anyone close?' had been her reply, its tartness telling me that that was all she'd be saying on the matter.

SEVEN

BY THE TIME THIRZA JOINED The Probe I had been soaking up Big Al's tales of Fleet Street legends and lunchtime lunacy for over a year. His stories described lives that seemed to have been lived on a different planet, and left me wanting desperately to journey there myself.

His most outlandish tale involved a sub-editor who had been taken to A&E, having split his head open after falling down drunk on a midday bender. Patched up, on his way out of the hospital he'd stolen a drip, complete with stand, and had wheeled it back to the office, stopping en route at an off-licence to buy some vodka. He'd then returned to his desk, plumbed in to a quart of IV ethanol.

'The dozy bastard was back in the same A&E two hours later with alcohol poisoning,' Big Al revealed.

But as well as tales of lunacy, I loved hearing about the work itself, on the big stories of the day, such as the Profumo Affair, the Moon landing and the Jeremy Thorpe murder trial. Big Al had been in the thick of them all, hacking mountains of copy from dozens of sources, cheerily slaloming his way through confusion, contradiction and legal minefields to produce tomorrow's news.

'You never did tell me about the pissing in the cup incident,' I'd remind him from time to time.

'You don't wanna believe everything you hear,' he'd always say.

In one sense I was already living the Fleet Street dream, albeit vicariously through Big Al, who brought the same passion and skill to The Probe that had served him so well on the nationals. But it wasn't enough; I wanted the real thing. I wanted my stories to be propped up against cereal boxes rather than wrapped around haddock and chips. I even went on a weekend pilgrimage to Fleet Street. It didn't matter to me that most of the papers had already moved out because the landmarks – the pubs and the art deco office buildings – were exactly as painted in Big Al's stories. I was transported back to another age, and I returned to Portsmouth more determined than ever to claim a little bit of that history for myself.

It got so that everything I did at work became geared to making this dream a reality. Probe press day was Thursday and in the afternoons I'd spend a couple of hours on the phone to the national tabloid newsdesks, flogging my best stories from that week. I had a pretty good strike rate for a reporter on a weekly freesheet. My tale about the short-sighted OAP shopper – who'd forgotten her glasses and had returned home to find she'd bought a jumbo box of condoms instead of tea bags – was a massive hit. Most weeks I was able to sell them something, and after a few months of this I was on first-name terms with at least one newsdesk person on all of the red tops. The ultimate goal was to become known and trusted enough for one of the nationals to offer me freelance weekend reporting shifts. The trouble was that every other ambitious provincial reporter in the country was doing the same thing, which made landing a shift ridiculously tough. But I had a secret weapon that all those other suckers lacked: Big Al. I knew that just one word from him in a well-placed ear would be enough.

'All in good time Bandit,' he'd say, whenever I begged him to put in that word for me, which was at least once every couple of weeks. 'You're a lovely boy but you're not ready to swim with those sharks just yet. Give it a few months.'

I'd almost given up hope of getting a shot at the nationals when, out of the blue, not long after Thirza had joined, Big Al picked up the phone.

'Is that Kevo?' he said. 'Al Barrett here. How are you, you old bastard? You off the sauce these days? No more drips I hope.'

The mention of drips stopped me dead – and Thirza too, who'd also heard the IV ethanol story.

'Listen Kevo, I've got this lovely herbert here, Bandit, who's got all the tackle.'

Tackle was Big Al's term for encapsulating everything a reporter needed in order to be a player.

'You'll know him by another name – Llew Sabler. Yeah that's right, the yarn about the old bird who bought Durex instead of PG Tips. Here,

Kevo, I reckon Bandit's ready for a shot at the big league … you will? That's great. Thanks mate … you too, and stay off the grog you dopey old sod.'

By the time Big Al replaced the receiver in the cradle, I was standing and staring at him like he had sprouted feathers.

'What'chu doing Saturday Bandit?'

'Er…'

'Whatever it is, cancel it. You're wanted at the Daily Ripple,' he added.

Thirza breezed over and gave me a hug so tight that her breasts cushioned up against me. Suddenly, reporting shifts on The Ripple felt like a runner-up prize.

*

It didn't matter to me that The Ripple's offices were nearer Kent than they were Fleet Street, nor that the building was no art deco beauty but a characterless grey box that was ugly enough to earn itself a berth on Thirza's wall next to the Tricon. Nor even that its newsroom was cavernous and sterile, and that I was given nothing at all to do on that first day – not a single thing. I half expected someone to hand me a telephone directory and tell me to work my way through it.

'They're testing you,' Big Al explained. 'They do it to everyone. Just sit tight and when they do give you something just make sure you're ready.'

'Plus the editor's a tyrant,' I said. 'He called some poor girl from the art department a cunt just because she'd used the wrong spot-colour on the TV listings. Who calls a girl that?'

'I'd fucking kill him if he said that to me,' hissed Thirza.

'I'd love to see that,' I said.

Ignore him,' Big Al counselled. 'Just keep your head down.'

He was right. I sat tight and when my chance came, I took it. It was only a two-paragraph nib about some soap star being killed off but they liked the job I did, and after that things slowly took off for me on The Ripple. After a few months they were sending me out to do legwork on some of the bigger stories. I began to feel like I belonged and that I was in the process of becoming a small footnote in the addendum of Fleet Street's history.

But no one ever rests easy on a paper like The Ripple – its demonic editor saw to that. Every time he came stalking out of his glass-fronted office, zeroing-in on his latest victim like a raging Pamplona bull, I would cower behind my monitor, fearful his eye might meet mine and that I would become the target of his next froth-flecked diatribe. My time would come, and in spectacular fashion.

EIGHT

It was after the mermaid incident that things started to sour between Thirza and me. I blame Big Al. He swept into the office one day and announced he was off to Corsica for a fortnight and that he was leaving me in charge of the paper. What was he thinking?

'Don't worry,' he'd said, smoke from his bobbing Marlboro corkscrewing into my frowning face. 'You've got John, and she's smarter than the pair of us put together – plus there's that work experience girl coming in who'll help with odds and sods.'

'John' was Thirza. Big Al called most women 'John', or at least those of them he liked, although I never thought to ask why; he made doing so seem like the most logical thing in the world. The work experience girl he'd mentioned was Fran, the daughter of a prominent Portsmouth businessman who ran a city-wide chain of used-car lots. Edwin, The Probe's ad manager, had been buttering him up for months in a bid to screw some advertising from him, and his charm offensive had included promising Fran a two-week work experience placement. I wasn't exactly expecting great things from her; at interview she'd proudly produced her cycling proficiency certificate.

'Just remember,' Big Al had continued, 'keep Emu sweet because he's a tosser and he'll make life difficult for you if you give him the chance, so don't give him one.' Emu was what Big Al called Edwin – after Emu, of Rod Hull fame.

'He lopes about like he's got someone's hand up his arse', Big Al liked to say. The avarian likenesses didn't end there because Edwin was also gawky and he had a beaky nose, which was all the beakier for being perched above an apology of a lower jaw that receded into a wattled neck.

None of us liked Edwin. He was a flat-track bully who browbeat his poor sales team, most of whom were young girls who had been handpicked by him for their browbeatability. Big Al had been right to warn me about Edwin. I should have listened to him.

My first week in charge went like a dream. We ran a terrific front-page yarn about Gosport father-of-three, Albert Watkins, who was obliged to go about his daily life wearing a gas mask, having developed an allergy to pretty much everything to be found in air. To her credit it was work-experience Fran who brought in the story. On her way to work one morning she'd seen Albert being wrestled to the ground outside a Budgens mini-market, after the store manager had mistaken him for a stick-up merchant.

'I was only trying to buy a jar of instant coffee,' Albert told Thirza and me (by writing it down, because he couldn't remove his mask, even to speak). 'Most shopkeepers don't even allow me inside,' he jotted, 'and you can imagine people's reaction on the streets.'

Poor Frank was also on permanent sick leave from his job, as a small-loans manager with a bank, because customers were reluctant to have their financial affairs overseen by Darth Vader, in tweed jacket and twill slacks.

As for my second week in charge, the sad truth is that I began acting out my childhood Lou Grant fantasies, the big difference being that I was no longer posturing before a mirror but in front of a newsroom comprising Thirza, Fran and our photographer, Mike. I don't know Lou Grant personally, mainly because he doesn't exist, but I'm fairly certain Lou would not have dressed his work experience girl in a mermaid costume and then sent her into the wintry waters of the Solent at 7am, topless, with a view to concocting a story about a mermaid sighting.

'Don't be such a fucking knobhead,' Thirza snapped when I first floated my mermaid plans on the Monday morning of the second week. The idea had come to me during the weekend, when I'd spotted a bus-stop ad for Copenhagen that featured the Little Mermaid.

'Come on,' I urged, punching her arm playfully. 'It'll be a laugh.'

She hauled me into the office kitchen.

'A laugh? Not for fucking Fran it won't, you twat.'

'She'd only be in the water for a minute or so,' I protested. 'I've seen plenty of folk swimming in the Solent in winter. It's warmer than you think. Seawater cools slower than freshwater. It's the salt.'

'Are you for fucking real? A moron could come up with a better story than that. It'll cause a world of trouble with Edwin and besides, we've already agreed to lead with my piece about Nicola. That's a real story, about a real person with real problems.'

Thirza was referring to a widowed mum-of-one, who had terminal cancer and was frantically seeking suitable adoptive parents for her soon-to-be-orphaned five-year-old daughter.

'Another week won't make much difference to her,' I said, 'and anyway, I'm the editor, not you and I say we go with the mermaid story. It's got legs. We can run Cancer Mum next week.'

Thirza grabbed two fistfuls of my shirt and slammed me up against the wall, so hard it sucked the breath from me.

'First,' she snapped, as I gasped for air, 'mermaids are not stories, they're fucking fairy tales. Second, they don't have legs you twat. Third, in case you'd forgotten, Cancer Mum has a name, Nicola, and time is the one thing she doesn't have. I'm telling you now if you run this mermaid shite then you and me, we're done.'

'Done how?'

'Just fucking done.'

*

It was touch and go with Fran for a couple of days. After her early morning topless dip in the November Solent she contracted double pneumonia. An asthmatic, she spent two nights in intensive care before her teenage body rallied enough for her to be transferred to a low-dependency unit. She might have told me she had a weak chest. How was I to know?

My mermaid story was headlined 'Stu snaps a mermaid', and told how amateur photographer Stu Brough had been out shooting some early morning mood shots on Southsea beach 'when this sexy fish girl appeared to me from nowhere'. At least Stu actually existed, sort of. He was actually seventy-nine-year-old Probe delivery 'boy', Den. I had persuaded him to pose as our amateur photographer, slipping him £15 for his trouble, which I put through expenses. For the stage-managed photo of Den that we used on the front page I had hung one of Mike's long-lens cameras around Den's neck and told him to point randomly at the sea as Mike fired off shots, as if he were showing us the precise spot the mermaid had emerged from the waves.

The days leading up to publication had been fraught, with Thirza refusing to acknowledge my existence. Things had become so tense I'd almost backed down and run with Cancer Mum – sorry, Nicola. But stupid pride had kicked in and I'd somehow convinced myself I didn't care to be lectured by Thirza, even if she was right. And as if almost killing Fran wasn't bad enough I had also misled Edwin into believing we were running Nicola's story.

On the morning the mermaid story hit the streets I arrived at work super early, so I could be alone for a time, to steel myself for the storm I knew was brewing – only to find Bob from Circulation already at his desk. I did a double-take; Bob was always late. His wreckage of a drinker's face was even ruddier than usual and his suit was comically crumpled. Had he slept rough?

'You're for the high jump you are,' he said, grinning and revealing a mouthful of tombstone teeth. He held up the mermaid front page for my viewing pleasure. 'Tell you what though,' he added, leering at the deliberately blurry picture of topless Fran that Mike had taken, thus rendering her unidentifiable, 'that work experience bird of yours has got a smashing pair of tits. Shame.'

He seemed to be suggesting that the worst thing about Fran being seriously ill was that he might be denied another opportunity to ogle her breasts. Before I could fashion a reply Thirza walked in. Luckily for Bob she can't have heard his comment, otherwise he'd have ended up in intensive care alongside Fran.

Thirza shot me a look I might have scraped ice off. She thudded her bag down on her desk and dropped into her seat as if from a great height, before yanking drawers open with the sole purpose of being able to slam them shut. She then stomped off to the kitchen, returning with a cup of coffee that she even managed to slurp furiously. But her ire found best expression in typing: she pounded the keys so hard the hammers sounded like small-arms fire, and her carriage returns were so violent that each of them shunted the typewriter closer to the edge of the desk. It was almost with relief that I looked up to see a puce-faced Edwin marching towards me.

'Sabler, what's this?' he barked, slapping that week's paper on my desk. As I studied the front page, mermaid Fran's blurry eyes seem to track mine, like the Mona Lisa's.

'Where's the story about the mum with cancer?' he asked. His nearly-chin wasn't quivering like it usually did when he was angry but instead was set firm, which had to be a bad sign.

I swung a half-circle in Big Al's high-backed editor's seat. I loved that seat. 'Er, yeah, late change of plan, Edwin,' I said. 'I tried to reach you last night but you'd already gone home.'

Like all credible lies mine had been rooted in truth: Edwin had gone home early, after his son had been taken ill at school.

'But don't worry,' I added, 'we're getting positive feedback. I faxed the story to TV South last night and they want me to appear on tonight's evening news programme. Fred Dinage'll be interviewing me,' I added with genuine excitement and another half-turn in my seat. Thirza snorted.

'Well how's this for positive feedback,' said Edwin. 'I've just had Fran's father on the phone. Before your little mermaid stunt he was about to take out a month of ads across all three editions, which would've been worth ten grand to this paper. But guess what? He's pulled the plug on it, and not only that he's also suing us for wilful neglect because you almost killed his daughter. I've got a meeting with the publisher this afternoon. He wants answers, and you're coming with me, to give them.'

Edwin turned to Thirza. 'The publisher wants you to take charge until Alan gets back. Are you okay with that?'

Ouch.

'Sure,' Thirza said. To be fair she ousted me as editor without a trace of smugness, although I think her anger was burning too bright to allow any other emotion a look in.

'We'll run the story about Nicola as our front page next week,' Thirza told Edwin. 'Llew wanted to throw it away on page three but I wouldn't let him.'

Double ouch.

'Great,' said Edwin. 'Right, you.' He aimed a quivering finger at me. 'Out of that seat.'

'It's alright,' Thirza said. 'He can stay there. I don't need a big chair to prove I'm in charge.'

Triple ouch.

*

Big Al returned the following Monday, by which time Fran's father had taken the story of his daughter's near-fatal work experience stint to Skinner's Tribune, and that bastard had lapped it up. 'Mermaid spoof nearly killed my girl', ran their front-page headline. They also quoted Fran's Mum as saying that I'd been 'irresponsible and puerile beyond measure'. Even Emu weighed in, telling The Tribune that 'disciplinary measures were being taken against Mr Sabler'.

The 'measures' Edwin had spoken of were two weeks' suspension without pay, pending an investigation, and effective immediately. Edwin left me to stew in my own juice at home, but predictably I chose to stew in something a little stronger.

I had but one visitor during my period of suspension: Big Al. He wore a grave expression when I opened the door to him.

'Bandit, Bandit, Bandit,' he said, with successive and solemn shakes of the head.

He left me hanging for a moment or two, before a fat grin split his face and a hyena-like cackle almost shook the Michael Caine specs from his nose.

'You lovely boy.' He was howling like a loon now. 'You lovely, lovely boy.'

I laughed with him, with the sheer surprise of it.

'Does this mean you're not gonna fire me?'

'Fire you? Why would I do that?'

'Because I almost killed our work experience girl, I cost the paper ten grand, I brought a lawsuit down on us and I got us plastered all over our biggest rival's front page.'

Saying it out loud like that made it sound serious enough to be fired four times over but Big Al dismissed it all with a waft of his hand.

'Granted,' he said, 'it'd've been tricky had the work experience girl died, but she didn't. As for Emu, don't you worry about him – he's all bluster. I know for a fact that that girl's dad was never going to advertise with us. He's golfing mates with that tosser Skinner, and they're probably Masons too, so his cash was always heading to The Tribune.'

'But he's still suing us, right?'

'Did you force Fran into the sea?'

'No, she was game from the off.'

'Did she tell you she had a weak chest?'

'No, else I wouldn't've done it.'

'Then he's got no case. There'll be an out-of-court settlement, nothing too crazy. You'll see.'

'But what about the story about me in The Tribune? Have you seen it?'

'Seen it? I'm framing it, Bandit. You really don't get it, do you? Everyone's talking about us. You got us on prime-time telly, for Pete's sake. D'you know how much an early evening TV ad slot is? We're the best-known local paper in the South East right now, and that means just one thing: ad sales. You watch, I'll have Emu eating out of my hand within a week.'

He jabbed a Marlboro at me, a sure sign he was about to get serious.

'But listen. You might be a lovely boy but John's lovelier, and you should've listened to her about that poor Nicola lady. There's enough great gear out there without making crap up. Okay, so it worked out well in the end but that wasn't by design was it. You got lucky, that's all.'

'Thirza's not talking to me,' I blurted. 'It's killing me.'

'Forget John for now. She's the least of your worries. Emu's after your arse but don't you worry, as I'll take care of him. Just keep your nose clean from here on in. Right, let's grab a pint.'

Big Al did take care of Emu – by demanding I was summarily dismissed.

'I knew whatever I said he'd demand the opposite,' Big Al explained. 'He's not just a bully, he's an idiot.'

So it was that I emerged from the mermaid fiasco relatively unscathed, professionally at least. I served two weeks' suspension without pay, and within a few weeks Fran had made a full recovery – unlike the mermaid fancy dress costume, which I had to replace at a cost of £75 because of salt-water damage. (My protests that a mermaid outfit that's not resistant to saltwater is hardly fit for purpose fell on deaf ears.) Commendably Fran bore me no ill will, and after a period of convalescence she even returned to complete her work experience – against the wishes of her father, who did indeed accept a modest undisclosed out-of-court settlement.

But that still left Thirza. A month on from Mermaidgate and she was showing no sign of thawing. She addressed me only when work demanded but otherwise blanked me, and I saw nothing of her outside the office. It felt like a bereavement, which caused me to wonder: what does this beautiful, captivating and combustible girl really mean to me?

NINE

I HAD HOPED THIRZA'S ANGER might have cooled during my suspension, yet upon returning to work the reception she'd given me had been glacial.

'I can't stand it any more,' I told Big Al at the end of my first week back. 'It's killing me. I'll have to quit if it carries on like this.'

'Don't do anything rash, Bandit. She'll come round. She just thinks you're a twat, that's all.'

'She's always called me a twat.'

'Yeah, but now she actually means it. Have you apologised?'

'I've given up apologising. She doesn't want to hear it.'

'Yeah, well, not speaking never solved anything. Go round to her gaff and refuse to leave until she opens the door. Camp in the hallway if you have to. What's the worst that can happen?'

She could kick my testicles back up into my abdomen, I thought. But I knew he was right, and that if my efforts at peacemaking didn't pan out then at least I could leave knowing I had tried everything.

It took a gallon of Dutch courage to force my legs to carry me the half-mile from my place to Thirza's. I arrived around 10.30 p.m., armed with a bunch of red roses. The front door to the Victorian tenement was unlocked. Someone had snapped off their key in the lock and the landlord had yet to replace it with a new one, despite robust encouragement from Thirza to do so. I entered the building. It had once been a large townhouse but had long since been carved up into bedsits. I climbed a single flight of stairs, ending up in a short, gloomy hallway, at the end of which was Thirza's door. I stood outside it for an age, tracing a finger up and down patterns in the wood grain, my pounding heart threatening to draw a tune from my ribs. I was about to knock when Thirza began playing music. The first couple of tracks I didn't recognise, but then came Whitesnake's cover of 'Ain't no

Love in the Heart of the City', followed by Pink Floyd's 'Money' and Lou Reed's 'Sweet Jane'. It had to be a compilation; there was no lag between the songs. Taped compilations were Thirza's one concession to obsession, and she was forever devising new themes – some inspired (Best Drum Solos) others lame (Songs With Pigs in The Lyrics). With practice, I got pretty adept at guessing her compilation themes within a few songs, but I had no idea what this one might be. Songs to Kill That Twat Llew To, perhaps?

I gave my roses a last-second preen and knocked. Thirza appeared at the door with a mug of tea in her hand and dressed as she had been at work, right down to her yellow building-site boots.

'What the fuck do you want?'

'Um, I—'

'And what the fuck are these?' She snatched the roses and slammed the door in my face. I heard a pedal bin snap shut, doubtless swallowing my peace offering whole. Led Zep was playing now. She turned the music up so loud it sounded like Jon Bonham was in there with her, pounding the skins like a lunatic.

A door opened behind me, from which emerged a chuntering neighbour, who was soon at my shoulder. He was a tiny, tidy man in his late forties. He was wrapped in a silk dressing gown and wore maroon velvet slippers. He could've found work as a Noël Coward look-alike.

'She woke you up too, did she?' Noël said, adjusting the cord of his gown. 'Have you just moved in?'

'Er, kind of.'

Noël knocked on Thirza's door.

'Fuck off,' she called, shouting over Robert Plant singing at full throttle. 'I don't wanna talk to you.

Noël thumped the door now, repeatedly, until it swung open.

'I said fuck—'.

'If you don't turn that music down I'll have the landlord serve you notice,' said Noël. 'He's my brother-in-law, you know, and this isn't the first time you've woken us up, is it?'

I don't know what I had expected Thirza to do. Punch him in the solar plexus, perhaps? As it was she surprised me, by apologising.

'I work nights, you know,' Noël added plaintively, hands upturned, like God.

I glanced at my watch. It was 10.55pm. I turned to Noël, tapping the dial of my Timex.

'Nights? Shouldn't you be on your way to work?'

'What?' he spluttered. 'Yes, I am running a little late as it happens, not that it's any of your concern.'

'So she did you a favour, then,' I added, jerking a thumb at Thirza. 'Had it not been for Led Zep you'd have overslept. Listen,' I added, patting Noël's shoulder, 'she did say sorry and she did promise it won't happen again, didn't you, Thirza?' She looked at me with something other than contempt for the first time in an age.

'Well, just don't let it happen again,' Noël snapped at her, before vanishing down the corridor, back into the 1940s.

Thirza leaned on the door jamb, arms folded. This was my chance.

'Look, Thirza, I came here to say, one last time, that I'm so very sorry. If you still want nothing to do with me then I'll find another job. We can't carry on like this. It's not fair on Al.'

'You're a fucking prick.'

She jabbed me in the chest, hard enough to shunt me backwards, but at least the sting had been drawn from her tone.

'I made a mistake. I'm… sorry.'

The last word caught in my throat.

'Oh, for fuck's sake, don't tell me you're gonna cry. And you didn't make just one mistake, by the way, you made a shitload of them.'

I swiped the back of a hand across my leaking eyes.

'Come in, you twat,' she said, producing a tissue from her sleeve, as women do. It may as well have been a white dove and, fittingly, Lynyrd Skynyrd's 'Freebird' began playing, at a volume unlikely to trouble Noël Coward.

'Is this a compilation?' I asked. 'What's the theme? I can't work it out.'

She looked me up and down, as if we'd never met.

'You're not getting off that easy. Explain yourself.'

'You mean about the mermaid?'

'Yes, about the fucking mermaid.'

'Look, I kind of let Big Al's big chair go to my head. I admit that.'

'That's kind of pathetic, don't you think?'

'I guess.'

'Most of what I warned you would happen, happened. So why didn't you listen to me?'

'I don't know. I just kind of got the mermaid idea in my head and couldn't let go of it.'

'D'you know something? You're an A-One fucking knobhead.'

'Yeah, I know.'

'So say it.'

'What?'

'Say, 'I'm an A-One fucking knobhead.''

'Are you serious?' But I could see she was. 'All right, if you insist.'

'I fucking do.'

'I'm an A-One fucking knobhead.'

'Good. Now fuck off. I'll see you tomorrow, you twat.'

TEN

'NEVER GUESS WHERE I'VE LANDED a job,' Emdel said down the phone. 'Portsmouth,' he added excitedly, before giving me a chance to speak.

'No way. That's brilliant. Who with?'

JCN Business Systems, in North Harbour? D'you know it?'

'Course. It's that massive modern building by the Pompey exit of the motorway. They must have hundreds of staff in there.'

'One thousand two hundred and sixty three. Listen,' Emdel added, 'I'm hiring a truck on Saturday and'll be down there about midday. Can I crash at yours until I find somewhere?'

'Yeah sure, but why d'you need a truck? You haven't got that much stuff have you?'

'Er, well...'

'Hang on a second. Don't tell me you're bringing your porn.' His silence was all the confirmation I needed. 'I won't have room for it here. It's only a bedsit. It's cramped enough as it is.'

'It'd just be for a few days,' he pleaded. 'It's only a bit of porn.'

A bit of porn? Emdel had amassed a pornography collection extensive enough to open a private shop. I once asked him how much he figured he had spent on it down the years.

'About £14,000, give or take,' he said.

'Jesus.'

'Yeah but remember, I've been buying it since I was thirteen.'

'How the hell did you buy porn at that age? You could barely see over the newsagent counter.'

I might have added that little had changed on that front.

'Mail-order,' he revealed.

'But how could you afford it?'

'Paper rounds.'

'Most kids with paper rounds save up for a bike.'

'Now you know why I didn't have a bike.'

'But didn't your folks suspect anything, what with all those packages coming through the door?'

Emdel had gone on to explain that he'd told his parents he was collecting part-works by mail-order, and that to make his story more believable he had scoured jumble sales and fetes for the kind of part-works they would expect him to be interested in, such as Carl Sagan's Cosmos. But because Emdel lived in a council house that was only twenty-two bricks wide (I once counted them) his burgeoning porn collection had soon outgrown his many hiding places, and so he'd struck a deal with a neighbour, to store the collection in his garage.

'I gave him free access to the stuff, as rent,' Emdel explained.

'You mean you let a neighbour wank over your porn?' I said. 'That's disgusting.'

'You've wanked over it,' he countered.

I glanced around my bedsit and sighed, as I visualised the place rammed with Emdel's crates of hardcore. In that moment it struck me that he had been in thrall to porn for the thick end of a decade, and that he'd never grow out of it until he found himself a girlfriend. Like pubescent boys the world over, we'd been obsessed with porn because it afforded us a tantalizing glimpse of the Promised Land. But while I (and most everyone else in our circle) gradually began fumbling and groping our way towards said Promised Land, Emdel got left behind, with the brochures.

His problem has always been confidence. Bespectacled, prematurely balding and standing at five-foot-three in his Tuf utility shoes, Emdel is a confidence-free zone around women. The crazy thing is there were girls who liked him, but he simply refused to believe that any female could possibly find him attractive, even in the face of strong evidence to the contrary. All he can ever see is potential rejection. It's very un-Emdel-like behaviour, because in every other area of his life he is Mr Empirical, adopting an evidence-based approach and adjusting his behaviour and views accordingly. Now in his early twenties, he is so set in his ways, so trammelled by his negative self-image, so drowning in hard-core pornography, that he is never going to get himself laid without paying for it

– which he'll never do, because he believes prostitution is reprehensible. (I think it's some kind of residual moral crap he's been saddled with following ten years of Catholic schooling, in the same way that I still feel guilty about masturbating.)

*

'Jesus Christ,' I shouted, hopping on one foot and cradling my big toe, having stubbed it on one of Emdel's seventeen crates of porn. 'If we haven't found a new gaff by the end of the week then your porn's out on the street. I'm serious.'

'What about this place?' Emdel said, tapping an open copy of that day's Tribune. 'There's a gaff for rent in Silver Street, Southsea. An old pub, it says. Is that near here?'

'It's just down the road. Give us a look.'

He handed me the paper, and I scanned the ad.

'It's perfect, but we'd better move fast.'

*

The pub, the estate agent had said, had been called The William The Conqueror, and had been converted into upstairs and downstairs flats in the 1970s. We would be in the spacious two-bedroom downstairs flat. We tossed a coin for the bedrooms, and I landed the larger of the two, the old saloon bar. It came with a trap door, which fed into the beer cellar. Exploring, we found a set of ivory hand-pumps down there and a crate of ancient brown ale. (I can report that, unlike red wine, brown ale does not improve with age.)

At JCN, Emdel was earning more than double my Probe salary, and judging by the mail that we received daily at our new address, he was spending most of it on mail-order hard-core magazines and videos. It was a month before he was fully settled into his bedroom, which is how long it took him to put up enough shelving to house his mountain of porn. When he had finished, his room resembled a porn lending library. Stock was arranged by genre, with each section demarcated by a sheet of coloured card. Genres included: Anal, Black on Black, Black on White,

BBW (Big Beautiful Women), BBC (Big Black Cocks), Big Breasts (the largest section, by some distance), Group Sex, Hairy, Lesbo, and MILF.

Emdel also possessed dozens of lever-arch files, each bloated with pages that he'd cannibalised from his magazines. On the window-ledge sat a pint pot, brimful of bent staples, taken from a decade's worth of mags that he had disassembled, to remove specific pages without tearing them. The spine of each file bore small coloured circular stickers, like those you see on books in normal libraries. I have no idea what the colours represented. Those files probably contained more of Emdel's genetic material than Emdel himself, and I was going nowhere near them.

ELEVEN

You'd be amazed at what you can see when spying through a punch hole in a sheet of foolscap in the offices of a Portsmouth weekly newspaper. It's like being a wildlife cameraman hidden in the bush. There's Edwin, the ad manager, rearranging his desktop furniture according to a Euclidean formula known only to him. There's circulation manager, Bob, conducting covert scratch-and-sniff sorties that are a thing of fetid horror. And then there is Thirza, who is typing a story, and whose protruding tongue slides across her lips from one side to the other, mirroring the carriage of her typewriter. I was studying Thirza covertly because otherwise I would be openly staring at her, which would have been too weird for words. I wasn't snatching sneaky glimpses either, but sucking up the sight of her, guzzling like a calf on the teat.

'Is that sheet of paper glued to your fucking nose or what?' Thirza asked. 'You've had your face in it for an age.'

'Council minutes,' I said, with as much faux nonchalance as I could muster, continuing to hide behind the paper, but now to mask my cheeks, which were burning hotter than a picket-line brazier.

It was official: I had a Thirza problem. My appetite was shot and my powers of concentration had nosedived, but most tellingly I had given up Saturday reporting shifts on the Insider. When the news editor had offered to take me on permanently, I had quit on the spot, such was my anguish at the prospect of having to leave Thirza behind for good. I hadn't even bothered asking if I could carry on working casual Saturday shifts, because the truth was, I was desperate to again spend Saturdays with Thirza, drinking, smoking and gigging.

'What d'you mean?' the news editor had said, non-comprehending, as if I'd set a complex Pythagorean problem before him. 'You're doing a great job, fella. I'm offering you a job. Why the hell would you quit?'

'The editor scares me,' I said, using a truth-hood to shoulder the weight of my lie. 'I know it's just a question of time before it's me he's screaming at.'

'Don't be daft,' he said, with a raspy smoker's laugh. 'He's all bluster. Don't mind him. We'll see you next week, right?'

'No, sorry, my mind's made up. But thanks for the opportunity.'

He had shrugged. 'It's you who'll be sorry, fella. There'll be no way back – you know that, right.'

'You're a fucking idiot,' Thirza said when I told her what I'd done. When I pointed out that it meant we could again spend Saturdays together, she added: 'Like I say, you're a fucking idiot.'

It was not the reaction I was hoping for. As for Big Al, he was too disappointed for words. He had vouched for me, and I had let him down badly.

But within a couple of weeks of me quitting The Insider, things at work settled back into the old rhythms, the one difference being that my feelings for Thirza had gone on to commandeer so much of my brain that there was precious little of it left for facilities such as listening and conversing.

'What's up with you tonight?' Thirza asked me one night in the Mow. 'I might as well be sat with Harpo fucking Marx for all I'm getting out of you.'

Worse, because my love for Thirza had nowhere to go it was like a never-ending build-up of static electricity, which left me fizzing and wired – especially at night. I'd lie awake, cursing love the way Thirza cursed Clintons. I was learning the hard way just how right she was: love most definitely is neither pink, fluffy nor sweet. It is no more pink, fluffy or sweet than serious road-traffic accidents, ArmaLite rifles or degenerative diseases. Love is dangerous and damaging, and should be handled with tongs, like plutonium.

Actually, when I say my love for Thirza had nowhere to go that isn't entirely true, because it decanted itself from my brain, ran down my arm, through my Parker ballpoint and on to endless sheets of A4, in the form of doggerel.

Have you ever noticed how the only things people ever write poetry about are Mother Nature, mortality and love, of the fulfilled and unrequited varieties? Never friendship. When Thirza and I were friends, poetry was the furthest thing from my mind, and yet the moment our relationship tipped over into something else – for me at least – tortured verse began issuing from me like a Trevi Fountain of angst. I wrote reams of wretched verse, gripping my pen so tightly that I developed a callus on the first knuckle of my right index finger and a bulging muscle at the top of my right forearm. I suppose you could call it a love muscle.

I explored my feelings for Thirza so exhaustively I became lost in a labyrinth of my own making.

Is my love for her so intense only because she's not loving me back?

What if she was to love me back? Would the feelings get weaker or stronger?

Do I love her at all? What if it's just infatuation?

What even is infatuation? How is it different to love?

Round and round and round I went, even questioning whether or not it was her magnificent breasts I was actually yearning after.

For his part, Emdel has always insisted that love is little more than a string of neurochemicals, designed to encourage homo sapiens to propagate the species, and that romance exists only in the crushed taffeta brains of writers, such as Barbara Cartland.

'That's pure rubbish,' he once told a misty-eyed fifteen-year-old girl in our form at school, after she'd claimed her parents had experienced love at first sight.

'Every time your mum and dad recall the first time they met,' Emdel had gone on to tell the girl, 'their recollections are coloured by their subsequent happy relationship, which means their emotions about that first meeting are bogus. They were attracted to each other by nothing more than chemicals, principally dopamine and oxytocin. Fact.'

Try putting that in a Clintons valentines card.

But here's the thing about Emdel: for ninety-eight per cent of his life, he has never had a girlfriend, and nor has he even been in the same postal district as the opportunity, so it's easy for him to dismiss love as something that happens only in the presence of a Bunsen burner.

As for the other two per cent? Well, he and Thirza spent that breaking my heart.

TWELVE

'For chrissake Al,' I grumbled from the depths of a Santa suit that appeared to have been tailored for a morbidly obese basketball player, 'they could've at least sent one that fits. I've had to roll up each leg four times just to get to my feet.'

'Don't turn the trousers up on the outside, you knobhead,' Thirza said. 'You look like a simpleton Santa.'

At that, Big Al and Thirza hooted in unison.

'Whatever happens don't let anyone see that T-shirt,' Big Al warned. 'Santa on a crucifix? Where the hell did you get that?'

I pointed at Thirza. 'From our resident heathen here. I tell you this for nothing,' I added, 'I'd rather be nailed to a bloody cross than be Santa in Debenhams. It's a stupid story idea, Al.'

Thirza snorted. 'Not like forcing Fran into the Solent dressed as a mermaid so she got double fucking pneumonia, then?'

The mermaid episode. Again. And, one, two, three ... cue Big Al.

'Not your finest hour was it, Bandit?'

'Why can't you be Santa?' I asked him. 'You'd be perfect, what with that big gut of yours. I'm so thin I could tread water in a test tube.'

'Roll your coat up and stuff it inside your tunic,' Big Al said, lovingly patting his paunch with both hands, like an expectant mother.

'Whatever you do don't get a hard on,' chimed Bob from Circulation, matter-of-factly, as if grotto-based arousal was a widely recognised hazard of the job. 'When I was growing up in Gosport there was this Santa that liked his job a little bit too much, if you know what I mean. Three years he got.'

'Bob,' I said. 'Do us a favour. Piss off.'

I turned to our photographer, Mike. 'C'mon Mike, let's get this over with.'

In a fit of pique I attempted to storm out of the office but discovered that there's no storming anywhere in an ill-fitting Santa suit. I tripped over a foot-long flap of trouser leg that had worked itself free, and crashed into Edwin's desk.

'Watch it Sabler,' he snapped.

I picked myself up and left the office to the sound of laughter tolling in my ears, like so many malevolent Christmas bells.

'You forgot your beard, you twat,' Thirza called after me, but I ignored her, too irate and embarrassed to care.

When Mike and I arrived at Debenhams we were shown into a back room, where one of the store's salaried Santas was stripping back to civvies.

'You got a spare beard?' I asked. 'I forgot mine.'

'Here.' He tossed what appeared to be albino roadkill across the room. I hooked the beard around my ears, and promptly gagged.

'It's soaked with your spit,' I said, tearing it off. 'I can't wear this.'

The other Santa shrugged. 'I'm off for lunch. You've got an hour. Grotto's on the fifth floor.' He farted shamelessly, leaving his curry air-buffet as a parting gift. I tossed the mucus-slicked beard in a bin.

'You can't be Santa without a beard,' said Mike. 'You look about twelve. Wear it inside- out.'

I followed his advice, and looked in the mirror. 'There's no hair on that side. It looks like I'm wearing carpet underlay.'

'It's better than nothing. C'mon let's go. Fourth floor he said, didn't he.'

'Yeah, think so.'

Five minutes later we were still grottoless. We wound our way through Cosmetics, Home Furnishings and Womenswear, by which time we'd acquired a train of excitable young children, who were ghosting our every step, perhaps hoping I might start tossing presents over my shoulder, even though I had no sack. It was all too much.

'For fuck's sake Mike, go and ask someone where the grotto is.'

'Santa said a bad word,' gasped a little girl from our retinue.

I leaned into Mike and growled: 'Quick, leg-it up the escalators. Let's shake this lot off.'

So we bolted upstairs, too fast for little legs to follow, and we found a kindly soul in Menswear, who pointed us to the fifth floor, and the grotto.

The grotto was hotter than an old people's home and reeked of curry farts.

'Fifteen minutes tops, and then we're off,' I muttered to Mike through the underlay. 'Get your shots, then we're gone. It's disgusting in here.'

Mike took light readings, and the children who'd been following us formed a queue outside. First into the grotto was the little girl who'd pulled Santa up for swearing.

'Hello,' I said, searching for a Father Christmas baritone but sounding more like a nuisance caller. 'And what's your name?'

'You said a bad word,' she admonished me. 'Santa doesn't say bad words.'

'That was another Santa,' I explained. 'He's been sent to wash down the reindeers because he was very naughty. I had to race here from Iceland at the last second, to replace him.'

'But Santa's from Lapland.'

'Llew, she's gotta go up on your lap, for the picture,' urged Mike.

'Who's Loo?' the little girl asked.

More firefighting.

'Er, that's Mrs Santa's special name for Santa,' I said, 'because she loves him very much.' I shot a look at Mike. 'Silly Mike, only Mrs Santa gets to call me Loo.'

I hoisted her on to my lap.

'Why's your beard funny?'

'Mike, have you got your snap?'

He nodded, so I slid the girl off my knee and packed her off with some gift-wrapped tat. I was broiling alive by now, and my agitation levels were in the red.

I nodded at Mike. 'Right, let's foxtrot oscar.'

'But you've only done one kid,' he said. 'I need some insurance in case those pictures are shit.'

'He said another bad word,' gasped the little girl, who hadn't quite exited the grotto.

'I said "ship", sweetheart,' blustered Mike. 'It's a photography term.'

The girl traipsed out, her present dangling from her hand by a ribbon, forgotten.

'Mike, guard the entrance. We're done here. I'm getting out of this clobber and I don't want any kids seeing me undress. We've shattered enough Christmas dreams already.'

'But what about all the little ones queuing to see you?'

'They'll have to wait for Stinky Santa to get back from his lunch.'

I had the tunic off and the trousers down by my ankles, when a blimp of a woman in sherbet leisurewear stormed into the grotto, dragging behind her the little girl whose Christmas Mike and I had subverted.

'Are you the bastard what swore in front of my kid?' she spat. 'I'll have your guts for fucking garters.'

Mike, the moron, fired off a shot, capturing Sherbet Mum confronting me, in my underlay beard and crucified Santa T-shirt. His picture ended up on the front page of The Tribune, accompanied by the headline, Probe reporter's Santa shame.

*

The knot of Christian protesters on the pavement outside the Probe offices was a mix of middle-aged women and pensioners of both sexes. Big Al peered down at them from between the slats of the Venetian blind that hugged the window next to his desk.

'What did I tell you about that T-shirt, Bandit,' he said, without looking away from the window. 'Still, I s'pose it's quite festive, what with all their candles and carols.'

'I wasn't exactly expecting that bozo to photograph me, was I, for chrissake,' I said, pointing at Mike.

'It was instinct,' Mike protested. 'I can't turn my talent on and off like a tap.'

'Taking the photo might've been instinct but developing it and then leaving it lying around?' Thirza cut in. 'That was pure fucking stupidity.'

'How was I to know Edwin would nick it and hand it to the Tribune?' Mike protested, arms outstretched.

Everyone knew Edwin was the traitor in our midst. After the mermaid episode, he'd made it clear he wanted me out of the door. But his treachery backfired badly, leading not to my downfall, but his. The entire Probe payroll sent him to Coventry for handing Mike's picture to our bitter rival. Edwin tried to bribe his way back into the circle of trust, with trays of donuts and pastries, rounds of drinks in the pub next door and out-of-character chit chat, but his cakes went uneaten, his drinks unsupped and his forced pleasantries unanswered. I almost felt sorry for him. Almost. After a week of being frozen out, Edwin realised his number was up, and he took a position as a second-hand car salesman at one of Fran's dad's dealerships.

'There's thirty-two of them tonight,' said Big Al, still studying the Christians down below. 'That's the record so far. What'll you say to them when you leave, Bandit. The usual?'

'Yeah,' I said. 'S'pose.'

'You need a new line,' said Thirza. 'You can't keep saying you meant no offence – that's lame. Why don't you tell them that Jesus is basically Santa, only for grown-ups.'

'Oh yeah, that'll really help,' I scoffed.

'You could always say that Santa's an anagram of Satan,' Big Al suggested, 'and that you were giving the public a coded message.'

'What kind of coded message?' I asked, in all earnestness.

The pair of them grinned at one another, intolerably pleased with themselves.

'Yeah, yeah, yeah,' I said. 'Very funny.'

On and on they laughed.

'I told him about that T-shirt,' Big Al said, removing his Michael Caine specs to wipe his eyes. 'I told him.'

THIRTEEN

'Cool name' was the first ever thing Thirza ever said to Emdel, after I'd introduced them one night in our living room. 'Where's it from?' she added. 'The Middle East?'

I laughed. Although Emdel had olive skin and dark hair (what was left of it), his mother was Irish and his father was about as Wycombe as it was possible to get, right down to his old-world yokel burr.

'For gawd's sake don't ask about his name,' I told her. 'We'll be here all night.'

'Perfect,' said Thirza. 'Because I've got all night.'

And so Emdel regaled her with his Theory of Names, and how there was one given name above all others that proved said theory to be true: his own. Malcolm.

Even now I sometimes think of him as Malcolm, because for the first eleven years of our friendship that's what I'd known him as. He was never wild about the name, but as long as it had a 'neutral' bearing on his life, he tolerated it. But that all changed in the late 1970s, thanks to a TV advert for Vicks Sinex, the decongestant nasal spray. In the ad, a comically bunged-up youth called Malcolm tells his mum he's unable to sit his school exams that day because of nasal congestion. 'Course you can, Malcolm,' declares the mum, handing over a bottle of Sinex, which he duly squirts up both nostrils. The ad then cuts to a beaming and decongested Malcolm returning home to announce his exam prowess with some nasal showboating. It was one of those ads that entered the public consciousness, and Emdel grew weary of people gurning in his face and quipping, 'Course you can, Malcolm.'

'I'm changing my name,' he announced one day.

'What to?' I asked.

'M. Derek.'

'What? That's ridiculous. That's far worse than Malcolm. You'll get slaughtered.'

'Will I?' He'd given me another of those looks. 'I bet you twenty-five pounds I'll have the name I want by the day of my eighteenth birthday.'

'And what name do you want?'

'Emdel.'

He had just under eighteen months to play with.

'You're on,' I'd said, and we'd shaken on it.

On 5 April 1990, Emdel's eighteenth birthday, we were perched at the bar of our local. He held out a palm.

'Hand it over. That's twenty-five nicker you owe me.'

Not only had he won the wager but he'd done so with time to spare, having been known as 'Emdel' for six months already. Only his parents and teachers still called him Malcolm.

I shook my head in admiration. 'Are you going to tell me now how you did it?'

'It's simple.' (Everything is simple to Emdel.) 'If a name has more than one syllable then people will shorten it. Take your name. Who ever calls you Llewellyn?'

'Only Mum, when she's pissed off with me.'

'Exactly. So you're Llew, just like I was Malc – to friends anyway.'

'But I still don't get what was wrong with Malc as a name.'

Emdel sighed. 'If you hate peas and someone gives you a plateful of them, do you hate them any less if they make you eat just half?'

'Fair enough, but you spent months telling people your new name was M. Derek, which is a thousand times worse than Malcolm, or Malc for that matter. What if you'd ended up saddled with it?'

'That was never going to happen. I knew people would shorten Derek to Del, just like they shorten Malcolm to Malc and Llewellyn to Llew. Hence M. Del.'

'So why didn't just ask to be called Emdel in the first place?'

'You can't choose your own nickname. That's just weird – and sad.'

Emdel had waved my money at the bartender. 'A pint of snakebite and Pernod and a pint of bitter for the sucker here. You want crisps?' he had asked me.

'Course I do, Malcolm,' I'd quipped.

'That's an amazing story,' Thirza told Emdel, two spliffs and countless digressions later. 'And one fucking cool name.'

After she met Emdel, things changed between her and me, because what had before been a cosy twosome, became a crowded threesome. I didn't mind at first because after all, Emdel is my oldest friend. And besides, I still had Cinema Night when – every Thursday – I'd get to nestle next to her in the dark for a couple of hours, which was inordinately pleasing. I'd been working up the courage for months to slip a nonchalant arm around her shoulders.

'Will you stop fucking fidgeting? Thirza had snapped halfway through the execrable Nuns on the Run, just as was about to make my move. 'Have you got fucking Parkinsons, or what?'

I wasn't to get another opportunity, because after that film, Thirza pulled the plug on Cinema Night.

'That's the third turkey we've seen in as many weeks,' she moaned as we walked home. She then took the unilateral decision that henceforth Cinema Night would become Video Night, to be hosted by me and Emdel, at our gaff.

After that, every Thursday after work we'd head to the local Blockbuster to trawl rental movies. Even though I was far more knowledgeable about film than her, this did not make me senior partner in the venture.

'No more subtitled shite,' she'd snap if she spied me drifting too close to the Overseas Films section.

But generally we liked the same kind of movies – character-based dramas and gangster yarns, with occasional sci-fi titles thrown in to keep Emdel sweet. After Blockbuster, we'd meet Emdel down the Mow for a few jars, before hunkering down to watch that week's purchase, armed with a pile of tinnies, a few spliffs and a mountain of munchies. Post-film, we'd chew the fat, and sometimes also the gristle and bone.

One night, the movie had been about a priest and a rabbi who'd become friends. I don't recall the title but I do remember the conversation it sparked because that was the first time I had a sense there was something starting to crackle between Thirza and Emdel.

'It's fucking bullshit, religion is,' Thirza declared as the titles scrolled. 'There's more chance of your telly floating out the window than there is of there being a god.'

'You're actually right in saying that, mathematically speaking,' Emdel replied.

'What?' I said. This, I had to hear.

'Gravity,' he continued, 'is all that's keeping anything or anyone on the surface of the Earth, and gravity is a function of the Earth's rotation, so if the Earth were to cease rotating then our telly would float. Fact. Now answer me this: under what conditions can God be said to exist, without question?'

'Fucking none,' Thirza shot, licking and sealing another spliff.

'I've never fucked a nun,' I said, drawing stereo laughs from the pair of them, which was gratifying. 'But seriously Emdel, you're missing the point,' I added. 'Religious belief is about faith, not science.'

Emdel leaned forward, palms upturned. 'So what's your working definition of faith?'

'When you, um, believe something is worth, er, believing.'

Thirza laughed and coughed out a cloud of blue smoke. 'That's fucking feeble, Llew.'

'I'll tell you exactly what faith is,' said Emdel, accepting the spliff from her. 'It's a desire gap.'

How can one head be so full of stuff I've never heard before? I thought.

'You're making this up as you go along,' I said.

'No I'm not. A desire gap is the gap between what is real and what people would like to be real.'

'Okay Einstein,' I said, 'let's say I have faith our telly's going to levitate before the night's out. You know it ain't gonna happen, I know it ain't gonna happen, and why would I even want it to happen? Where's your desire gap there?'

'You might want it to levitate for any number of reasons,' he replied, with the manner of one lining up all his ducks. 'Perhaps for example you'd like to move the TV upstairs without having to lift it, or you'd like it to be at a more comfortable height, for ease of viewing.'

'But those are ridiculous things to want.'

'You're missing the point.'

'What's new,' chirruped Thirza, now stretched out across the floor on a cushion.

'Forget the TV,' Emdel said. 'That's just a control argument. The point is that religious faith involves an immeasurably large gap between what is almost certainly true and what people would like to be true. Namely, Heaven.'

'What about Heaven?'

'Oh for fuck's sake, keep up,' Thirza said. 'It's obvious isn't it? Eternal life and the chance to see dead loved ones again – that's how they sell Heaven. Of course people want those things, just like people want to be rich, but the difference with Heaven is that people want it so bad that hundreds of millions of the suckers end up actually believing it's real.'

'Exactly,' said Emdel, sharing a smile with Thirza that I sensed had no room for me. 'And faith,' he added, 'is actually the flip-side of fear.'

'Really?'

'Of course. You never hear people say that they have faith that there's a Hell, do you, but you hear plenty of people say that they fear there's one.'

'So you're saying faith is for believing good things, and fear is for believing bad things, but that either way there's a desire gap for both?'

'Hallelujah! He's got it.'

Thirza was beginning to gnaw at my nerves with her insistent sniping, but I bit my lip, because ... well, I'm scared of her.

'Yeah,' Emdel confirmed. 'Faith is the gap between reality and the good things we want to happen, while fear is the gap between reality and the bad things we don't want to happen.'

'This eternal life thing, it's conceited fucking bullshit,' spat Thirza, sitting up from a slouch, to get her shoulder squarely behind her point. 'Humans are part of the animal kingdom. Fact.'

Jesus, she's starting to sound like Emdel.

'And,' she continued, 'that makes us animals, no better or worse than badgers, ants or sparrows. Does a sparrow think it'll live forever in some disembodied state of eternal bliss? Of course it fucking doesn't, so what makes us think we're so special? Pure fucking arrogance, that's what. No wonder the world's such a pile of shite.'

'OK,' I said, feeling I had to mount some form of counter-offensive. 'How come it's possible to be spiritual without being religious? Where's your desire gap there?'

Thirza swiped a bottle of Jack Daniels from the table. 'I'll show you spiritual.'

She took an almighty swig and let rip a rasping belch. As I watched the pair of them guffaw in stereo, a pang of jealousy tugged at my guts.

*

One Video Night, Emdel brought along his work colleague, Glen. As far as I knew, Glen was the only one of Emdel's many JCN friends who'd had any kind of sexual experience at all. Apparently he'd had once gone out with a girl named Denise for three weeks, only to discover the hard way that Denise was in fact Denis. He'd been so traumatised by the experience that he no longer spoke to women, in case they were men. (I had some sympathy with him here, having fancied Boy George by mistake for a fortnight in the 1980s.) Quite how Glen would fare around Thirza, I could not imagine.

'Why'd you invite him?' I'd protested, when Emdel revealed Glen was coming. 'It's like talking to an android.'

'All I did was mention we were watching Up in Smoke tonight and he kind of invited himself. He's a Cheech and Chong nutter. He's seen it twenty-four times.'

'Of course he has. Like I said, the guy's an android.'

I had hoped Glen's visit would be a one-off, but no; he ended up coming every week. Worse, he began bringing another workmate with him – Jason. Every Thursday at 8pm on the button, Jason would pull up outside my bedroom window in a Rolls Royce.

Asked to envisage a young man driving a Rolls Royce you might picture, say, a debonair toff about town, or perhaps a precocious entrepreneur riding the coat-tails of the computer age. But no, Jason was neither of these things. He was a mailroom boy, and his Rolls Royce was less Silver Shadow and more Mud-Green Pall, its once-white bodywork an essay in rust and algae. But being a Rolls it still ran. Just.

Jason had big plans for it, which he never tired of telling us, but on his paltry wage he'd gotten no further than replacing the driver's-side door, which was crimson. Not only was it a different colour to the rest of the car but – because it was also the only part worth polishing – he had T-cut it to within a micron of its life, so that it sparkled like a ruby in a rusty iron crown. The only other modifications he could afford were stickers, and so each flank had an acrylic flame licking across its decrepit coachwork. The side windows, meanwhile, were covered with mirror-finish adhesive sheeting, which could not have been more bubbled and creased had he applied it with his feet. Then there was the lettering he'd stuck across the top of the windscreen: Jason and Maureen. No one had ever met Maureen, and in time I would come to wonder if Maureen had even met Maureen. The only person I ever saw ride in that car with Jason was Glen. It should've been Glen's name up there, not Maureen's.

So it was that, by dint of sheer intransigence, Glen and Jason became Video Night regulars. They were harmless enough, I guess, and after Jason had run out of things to say about Maureen they spoke so rarely it was like they weren't there anyway. For weeks I thought them just painfully shy, but in time it became clear that their silence had its genesis in awe – their awe of Thirza. They were forever stealing glances at her (as I also did, in fairness, through foolscap) and when she spoke, their eyes never left her. And like Emdel, they also laughed at all her jokes, even the unfunny ones, of which there were plenty.

With Glen in particular I had the sense that, feeding his awe, was a magma chamber of suppressed emotion that might blow at any second.

'What is it with those two?' Thirza asked one night after Glen and Jason had left. 'They make Helen Keller sound like a town crier.'

That set Emdel off, which in turn sent Thirza into meltdown. When they were finally done, the pair of them gasping like a brace of landed fish, I saw Thirza consider Emdel with a softness she had never seen fit to bestow upon me.

*

Video Night dynamics changed irrevocably when Glen first brought along his guitar. He looked every inch the Bargain Bucket Keith Richards, whose shagginess and cragginess he shared, thanks to his acne scars and thick, long dark hair.

After the film, Glen stunned us, and himself probably, by actually speaking to Thirza.

'I saw you wearing that Stone Roses top last week,' he said, gently hoisting his guitar from its case, 'so I thought you might like this.'

That was his cue to launch into an acoustic cover of the Roses' 'This Is the One'. I had been right about that magma chamber because Glen rained down upon Thirza a skyful of impassioned soulfulness that left her eyes brimming with tears.

When he finished, Glen was greeted by a near-reverential hush. Thirza padded towards him, swabbing her cheeks with a sleeve, and she bent down to place a kiss on his cheek. He could not have looked more surprised had she whipped out his glans and popped it in her mouth, and frankly neither could we.

'Glen, that's one of the most beautiful things I've ever heard,' she said. 'Thank you.'

Glen blushed, nodded and slipped back into mute mode. But after that both he and Jason were far more relaxed around Thirza, as if somehow they now felt truly worthy of being in her company. Glen went on to serenade Thirza a few more times with Roses numbers but as impassioned and impressive as he was, he never again touched her the way he had that first time, at least not enough to make her cry, or to earn a kiss.

*

There could be little doubt about it: Thirza and Emdel had begun to riff off one another like it was jazz improv. As close as I was to Thirza, we didn't riff, we shared. Plus, I had noted how Thirza never gave Emdel a hard time as she did me; I can't once remember her calling him a twat or chastising him for anything. And she'd listen to him, rapt, as he served up theory upon theory, on miscellaneous matters that require scientific scrutiny – such as why headphone cables tangle the second your back is turned.

'For fuck's sake,' Thirza cursed one Video Night, fishing around in her bag for some matches to relight the spliff I'd passed her, but instead yanking out a bird's nest of cables that were attached to her Walkman headphones. Glen sprang from his beanbag and offered her a light. I swear, no man has ever moved faster over two yards.

'These things have got a life of their fucking own,' she griped, tossing the headphones on the floor. 'I only untangled them a few hours ago.'

'Actually, they do have a life of their own,' Emdel said. 'It's called Knot Theory, which explains why, when a cable or a length of string is jostled, knots form spontaneously. Here.' He leaned across Thirza's lap, with a tad too much familiarity for my liking, and took the headphones. He untangled them, decanted some shrivelled apples from our fruit bowl and dropped the headphones in. 'Right, shake this bowl for a minute or so,' he told Thirza.

'No fucking way,' she said, after much shaking. 'They're tangled again.'

'That's because your headphone cables have critical length, which means they'll always tangle when shaken. If they were shorter, they wouldn't.'

After the Knot Theory episode it became Thirza's habit, post-film, to turn Thursday nights into a version of Stump the Scientist, the 70s TV show hosted by James Burke, in which boffins fielded tough questions from an audience of schoolchildren. Unlike the show's scientists, Emdel had no prior warning of any questions, and yet not once did Thirza catch him out. She even started hitting Southsea Library on Thursday lunchtimes, in a bid to unearth problems that might defeat him. Some of her questions included: Why is the sky blue? (Air molecules scatter blue light from the sun more readily than red light, apparently); Why is water transparent? (Electrons in water allow light through); and why does a machine-washed duvet-cover swallow every other item of laundry? Actually that last one was mine. It was something I'd been wondering about for years.

'It's the Coriolis force,' Emdel explained. 'That's why everything ends up inside your quilt.'

'Of course it is,' I replied, smacking the flat of my hand to my forehead.

Emdel wrote down the Coriolis Force formula on the inside of a pizza box lid and walked us through each step, but only Glen was able to follow, even correcting him at one point. It was the kind of thing you usually witnesses only when watching Open University, stoned, at 2.30am Before leaving, Thirza tore the lid from the box and took it with her, which I thought odd. I would go on to curse the very existence of that scrap of grease-stained pizza lid, as well as the person who had scrawled upon it.

FOURTEEN

'On your lonesome today Llew?' Blanche asked, plonking a post-work pint of bitter on the bar. Unusually, I was the only one in there.

'Yeah,' I said. 'Thirza's gone home for the week. Her dad's got 'flu, and needs some help with the pigs.'

'Oooh,' Blanched mouthed. 'That won't have pleased her, going back to Farmland.'

'Tell me about it. She's been bitching about it all week.'

'She's a city girl at heart, our Thirza,' Blanche said, smiling. 'That picture she has of the Tricorn cracks me up.'

That picture is above Thirza's bed, I thought. When would Blanche have seen it?

'What's up? she asked. 'You've got a faraway look all of a sudden.'

'Nothing.'

'So where's your little mate today, the brainbox?'

'He's gone home too. His great aunt died.'

The news seemed to cause Blanche to stiffen.

'Now you've got a faraway look. What's up?'

'Nothing,' she said, focusing all her attention on wiping the already clean bar.

Why did she react like that? I wondered.

At that moment, Blanche's brother, David, appeared with a mop and bucket and began swabbing the floor. It was the first time I'd seen him in an age.

'Thank you, David,' Blanche shouted across to him.

David smiled first at her, then me. He had a sad smile, I thought.

Blanche didn't like to talk about David, I knew. I'd heard her stonewall curious customers on the subject before, but I know a thing or two about winkling information from people, plus I'm a nosy bastard, and so after David had glided back upstairs I decided to see what I could prise from her.

'If you don't mind me asking, Blanche, which you probably do, what's the story with David?'

Trick One: telling people they are unlikely to do what it is you want of them makes them more likely to do it, because we're contrary buggers at heart.

'There's no story, at least not for the likes of you.'

'It's just he never seems to go out,' I persisted. 'I've not seen him around once, and I live and work virtually next door to this place.'

'If you must know he only goes out for appointments, to the dentist or doctor, that kind of thing, and I have to go with him.'

'He seems like a gentle soul.'

Trick Two: empathise, to keep them talking.

'There's no one gentler.'

'Has he always been that way?'

'He's always been gentle, if that's what you mean.'

'But reclusive? Was he like that as a kid?'

'What, you're a shrink now are you, as well as a journalist?'

'Sorry. Didn't mean to pry.'

Trick Three: when apologising do so with an obverse version of the truth. It's like honesty, only for fibbers.

'Anyway, no, to answer your question. As a boy he was the life and soul.'

'So what changed?'

'It's not my place to say.'

'I understand.'

More empathy.

'If you must know, he was bullied something rotten when he was young. Camp David they called him. He got beaten up so often that in the end he refused to go to school. Dad had already died by then, from a heart attack, and Mum tried everything to get David back into the classroom but nothing worked. In the end she had to home-school him in between cleaning jobs.'

'God. Poor guy.'

'Don't feel sorry for him – he got a better education than me. Mum did a brilliant job. Amazing woman she was.' A far-away smile softened

Blanche's face. 'After Mum died from cancer, it was just me and David,' she continued. 'He was fifteen and I was a few years older. I became his legal guardian. That was when things got really bad.'

'Because of the grief?'

Trick Four: the deliberate misread. This is my signature ploy as a harvester of sensitive information. People nearly always correct you if you're wrong, they just can't help themselves. I'd sensed there was more to David's story than him losing his mother.

'No, though that didn't help. It was … something else.'

'Something else?'

Trick Five: mirror the other person's language. It makes you sound like them, and we all love ourselves, right?

'It was odd,' she said. 'For a couple of years after Mum died, David hardly left the house at all, a bit like now. But then all of a sudden he started going out again, and for a time he seemed really happy, almost like the smiley little boy he'd once been. This went on for a few months, but then he started coming back later and later, and sometimes not at all, and he became more withdrawn than ever. He flat-out refused to tell me where he was going and so one night I followed him. I was worried about him. I knew he was gay and very vulnerable.'

'So where was he going?'

'To some big posh house over Farlington way, near the marshes. I looked up the address on the electoral roll and found it belonged to John Skinner. You wrote a story on him, right?'

'Skinner? Jesus. The guy's a scumbag. What on earth was David was doing there?'

'He wouldn't say. He was furious I'd followed him. I've never seen him so angry about anything. I thought he was going to hit me. It was scary. Something was going on in that house that he wanted no one to know about, I'm sure of it.'

'Did he carry on going to Skinner's, after you'd confronted him?'

Blanche nodded. 'For a time, but then he stopped, and after that he basically just lived in his room, until I took tenancy of this pub, and he moved here with me.'

'He must get lonely up there,' I said, nodding up at the ceiling, at Blanche's flat.

'He keeps himself busy. He's been writing something for years.'

'What, a novel?'

'No idea. I've given up asking.'

'So what happens if you get married, Blanche? Where'll he go then?'

She stroked my cheek. 'Ah, Llew, pet, are you proposing?'

I felt my cheeks redden.

She laughed. 'You love playing the hard-boiled hack but d'you know what? You're a pushover. A mummy's boy.'

Blanche didn't know the half of it. I still took my washing home once a month, and Mum was forever posting survival packages, the most recent of which was a single sock she'd found under my bed, having mailed its partner a month earlier.

'David likes you, by the way,' she added, out of nowhere.

'What?'

'It's true. He's asked me a few times about you – your work, what you're like, whether you're gay.'

'What!'

She winked. 'Got you again.'

That's when she gave me the siren eyes; it's a superpower some women have.

'He gets so lonely,' she sighed. 'He'd love nothing more than to chat for hours when I go up at night, but after a long day down here all I want is to catch up on my soaps, so he doesn't get much in the way of company. It'd be nice for him to have someone to talk to, just occasionally, Llew.'

Blanche dialled up the invisible mind-altering psy-beams. Resistance was futile.

'I'd be happy to pop upstairs to give him a bit of company,' I heard myself saying.

'Would you? Really? Bless you. You are a darling.'

'Yeah, that's me.'

'I'll let him know to expect you, shall I. Next Wednesday okay?'

'T'rrific.'

I had set out to play Blanche for information but had ended up being finger-picked myself, like a redneck's banjo.

FIFTEEN

Blanche lifted the bar hatch and ushered me through. I paused before the door that led up to her flat above the Mow. I'd been putting off my promised visit with David for weeks, even taking to drinking in another pub in order to avoid Blanche. But I'd bumped into her in a corner shop and – with a single piercing look – she'd guilted me into keeping my word. But what could I possibly have in common with a homosexual hermit? It would be pure torture. And what if he came on to me? This was, after all, a man who'd last had sex back when I had the reading age of an eight year old.

'Go on,' she urged, wafting a tea towel in my direction. 'He's not going to bite you.'

I plodded upstairs with the heavy step of a condemned man. The walls were lined with posters of Hollywood musicals. I groaned inwardly as my eye moved from Gigi, to Guys and Dolls and – horror of horrors – to Seven Brides for Seven Brothers. One Christmas long ago Mum had forced Dad and me to sit through Seven Brides, when Zulu had been on the other side. Every Yuletide since, one of us would remind her of the televisual trauma she had inflicted upon us.

Great, I thought. Not only might David's soft spot for me become a hard spot but I'll also have to listen to him drone on about musicals.

'Hello,' I called feebly at the top of the stairs, in the hope he mightn't hear.

But he emerged, floating towards me in the same way his sister did behind the bar.

'Hi Llew.' His words came wispy and soft, like smoke. 'Nice to meet you. Properly, I mean.'

'Yeah, you too. I see you like musicals.'

'I adore them, yes.'

Of course you do. 'What's your favourite?' Stop, you idiot. You'll only encourage him.

'Seven Brides ...'

Of course it is.

He clasped his hands at his chest and looked heavenwards, eyes closed.

'I find it soooo uplifting.'

'Maybe we could watch it together.' *What*! I howled, inwardly. Where the hell did that come from? It's like my free will has been annexed by Nazis, like the Sudetenland.

'Oh, how wonderful!' he gushed. 'I have them all you know. Every single musical ever made. Come see.'

He led me into Blanche's sitting room. One look was enough to confirm that it was official: I was in hell. There was shelf upon groaning shelf of videos, all of them musicals. I'd have been groaning too had I been one of those shelves.

'Do you like musicals, Llew?'

'Love 'em.' Okay, this is officially getting scary now.

'D'you have a favourite?'

Having so recently thought of Nazis, I told him it was The Sound of Music.

'How delightful! Why don't we watch that tonight?'

'T'rrific.'

He clapped with excitement. He actually clapped.

'Wonderful,' he added. I'll wear my lederhosen!'

And I'll wear my SS Gruppenführer uniform complete with sidearm, to end my misery.

'We're going to get on well you and I,' he chirruped, 'I just know it.' He jumped excitedly, like a child on Christmas morning.

Who is this guy? I wondered. Does he have a twin? Where's the wispy wafty Trappist who ghosts around with a mop downstairs? I want that version.

I gathered my senses, and realised I had best steer talk away from musicals before I found myself agreeing to a costumed run-through of Oklahoma!

'Blanche told me you write,' I ventured. 'Do you mind me asking what about?'

And with that, I had my wish: he became the David of downstairs. His chirpiness was dampened and the energy that had so animated him drained away. His eyes were downturned and he grew hunched, as if trying to vanish inside himself.

'It's kind of you to come, Llew,' he half-whispered. 'I imagine you don't really want to be here. It's only because Blanche asked, isn't it? I know she worries about me.'

'I do want to be here,' I protested, and in that moment I really did. He was vulnerable suddenly, and lost, and I felt for him. 'I'm sorry for asking about your writing. I didn't mean to pry.'

'I'll be back in a second.'

He left the room, returning with a bulging backpack, which he handed me. I was unprepared for its weight.

'I'd welcome your thoughts on this,' he said. 'I've been working on it for some time.'

'What is it?'

'A novel.'

It felt more like an anvil. I wondered if I hadn't stumbled upon Portsmouth's answer to Proust.

'No one has ever read it, not even Blanche, so please don't say anything to her about me giving it to you. She might be hurt that I didn't show it to her first.'

'Of course. I'm honoured.'

'Hey, you're a writer, so maybe you can give me some tips?'

'I don't write fiction, David. That's a different game altogether.'

He patted the sofa.

'Oh, okay. Anyway, take a seat, make yourself comfortable. I'll fix us a drink and then we can settle down to some Julie Andrews and Christopher Plummer.'

'T'rrific.'

Not even Nazis were able to redeem The Sound of Music, because they'd been sugar-frosted along with everything else, so that rather than hunting down the absconding Von Trapp family like swine – and summarily executing a few of the younger ones by way of example – they ponced about like schoolboys playing hide and seek, leaving the family to flee. But at least they didn't sing or dance. Unlike David.

*

David was not Portsmouth's answer to Proust. Yes, his novel was expansive but only in the way cancer is. It ran to over 1,200 sheets of A4, mainly because as a writer he was incontinent, describing everything in preposterous detail, with neither discretion nor design. His manuscript could have had every other page removed with no impact on flow. I didn't give it a close read; I'd still be macheteing my way through it now had I done so. Rather I scanned it, with a growing sense of dread about what I could possibly say when he sought my opinion of his work.

'It shows promise.'

Patronising and wholly untrue.

'I really liked it.'

I liked it less, even, than Seven Brides ...

'You have an eye for detail.'

You spent three pages describing a rusting Rolls Royce in a front garden and two pages apiece on waves crashing up a shingle beach and the hypnotic effect of flames in a grate.

'I can tell you've put a lot into this.'

Maybe I'd go with that. It was truthful, but in a way that would spare his feelings.

That said, David's story did end up grabbing me by the throat, when his antagonist finally emerged, four-hundred pages in. He was a local businessman called Mark, who'd made his fortune from pornography. One section described how David's protagonist, Peter – a thinly disguised version of David – had enjoyed sex sessions with an older man named Drew at a series of debauched gay parties hosted by Mark at his house. Mark then goes on to blackmail Peter and Drew into appearing in a series of extreme hard-core gay movies, having earlier secretly filmed them having sex. From that point on, I read David's manuscript not as a despairing critic but as a salivating journalist.

At work I photocopied those parts of the story featuring Mark, and showed them to Big Al. I'd already told him how, years ago, a concerned

Blanche had followed David one night and discovered he was secretly visiting Skinner's place in Farlington, and that Blanche also believed something terrible happened to David in that house.

'Holy shit, Bandit, I think you're right,' he said, having scanned through the wad of pages. 'This is no work of fiction. This is Skinner he's writing about. Those parties were real. I bet the blackmail's real too. S'gotta be.'

'Let's say it is true,' I said. What do we do?'

'We nail the filthy fucker,' Thirza said. 'Send me, Al,' she implored, standing. 'I'll doorstep him, no problem. He doesn't scare me.'

'Yeah but you might scare him, John,' Big Al answered. 'Then we'll be left with nothing. No, we'll tread softly on this one.'

He lit one cigarette from another and smoked it down to the filter in silence, staring into the mid-distance while stroking his chin, like some academic pondering an impenetrable theorem. Thirza and I knew not to disrupt his train of thought in such moments.

'Right,' he announced, jabbing the smouldering butt in my direction. 'Bandit, next time that scumbag Skinner phones you with a job offer you tell him that you're interested, and then angle for a meet-up. In the meantime see what else you can get from your man David. We need confirmation. Names, dates, places. You know the score, you lovely boy.'

*

Wednesday evenings became Musicals Night, a prospect that in the normal course of events might have had me seeking blessed solace in a gas oven, perhaps, or a noose. But events were far from normal; David might be the key to us bringing down Skinner, and so I approached Wednesday nights like a professional. If that meant I had to don a diamante stetson and power-mince around David's living room, belting out songs from the shows, then so be it. At least Blanche allowed me to drink as much as I wanted on those nights, so grateful was she that David finally had some company that wasn't her. That helped take the edge off.

'Did you have a chance to read my book?' David asked casually on my second visit, as the end-titles to Paint Your Wagon rolled.

'Can I ask you a question?' I replied, happy to deflect his request for a literary critique.

'Of course.'

'Your character, Mark. Is he based on John Skinner?'

David opened his mouth, as if to speak, but got no further than a passable impression of a landed fish.

'It's just I've been digging into Skinner's past,' I added, as he continued gulping like a carp. 'You might have read my piece on Skinner's porn shops a while back.'

David gave a faraway nod.

'I did some deep backgrounding on that piece, and there was some stuff we couldn't use because we had no proof. Stuff like Skinner's parties for example.'

'Who told you about the parties?' he asked, snapping back into the present.

I could hardly tell him that Blanche had spoken of his clandestine trips to Skinner's house, and that his manuscript had simply filled all the blanks. And so I went all Woodward and Bernstein on him, announcing I was unable to reveal my sources.

'I know the parties are real, David. But what about the blackmail? Is that real too?'

David nodded slowly, without looking up from his feet. Silent tears dripped from his nose. I patted his knee.

'You can help us get him, David. The Probe can make him pay for what he did.'

He began shaking, as if hypothermic. 'If I do that then he will destroy me. He made that very clear.'

I took his hand with the one that wasn't on his knee.

'David, he's already destroyed you. Look at the past ten or fifteen years and tell me that he hasn't.'

He started bobbing with emotion and buried his head in the crook of my shoulder, so that his warm tears dampened my skin.

'What could I possibly do to help, anyway?' he said, into my neck. 'Who'd listen to an old queen like me.'

'You're a witness. You saw everything, heard everything. And what about that older man from the parties that you describe in your book? Is he real? Did Skinner blackmail him too?'

I felt him nod, and through sniffles David revealed that the other man had been called Max, and that he and Max had grown close.

'Skinner used to hold fag parties at his house,' David said, pulling away, before going on to fill tissue after tissue with tears and snot. 'They became legendary,' he continued, about a quart of bodily fluids later. 'Men would travel from as far away as Bournemouth and Brighton. This was the 70s, don't forget. In those days queers met in public toilets, so you can imagine how we loved those parties. There was drink and drugs of all sorts. Some of the more outrageous queens thought nothing of cavorting in full view of everyone. It was quite debauched. Skinner wasn't interested in them, though. The ones he had his eye on were the respectable men. Teachers, bank managers and businessmen, with reputations to protect – and marriages as well, many of them. Skinner knew that if he had dirt on them then he could make them do anything.'

'What did he have on Max? Was he married?'

'No, his father was a Tory MP. The scandal would've done for his career.'

'And so what did he have on you?'

'He knew I lived in Leigh Park. He'd grown up there himself, and he knew that if people there found out I was gay then they'd've lynched me, if I was lucky.'

'So he secretly filmed you and Max, having sex in the bedroom?'

'Bed*rooms*,' he corrected me. 'There were five of them, maybe six. Skinner was already wealthy by then, from his shops.'

'And how many men did he film, d'you think?'

'Oh, I don't know. Dozens.'

'Over what kind of period?'

'A year, maybe more.'

'But how did he manage to film you secretly? I mean, videos cameras back then were as big as a breeze block.'

'The bedrooms all had mirrored wardrobes. He must've filmed from inside those somehow.'

'Did he pay you for being in his films?'

'Of course not.' David leaned into me and again cried hard into my neck. It was at least a minute before he could speak. 'He made us do unspeakable things, and not just with other men. There were animals.'

David sat up and worked his way through the rest of the tissues before being able to continue. He went on to tell me that Skinner had shot all the films in a purpose-built studio at the top of his garden, and had made David and Max appear in a total of seven movies.

'What I don't quite get is how he blackmailed you to do so many films,' I said. 'After the first one, what did he have on you any more? I mean, it was all out there already, in the public domain. How did he make you do the other six?'

'The films were for export,' he explained. 'They were way too extreme for the UK. They were all for mail-order, to places like America, Holland and Germany. He knew the chance of anyone recognising us in those places was practically zero, yet he could still post any of those films to loved ones, or to people who'd persecute us.'

We sat in numb silence for a time, until David slowly crumpled in on himself and began hyperventilating. I feared he might be having a heart attack.

'Should I get Blanche?'

'No,' he said, between gasps. 'I think I… just need to lie down… for a bit.'

Falteringly, he rose from the sofa. Afraid that he might keel over, I took his elbow and led him to his bedroom. The room was spartan and soulless, more of a cell than a room.

He peeled back the quilt and slid under, pulling it up over his head. I waited for him to speak, to say goodbye at least, but he said nothing, and so I slipped away, wordlessly, happy to be out of there.

SIXTEEN

I DIDN'T HAVE LONG TO wait for the next phone call from Skinner. Unlike previous occasions, I was happy to have his breathy obnoxiousness in my ear. Knowing what I did about his Seventies sex parties, and the ensuing blackmail campaign, gave me a sense of control and power that was intoxicating. Had he felt the same way when he had forced all those men to degrade themselves by appearing in his twisted films? It was a disquieting thought.

'Listen,' I said, after Skinner had made himself known to me, 'I'm going to have to call you back. I need some privacy,' I added, in a conspiratorial whisper. 'What number are you on?'

'Sounds promising, Mr Sabler,' Skinner said, having first given me the number.

I replaced the receiver, waited a couple of minutes, then picked it back up.

'Nice touch, Bandit,' Big Al said.

Thirza gave me a double thumbs-up as I dialled the number.

'I can speak freely now, Mr Skinner. Listen, first things first. I'm on a written warning thanks to you. After you splashed that Santa crap across your front page, those Christian protesters were outside our office for nearly a fortnight. Ad revenue nosedived because of it, and guess who our publisher blamed? Me.'

The truth was that ad revenue had actually gone up following the protests. Regional TV had picked up on the story and their coverage had given The Probe's profile wings. And while the publisher had indeed expressed his concern to me about the protesters, he'd merely reminded me that I had been hired to write the news, not to make it.

Skinner gave a malevolent chuckle that put me in mind of sundry Bond-film baddies. Did he have a trap door in his office that opened into a tank of sharks, I wondered, or perhaps on his payroll he had a rotund bowler hat-wearing oriental bodyguard?

'Yes, you're quite famous, Mr Sabler, thanks to me.'

'It's infamy actually, not fame.'

'As I've always said, it's far easier to work with me than against me. So how can I help you?'

'Look, I'll be honest, it's not just that life here is getting sticky, but the pay's also crap. I'm sick of living in a damp bedsit eating instant noodles for tea.'

Big Al grinned wildly at that and was up and out of his chair, Highland flinging his way across the room, smoke tracing his every move.

Skinner gave another of his villainous chuckles. 'Ah, money. It always comes down to that in the end. Principles are an expensive luxury, are they not?'

'Mr Skinner, let's get this straight: I don't like the way you run your paper or the way you do business, and that will never change.'

'I set the terms of employment, Mr Sabler, not you.'

'But it's you who's been chasing me, and for months now.'

'And why do you think that is?'

'I dunno. You tell me.'

'I will triple your current salary. What does that tell you?'

'You'll triple my salary?' I parroted, for the benefit of Big Al and Thirza.

Thirza began scribbling furiously, then held up a message: Get me a fucking job too.

'It tells me you've got a lot more cash than The Probe,' I said.

'It ought to tell you more than that. What would I expect of you for that kind of money, do you think.'

'Hard work?'

'Everyone expects that. No, I'd expect – I'd demand – something far more important: total and unwavering loyalty.'

'You mean that you'd have me working on stories to oil the wheels of your dodgy business deals and expect me to suck it up.'

'I think we should meet,' he said, taking the conversation in a fresh direction.

'He wants to meet me,' I mimed to Big Al, who gave a double fist pump.

'I'm having an executive barbecue at my house next Saturday,' Skinner continued. 'I'd like you to come.'

'Okay. I will. Thanks.'

'And Mr Sabler? Think very carefully in the meantime about what we've discussed today.'

'I will. Goodb—'

He hung up before I could finish. Big Al and Thirza were on top of me in a flash, hungry for details.

'Right, this is big league, Bandit. You'll need a camera, to snap the bedrooms and also the studio, if it's still there. We'll come up with a strategy, to help you get what you need on the day.'

'I know what my strategy'd be,' Thirza said. 'Take the fucking job and triple my salary.'

Big Al and I swapped quizzical glances.

'He's a pornographer, Thirza,' I pointed out. 'I thought you hated porn, and I thought you hated Skinner even more.'

'I do, fuck, yes. It disgusts me, he disgusts me, you know that. I'm only joking, you twat.'

But her burning cheeks suggested otherwise. The corrupting force of money had been laid bare before me. Thirza's head had been turned, merely by being in the vicinity of a triple-your-money offer to a colleague.

The realisation left me in no doubt that the best tack at the barbecue would be to schmooze with those who did Skinner's bidding, his colonels and generals. If I could connect with just one of those corrupted souls, then who knows what I might learn?

SEVENTEEN

HAVING NEVER BEFORE BEEN TO a pornographer's house I didn't know quite what to expect of Skinner's. Statues of Greek gods and an indoor fountain, perhaps? Dildo door handles? In the event it looked rather like the faux-Tudor pile owned by my Uncle Neil, my dad's cravat-wearing brother, who is a stockbroker and about as far removed from pornography as it's possible to be, if one discounts a 'nicely turned ankle', which seems to be his thing.

Skinner's place was not only big and timber-clad but it also had a horseshoe-shaped gravel drive, which put me in mind of a BBC Radio sound effect, as my car crunched across it. I drew to a halt between an Audi convertible and a BMW 7 Series, both of which were red and shinier, even, than the T-Cut maroon door on Jason's Rolls Royce. My shit-brown Allegro took on a reddish tinge from the cars either side of it, as if embarrassed.

Uncle Neil had more in common with Skinner than I'd expected, because Skinner answered the door wearing a paisley cravat, which was tucked into a crisp pink long-sleeved cufflinked shirt. I'd only ever seen him from across a crowded room before, and at that distance he had appeared remarkably unremarkable. Up close, however, I found his unremarkableness bewildering.

In his manuscript, David had described most everything and everyone in sub-nuclear detail, and yet he had not described Skinner's face at all, which had struck me as odd. But as he stood before me, I understood perfectly why this was. His face bore no lines or creases to betray evidence of worry or laughter, anger or concern, and there was nothing in his slow, cold eyes to suggest that things would ever be any different. His face was a blank, his features an irrelevance. As if to confirm as much, Skinner gave me an approximation of a smile as he shook my hand.

'Ah Mr Sabler, welcome. Come in.'

The entrance hall alone could have swallowed half of my flat, as could most of the other rooms it fed into. The decor and soft furnishings throughout spoke of an almost exclusively female touch, and it was difficult to imagine anything racier than a Tupperware party ever having taken place there.

'This is Daphne, my wife,' he said, introducing me to an impeccably packaged slip of a woman. She had a large glass of red wine in one hand and was pretty, if a little jaded. She must have been at least ten years his junior.

'Welcome to our home,' she said gesturing in a careworn manner at the rooms around us. Her words were a little blurred; it was clearly not her first glass of the day. Her handshake was one that the Queen might offer – all fingers, and no palm. 'I hear you might be joining us,' she added, holding on to my hand as she spoke.

Us? She made it sound like I was being considered for a position on the sofa, between her and her husband.

'That's one of the first things you'll discover about life on The Tribune,' said Skinner, catching my surprise. 'We're one big family.'

I noted how he hadn't used the word 'happy' in that statement.

'Yes, aren't we,' said Daphne, with a weary smile, before peeling away and heading upstairs.

Skinner watched her disappear, his eyes colder than before, I thought. 'Come,' he said, turning to me, 'let me introduce you to everyone.'

'Everyone' was all his executives and their wives. They were politely chirruping on an expanse of sunken patio, between sips of champagne, which was all anyone appeared to be drinking. The scent of marinated meat being barbequed wafted past my nostrils but I had no appetite, even though I'd not eaten all day. My guts were knotted with nerves.

'We'll talk later,' Skinner said, touching my elbow and leaving me in the company of his champagne-supping underlings. Most of the women had coiffured hair and wore sharply cut suits in primary colours, as well as bold jewellery. Any of them could have sat in front of an auto-cue and read the news without looking out of place. The men, meanwhile, were mostly dressed as if for Cowes Week – all chinos, deck shoes and polo tops. I flitted from couple to couple, trading introductions and small talk, until everyone morphed into an homogenised whole.

Eventually I was introduced to the editor, Nigel, a saturnine character who might have been classically handsome were it not for his monumental Freddie Mercuryesque gnashers. Had Nigel been a car, he might have been a Jaguar E-type that had been painted by a blind man, in vinyl matt.

'I hear you're thinking of joining us,' Nigel said, his tone neutral, suggesting he had no opinion either way on that prospect.

I tried hard to meet his eye but inexorably my gaze was drawn to his teeth, which could not have gleamed any brighter had it been a toothpaste commercial.

'Er, yeah. Thinking about it.'

He patted his trouser pocket.

'I'm sure he'll make it worth your while,' he said, matter-of-factly, following that up with a humourless wink.

'So I believe.'

'We're like one big family on The Tribune,' he added, poker-faced.

Everyone had said the same thing, all of them omitting the word 'happy'. They'd clearly been briefed by Skinner. It was certainly no family I wanted any part of, whatever the financial perks, and after an interminable hour of rictus smiles and one-size-fits-all pleasantries I knew I would get no information of value from any of them, and my mind turned to the camera in my inside jacket pocket.

David had spoken of a film studio at the top of Skinner's garden. I drifted away from the patio and up a few steps on to the huge expanse of lawn. It was screened on either side by almighty hedges of cypress trees, tall and dense enough to keep prying eyes and ears at bay, I guessed. At the top of the garden, running the width of the lawn, was another screen, this time of gently swishing bamboo, which had a narrow gap in its centre. I meandered lazily across the lawn towards the bamboo curtain, as if lost in thought – not wishing to appear overly purposeful to anyone who happened to be looking on, especially Skinner. Through the gap in the bamboo I glimpsed a large weather-board structure, with picture windows and a flat felt-covered roof. I glanced back at the house. No one was looking, so I slipped through and headed for Skinner's old porn studio. I tried the door; it was locked. I pressed my face up against a window, looking through cupped hands to block the light. It was rammed with boxes and old garden furniture but in the corner, looming above all else, was a big fat studio light on a stand. I wondered what manner of misery and suffering it had lit in its day – David's suffering, and Max's. I took the camera from my pocket and fired off some shots, before returning to the house, with as much insouciance as I could muster.

I snaked back through Skinner's people on the patio and on into the kitchen. I needed some photos of the bedrooms, where the blackmail had taken place. Skinner was in the kitchen, with his back to me, and was in reluctant conversation with a newscaster wife. He laughed at something she said. It was an ersatz laugh, like that of a ham actor. I drifted through into the hallway and tip-toed up the stairs, like an intruder in the dead of night.

At the top was another hallway, broad and full of statement furnishings, including a chest-high Chinese urn and a period presentation table, inlaid with pearl and gold leaf. Off the hall were eight doors, all of which were closed, except for one. Through it I could see the corner of a bed. I knocked gently, not expecting a reply.

'Yes?'

The female voice jolted me. It was Skinner's wife.

In for a penny...

I eased the door open, and there was Daphne, hunched over a large vanity table by the window. She span around, looked me up and down, smiled, and proffered a rolled-up banknote.

'Want some? It's the only way I can get through days like this. Come in. Shut the door.'

I found myself with a twenty-pound note up my left nostril, snorting cocaine with Skinner's wife. I'd had coke only once before, when someone had left a wrap of it on top of a toilet cistern at a house party, but whatever had been in that batch bore no comparison to the stuff Daphne had, because after thirty seconds one half of my face was numb. You could have taken a road drill to my molars on that side and I'd not have felt a thing.

'Jesus Christ,' I said. 'I can't feel my head.'

Daphne fixed me with a sombre expression.

'You can never be numb enough around him. You seem like a nice lad. Can I give you some advice?'

'Sure.'

'Go downstairs, walk out the front door, get in your car and never come back, otherwise you'll end up like that lot downstairs. Have you met them, his clones? They weren't always like that you know. Most of them started out as regular people, like you.'

'So what happened to them?'

'He got to them. He trapped them with money, like he's trying to trap you, and now they all do his bidding. What's he offered you, honey? Double what you're on?'

'Triple.'

'Oh, he must want you real bad.'

'But those people downstairs, they're free to leave The Tribune any time they want, surely?'

She shook her head slowly before patting my knee, a little patronisingly I felt. 'When you've bought a big house and have a whopping mortgage, and you've got school fees to pay on top of all that, where else are you gonna work? Not another regional paper, that's for sure. His lot earn more than most national journalists. The Tribune's not a newspaper, it's a giant gilded cage.'

'So how did you meet him, if you don't mind me asking?'

'I was a Tribune sales girl – young, single and pretty, like all the women he hires. I got talking to him at one of the endless social events he likes to hold.'

'He doesn't strike me as the sociable type.'

'He's not. He hates people. He's only nice when he wants something. The parties and events are his way of making sure that as many of his staff as possible are married to each other, as that way he's got more control over them.'

'Jesus Christ, it sounds like something from the Third Reich.'

'Those wives downstairs, dressed like Angela Rippon? They're all former Tribune sales girls, just like me.'

'But you must've been attracted to Skinner, to begin with at least?'

'My god you're nosey. I can see why you're a journalist. It's like I said, when he wants something he can turn on the charm and do a great impression of someone who cares. He treated me like a princess.'

'And when did that all change?'

'Not long after we were married. When I told him I wanted to have kids, d'you know what he said? That I might as well get a hysterectomy because I'd be getting no brats out of him. Soon enough we were sleeping in separate bedrooms, and it slowly dawned on me that I was only ever for show, so he could keep up appearances.'

'Appearances?'

'He's a fag, honey, and he worries that if people cottoned on to it then it'd be bad for business. Right,' she said, tapping my knee, 'your turn. Tell me about yourself. Are you really here for a job? After everything you wrote about him, I find that hard to believe.'

I looked hard into her drug-dilated eyes, seeking her truth. Should I risk everything by telling her why I was really at her husband's barbecue, or should I make my excuses, sneak into another of the bedrooms, get some pictures and get the hell out of there? I took a deep breath.

'I'm here because I want to bury your husband.'

It seemed a gamble worth taking. She had expressed nothing but contempt for Skinner, and if I could persuade her to be an ally then she'd be the ultimate insider – my very own Deep Throat.

She cocked her head and squinted at me, almost imperceptibly. 'Bury him? For what?'

'For the men he's blackmailed,' I said, with growing uncertainty. 'For the lives he's wrecked.'

She sat staring at me, impassively, long enough for me to fear she might spring to her feet and summon her husband. Instead she pointed at the fitted mirrored wardrobe that dominated the room.

'Go over to the wardrobe and open the second door to the left.'

I did.

'Look through it, from the inside I mean.'

'Jesus, I can see you and the room. It's transparent.'

'It's a one-way mirror, like they have in police stations. All the bedrooms have the same kind of wardrobe, with one door like that.'

'So this is how he filmed them,' I said, more to myself than her. 'Mind if I take some snaps?' I slid the camera from my jacket and waved it at her.

'Long as I'm not in them,' she said, ducking down behind the far side of the bed.

From inside the wardrobe, I got some shots through the door to get a blackmailer's-eye view of the bedroom.

'How did you know about the blackmail?' I asked her, emerging from the wardrobe. 'That was well before your time.'

'I know all his secrets, honey,' she said, snorting another line. I make it my job to. I'm sure to need that information one day.'

'Will you help us, Daphne, to nail him?'

'I thought I already was.' She stood, wiping her nose on a handkerchief that she produced from her sleeve. 'Listen, you should go. He'll be wondering where you are. He can't find you up here or we'll both be for it.'

'What would he do?'

'To you? Have you attacked. Break a few bones. That's what he was planning to do before he decided to lure you across to the dark side. Honey,' she added, patting my hand, 'after you blow him out, you be sure to watch your back.'

The menacing cyclist flashed past my eyes. He had uttered those same words. I shuddered.

'And what about you?' I asked, hearing the fear in my voice. 'What would he do to you if he found us up here?'

She shrugged. 'The usual. Give me a beating and then confine me to quarters, until the cuts and bruises have healed.'

She reached up to her mouth, and suddenly half her front teeth were missing. In her hand was a dental plate. She looked ten years older. 'This was his handiwork.'

'How can you bear it, being with him?'

'I'm biding my time, honey, and from what you say it sounds like that time may be coming. Now seriously, get the hell out of here. I mean it.'

'Has he still got the tapes?' I asked quickly, as she shooed me towards the door. 'The ones he used to blackmail those men?'

'Got them? Honey, he's still watching them, the pervert. I caught him once, cock in hand, when he thought I was out, shopping. I was shocked to see my own bedroom on the TV screen. Suddenly those weird mirrors made sense.'

'Did you know he'd blackmailed people with those films?'

'When he smashed my teeth in, I guessed as much. That was his way of telling me to keep my mouth shut.'

She had one hand on the door handle and the other on my shoulder.

'Where does he keep the tapes?'

'Not here any more, that's for sure. My guess is they're in his shop somewhere.'

Skinner still had one Private Shop , to the east of the city, in Leigh Park – Europe's largest council estate. It had been his first shop, and I had visited it for my Probe piece on him. It hadn't seemed very open to me, the front being slicked with algae and one of the windows boarded up with damp-blistered plywood. But of course he could still be using the place as an office, or for storage.

She eased the bedroom door open and peered out to check the coast was clear.

'Have you ever been inside that sho—'

She gave me a shove, and the door clicked shut behind me. Dribbling from my still-numb chops, I crept down the stairs and slipped silently from the house.

But there is no slipping off silently in an Allegro with a dodgy starter motor that is being driven across a three-inch-thick carpet of aggregate. As I waited for a break in the traffic to pull out of Skinner's driveway, my rear-view mirror showed the front door opening. There stood Skinner, his slow, cold eyes peering at me from that nothing face. He was wagging a finger.

EIGHTEEN

'What d'you mean, can I help you dump your porn down the cellar?' I asked Emdel. 'You hired a truck specifically to bring it down here, and now you say you're done with it?'

'Er, yeah.'

'Have you been neutered or something, like a dog?'

'I've just had enough of it that's all, okay?' he said pointedly and – I couldn't help but feel – not altogether honestly.

So, in a fog of incredulity, I helped him cart nineteen crates of porn down into the cellar (he'd purchased two more crates' worth in the time he'd been in Portsmouth, now that he was flush with cash). Emdel was uncharacteristically muted as we lumped and bumped. At first I tried to lift the mood with lame jokes – about him becoming a monk and wearing a habit, stuff like that, but I got no response from him.

When we were nearly done I could bear the silence no longer.

'What's this all about, really?' I asked at the foot of the cellar steps, mopping streams of sweat from my face with a sleeve. 'You spend a lifetime collecting porn, you go away for a few days and you come back behaving all weird and say you want to bin it all.'

He gestured at the stack of crates. 'I've grown out of it, that's all. I don't see what the big deal is.'

'You're were only gone seventy-two hours. You can't have grown up that much. Did something happen at your great aunt's funeral? Did God appear to you and warn you off masturbating?'

He coughed, superfluously. 'She was cremated. It was a humanist service.'

'Oh, well that explains everything then. Yeah, it all makes perfect sense now.'

'Are you gonna help me or not?'

'I am helping, in case you hadn't noticed.'

'Look, people change,' he said, clomping up the steps to fetch another crate. He stopped at the top and turned. 'I'll buy you a curry after,' he added. 'As a thank you.'

'Yeah, cheers.'

I hung back in the cellar and eyed the growing stack of porn-filled crates. The crates might stack up but I knew that something about this sudden change in Emdel didn't.

*

Three days after helping Emdel purge himself of porn, I found myself heading for Thirza's flat with the intention of declaring my love for her. Something in me had changed. I didn't know what exactly, only that I was done with tip-toeing around my feelings for her. Although I feared there was a healthy chance she might reject my love out of hand, and that it might end up harming our friendship, I no longer cared.

Before setting out on the short journey to Thirza's, I staged a ceremonial torching of all my love poems, choosing an evening that Emdel was out, over at Glen's, playing Dungeons and Dragons. I'd written hundreds of poems, all buttock-clinchingly dreadful. I tore every single one from a series of A4 pads and scrunched each up until I was surrounded by a knee-high mound of paper. I stuffed armfuls of them into the grate and set them ablaze with my Zippo lighter. The fire grew so fierce that flames began flicking out into the room, like fiery lizard tongues. On and on I lobbed poems into the grate until the heat became so intense it forced me to retreat back across the room. About ten minutes later there was a knock at the door. It was a neighbour, and he was pointing at the heavens.

'Mate, your chimney's on fire.'

I stepped outside and looked skywards, stunned to see five-foot-high flames dancing magnificently in the early evening Hampshire sky. I had to postpone my declaration of love by a couple of hours, while I waited on a fire crew to extinguish the blaze.

'What the bloody hell were you burning?' one of the firefighters asked once the blaze was out. 'It's not even cold tonight.'

'Love poems,' I told him, feeling too weary and put-upon to lie.

'Holy crap, fella, you must really love her,' he said, laughing.

I nodded and watched him clamber up into the cab of the tender alongside his waiting colleagues. As the engine pulled away I closed my front door and made for Thirza's bedsit. She lived just a half-mile away but the journey took an age, because unalloyed terror caused me to turn back, twice. As I walked back and forth, to and fro, from mine to hers, I imagined all possible outcomes: Thirza laughing in my face; Thirza wrapping me up in a passionate embrace, and us falling into bed; Thirza blowing me out, gently; and Thirza blowing me out with a savage punch to the solar plexus, before leaning over my stricken frame to shout the odds about what a twat I was for ruining our friendship. No one outcome seemed more or less likely than any other, although the violent one seemed to linger longest, which did little to settle my fizzing nerves or churning guts.

When finally I reached her place, I stood on the opposite side of the road, looking up at her gaff's two sash windows. The lights were on. I stared up at the windows long enough to give me neck ache, as if doing so might help me divine some form of universal truth about the nature of love, from thin air. Eventually I succeeded in forcing my legs to carry me across the street. The building's communal entrance was open, the lock still out of commission. Shortly before I reached Thirza's room I passed a door, from behind which came the sound of tinkling water, accompanied by Thirza singing a refrain from a song I didn't know. She knew tons of songs that were unfamiliar to me; I was still very much junior partner on the music front. I approached her front door; it was unlocked. I scuffed my feet on the hallway lino, unsure what to do next. Most of me was desperate to get the hell out of there before it was too late, but I stood firm, even though my stomach was lurching so violently I feared I might puke.

I peered into her bedsit. As ever, the Tricorn watercolour above her bed made me smile, and once more I wondered what Blanche had been doing in Thirza's place for her to see it. I hadn't thought about it since Blanche had made the original comment, but again it struck me as odd that Thirza would bring her back here, where there was barely enough space for one person. My eye was drawn to an open drawer in her bedside cabinet. A corner of cardboard was sticking out, and I recognized it as the pizza-box lid, of Coriolis force fame. Something compelled me to study it closer. I glanced over my shoulder, back down the hall. Thirza was still trilling away in the shower, so I snuck into her room and eased the pizza lid from the drawer. The Coriolis force scribblings were there, as expected, but at the base of the lid, also in Emdel's spidery hand, were some words I most certainly had not expected: 'Thank you for sharing the last few days with me. They were the best of my life. Can't wait to be together again. Love Emdel. x'

I stood staring at the grease-spotted cardboard, attempting to blink away Emdel's message of love, believing it some form of mirage, but every time I opened my eyes, there it was. I placed the pizza lid back in the drawer and turned to leave. But I stopped, returned to the drawer, removed the pizza lid, tore it in two, and tossed it on the bed.

I darted down the hallway and took the stairs two at a time. Out on to the street I plodded along as if the pavement were a gloopy farmer's field of mud sucking at my shoes. I had no sense of where I was or where I was headed. How blind I had been. Emdel hadn't been at a great aunt's funeral, and Thirza hadn't been back on the farm. They had been together, holed up in some love nest. And Emdel wanting to dump his porn? How could I have been so dumb? Thirza had a pathological hatred of pornography. We'd both witnessed her stinging anti-porn tirades, more than once.

'Porn turns women into spunk pots,' she'd say. 'I could never be with a man who used it. Never.'

Perhaps my conscious mind simply elected not to face the painful truth – unlike my subconscience, which dispatched me on a last-ditch, rear-guard mission to wrest Thirza from Emdel's sweaty paws.

I turned into a pub I'd never seen before and hit the optics, hard.

*

I awoke, shivering, just before daybreak in a grove of laurel bushes in the middle of a large roundabout on the main road out of Southsea. Vomit was crusted on the front of my lightweight jacket, which I'd at least had the good sense to zip up, I noted. At the moment of awakening I thought

I may still be dreaming, that I might awake again, in my bed this time. But my chattering teeth and pounding head, the vomit, and the sound and fumes from the pre-dawn traffic told me otherwise. I squinted at my Timex; it was a quarter to five in the morning.

Where to now? I wondered. Home, to that bastard Emdel, or hang out at a café until it's time to go to work, with that bitch Thirza? Fuck them both. Fuck everyone.

NINETEEN

My Dad would eat beans on toast every night of the week if Mum let him. As it is he only ever eats them on a Saturday. This is because during the week, every week, Mum prepares the same five meals, in the same order, and brooks no argument: Monday – toad in the hole, with peas and gravy; Tuesday – salmon fishcakes, with carrots and broccoli; Wednesday – Irish stew; Thursday – liver and bacon, with mash, peas and onion gravy; Friday – fish and chips with mushy peas. On Sunday it's always roast beef. Family meals have been that way since forever, and Dad and I have dubbed Mum's weekday fare the 'Big Five'. Oddly perhaps, neither of us has ever complained about the monotony of her menu. Maybe that's because her food is always top-notch, which I guess it should be, given the years of practise she's had at making each dish.

As a result of Mum's cyborg-like approach to domestic catering I am hard-wired to cook at least one of the Big Five every week. One is my default setting. However, if I am feeling particularly insecure or troubled then my consumption might rise to three a week. Rarely am I distressed enough to consume four. The last time the dial hit four was three years ago, when Dad was diagnosed with bowel cancer. Happily, he came through the other side, and I dropped back down to one a week.

In the hellish weeks following Pizza-box-lidgate, I found myself consuming all of the Big Five, and in the same order I'd been served them throughout my life, which was another first for me. I was taking comfort food to synaptic levels.

The fact was, discovering that Thirza and Emdel had become an item on the sly, had the effect of invalidating all of my existing feelings for each of them, which in Emdel's case meant a lifetime of feelings. Given that as people, we are little more than the sum of our feelings, I think it's safe to say that Emdel getting together with Thirza turned me into a different person. Not better or worse, just different. But I didn't want to be different. I wanted to be the same. And that's where the Big Five came in; they helped anchor me to a comfortable past, and prevented me from cartwheeling into a dimly lit future, full of shadowy and forbidding unknowns.

But I was cartwheeling nonetheless. Emdel and I no longer lived together. The day after I deposited the torn pizza-box lid on Thirza's bed, he'd moved out; she must have tipped him off. Actually, technically he didn't move out at all – he snuck out one afternoon while I was at work. I could tell he'd packed in a panic, doubtless fearful I might swing by unexpectedly. In his haste, he'd left one maroon sweater draped over a half-open drawer in his bedroom and another strewn on the carpet. Emdel, you should know, owns five identical maroon sweaters, five identical yellow plaid shirts, two pairs of blue jeans and one pair of black Tuf utility shoes. He'd read somewhere that Einstein's wardrobe consisted of five versions of the same outfit, because he'd not wished to squander brain energy on accessorising when it could be better used figuring out how the universe works. This affectation of Emdel's had always amused me, but as I studied the hastily abandoned maroon sweaters, the arrogance of it took my breath away.

Emdel also left a note, under a bottle of Jack in the kitchen, where he knew I'd find it: 'Am kipping at Glen's until things have calmed down a bit.'

Was he really at Glen's or was he shacked up with Thirza? I was pretty sure it was the latter. And what did he mean, about waiting for things to 'calm down'? I was heartbroken, not psychotic. He knew better than anyone that I had never subscribed to violence. Surely he knew that it would never even occur to me to wrap my hands about his throat until his stupid face turned the same shade of maroon as his preposterous Einstein sweaters.

At least Emdel sneaking off meant I was spared having to confront him; I am non-confrontational by nature. But there was no escaping Thirza, what with us being colleagues. In my naivety, I had believed that she and I would talk things through, that I would reveal my love for her and that thereafter she would be mindful of my broken heart, and treat me gently, like a chick with a broken wing or something. The plan was to then play the long game, by demonstrating my devotion to her in spectacularly touching ways that I was yet to determine, before going on to wrest her from Emdel's traitorous grasp, however long that might take.

Instead, Thirza behaved as if nothing had happened. At work she was unchanged – as chatty, impassioned and foul-mouthed as ever. The longer this went on the more I filled with resentment and anger, until I was no longer able to speak to her without wanting to scream. But instead of screaming, I channelled my feelings into making snidey comments at her expense. I knew this was like poking a hornet's nest with a stick but I didn't care – I wanted to provoke some kind of reaction from her, even if that reaction was for her to floor me with a roundhouse kick to the head. One way or another I would force her to acknowledge my pain, and thus I embarked upon a programme of passive-aggressive protest, never missing an opportunity to have a pop.

'What's the difference between licence with a c and license with an s?' she asked Big Al one day, around one week into my programme.

'Really?' I said. 'That's grammar basics. Secondary school stuff.'

'What's with you lately, Bandit?' Big Al said, having seen his work environment go from life-affirming to life-sapping in double-quick time.

Thirza leapt up, grabbed two fistfuls of my shirt and hauled me to my feet.

'Right, you fucking twat – outside. I'm done with your shite.'

Roundhouse kick it is then, I thought, as I followed her downstairs and out on to the street.

'What the fuck is eating you? she said, slapping my chest with the back of her hand. 'The only time you speak to me these days is when you're making some smart-arse comment or other. What's going on?'

'Oh come on,' I mock laughed. 'Like you don't know.'

She shoved me back with both hands against the office building. I hit it with a thud.

'If you've got something to say then fucking well say it. I'm done with your passive-aggressive bullshit.'

'Okay then, I will say it. I love you. There. Happy now?'

'What the fuck are you talking about, you love me? Don't be so fucking ridiculous.'

I exhaled sharply, open-mouthed.

'See, there's the problem,' I said, my wild gesturing fuelled by disbelief. 'I tell you that I love you and you make me feel like, I don't know … like that oik with the kebab. I'm not making some moronic comment about your breasts here. I'm telling you that I'm consumed by love for you. You're why I gave up my chance on The Insider for God's sake. I couldn't face not being around you.'

'Don't you be blaming that on me,' she said, wagging a finger in my face. 'I told you at the time you were a fucking idiot for passing up that opportunity.'

'I'm not blaming you, I'm just explaining how I feel about you, so that you know.'

'So now I know.'

'And that's it? That's all you've got to say?'

'I don't know what else to say. Look, I'm flattered, Llew, I am, but I don't know what to do with the information. You're my friend. My good friend. My very good friend.'

'Friends are as friends do.'

'And what the fuck is that supposed to mean?'

'You say you're my friend and yet you treat me like I'm some kind of idiot.'

She laughed, but not in a mocking way. It was the kind of laugh that, like a riptide, sucked me towards her – made me want to be part of her.

'Who was it that ended up plastered all over The Tribune after he almost killed the work experience girl,' she said, still laughing.

'Yeah but—'

'And who was it that got splashed across the same paper, pictured wearing a Santa-on-a-cross T-shirt in a fucking department store grotto.'

'You bought me that T-shirt.'

She laughed again.

'I didn't make you wear it though did I, you twat.'

'Still …'

'And who is it that loves Gary fucking Numan.'

'That makes me an idiot?'

'A musical idiot. Listen, Llew, you talk about love. Well I love being your friend. Isn't that enough? This other love of yours – I don't know what to do with it, I really don't. You're pouting again.'

'You knew what to do with Emdel's love though, didn't you. And behind my back as well.'

Her eyes grew sharp and flinty.

'My private life is none of your fucking business.'

'You and him stabbed me in the back. I'd say that's my business.'

'And there it is, finally. So that's what this is really all about.'

'What else could it possibly be about? And to make matters worse I've had to sit at my desk this past week, watching you pretend that nothing's wrong.'

'I'm not pretending, you fucking dimwit. Nothing is wrong, and no one's stabbed you anywhere. I've never wanted you in that way, and I'd say I've made that pretty fucking clear right from the off.'

'But—'

'What I do with Emdel is none of your fucking business, and if anyone should be annoyed then it should be me, at you, for creeping about my room like some kind of fucking stalker while I was in the shower.'

'I came to tell you I'm in love with you. Your door was open. I saw the pizza lid sticking out of the drawer.'

'And that's where you should've left it.'

'Tell me this then: if nothing's wrong, why do I feel so betrayed?'

'Because you've chosen to feel that way. What d'you think we are, me and Emdel, fucking mind-readers? How the fuck were we supposed to know you were in love with me? Not that it'd've made any difference to me if I had known, because like I say, I've never given you cause to think that I want you as anything but a friend.'

I tapped Thirza's chest with an index finger. She chopped away my hand with the blade of hers.

'Where I just touched you,' I said, rubbing my smarting wrist, 'that's where your heart should be. But d'you know what, I don't think you've got one. I think there's a house brick in there instead.'

'Oh, for fuck's sake,' she said, wheeling away towards the office entrance, before stopping, turning, and adding: 'I'm done with this hurt little boy routine of yours. D'you know what? It's actually a bit pathetic.'

Once more she made for the building.

'Hey,' I called at her back.

She turned. 'What?'

'We're done, you and me. This friendship's dead.' I wafted a hand at her, like a lord dismissing a serf, before brushing past her through the door.

'You're a fucking twat,' she called at my back.

Her voice had definitely cracked on the word 'twat'. I smiled, pleased that I at least meant enough to her for that final insult to catch in her throat. It was a small victory, amid the smouldering ruins of defeat.

TWENTY

The spasm of satisfaction I felt at hurting Thirza with my official termination of our friendship didn't even last as long as it took me to return to my desk, by which time I was already wondering what on earth I had just done. I did not have long to wait for an answer. When Thirza returned a minute or so later, she issued me a look of such withering contempt that it was practically radioactive. From that moment on, she could hardly have been any more gladiatorial had she come at me with a trident and a net.

'Fuckwit, it's for you,' became her preferred way of announcing she was about to pipe a call through from her phone to mine.

'Didn't make you one, twat face,' was how she liked to announce she'd made coffee for her, Al and Mike but not me. 'You can make your own, and I hope you fucking choke on it,' she might add, if she was in a good mood.

She also invested time and energy into dreaming up new ways to put me down. On one occasion, apropos of nothing, she tossed a copy of Dostoevsky's The Idiot onto my desk.

'Didn't know you'd written an autobiography,' she said.

She must have trawled every charity shop in Southsea in order to deliver that put-down because Thirza was given to reading airport novels, not Russian classics. (I actually read the book, as now I had time to kill most evenings, what with no Thirza or Emdel to go out with. The main character, some Russian prince, is so good-natured that everyone takes him for a fool, and I found myself identifying strongly with him.)

Ours was an open-plan office, but Thirza cared not a jot who heard her insults or what they thought, but she drew the line at people making smart-arse comments, especially Bob from Circulation. We both did.

'You lovebirds had a little tiff, have we?' he quipped one time, his grin exposing teeth so stained they appeared wooden.

'Shut the fuck up, Bob,' she and I chorused, in a rare show of unity.

Big Al tried everything to pacify her, even threatening her with a verbal warning unless she cooled it. Things calmed down for a day or two after that – until she blew-up again, with a little nudge from me.

'I see Numan's been inducted into the Rock and Roll Hall of Fame,' I said, to no one in particular. 'Long overdue.'

'Fuck Numan and fuck you, to death.'

While I might have fired the odd salvo here and there, the truth was Thirza was built for conflict and I wasn't, and before long our workplace war began to unpick my nerves. Every morning I'd have a sick feeling in the pit of my stomach at the prospect of another gruelling, bruising and lacerating day in the Coliseum. I knew I must escape Portsmouth – and Thirza – before I had some kind of breakdown.

*

'I'm telling you, Bandit, they'll never have you back,' Big Al said, before downing half of his pint in three gulps. 'I warned you about blowing out The Insider. You're dead to them now. End of story. Is this why you brought me to the pub? Well, you've wasted your time.'

'But what about all the other tabloids?' I pleaded. 'You've got contacts all over the shop. You could easily put in a word in for me someplace else. The sooner I get out of this place the better. This crap with Thirza's killing me.'

Big Al half-choked on his beer. 'It's killing *you*. What d'you think it's doing to me? I'd get more peace sat in the middle of the bloody Balkans conflict than I do working with you two.'

'Well surely that's even more reason to help me out, because once I'm gone things'll be peaceful again. I wouldn't let you down this time, Al. I promise,'

'You said that last time. Look, why don't you get yourself a job on a regional daily? With your portfolio they'd snap you up. You could be outta here in a couple of months.'

'I can't work for the regionals. I haven't got my shorthand. They're sticklers for it.'

'So go get your shorthand.'

'What? You've gotta be kidding me. That'd take years. I might've killed Thirza by then.'

'My money's on her killing you first.'

'Yeah but the tabloids don't care about shorthand, and you know that working on Fleet Street's always been my dream.'

'You *were* working on Fleet Street, you dope, and you blew it.'

'Come on, be fair, I was lovesick. It's a sort of illness, like blood poisoning or something.'

'No,' he insisted. 'For me it's a case of once burned, twice shy.'

'It really would be different this time, I promise. I'd be a million per cent focused. All it'd take is one word from you. Please, Al. I'm begging you. I've gotta get out of here.'

'So quit, and go freelance.'

'I don't wanna be a freelance. It'd be a disaster. I need to work in an office.' I chose not to say I suspected that as a freelance I might spend the best part of my working day lounging around in a dressing gown, masturbating flamboyantly. 'Please, Al.'

'Last time I vouched for you I ended up looking like a right berk. Never again.'

'I couldn't be more sorry about that, but you said yourself they liked me on The Ripple. You said your mate Kevo thought I'd done a great job.'

'Yeah, before you quit.'

He lit a fresh Marlboro and allowed his words to hang for a moment, before re-crossing his legs and pointing the lit end of his cigarette at me. 'Okay. I tell you what, Bandit, I'll make you an offer.'

'You will? Great. Thanks, Al.'

'Hang on a sec, you haven't heard it yet. If I'm to put in another word, you need to show me, long term, that you're properly ready for the big league this time. Mentally.'

'What, you mean you want me to trawl for more gear?'

'No, you're already a lovely boy for the gear. What I want is for you to show me you can sort out this crap with Thirza. Do whatever it takes, for my sake as much as yours. I'm not getting involved any more. It's down to you now. You succeed in that, and I might put a word in for you. Might.'

'But what do I do? She hates my guts.'

'Bandit, if you really believe that then Thirza might be right about you being a twat. You're the one who told her the friendship was dead. Never forget that.'

'But I love her, Al, and she shagged my best mate behind my back.'

'I'm not getting into all that. Just find a way to make and keep the peace, or you can forget Fleet Street.'

*

Entering Clinton Cards, I knew exactly the kind of product I was after: a padded and outsized greetings card that comes not in an envelope, but a box. Everything about such cards drove Thirza absolutely wild. I found just what I was looking for, and even better this particular outsized card sported precisely the kind of tableau she abhorred: a knot of self-aggrandized and bewhiskered Georgian gentlemen golfers, who were gathered about a vintage Rolls Royce and pointing at something out of frame that clearly pleased them mightily. A suffragette chained to the clubhouse railings being ravaged by a group of police constables, perhaps?

I was in Clintons because earlier that day, Thirza had asked why my parents had not had me adopted or euthanized, given I was little more than 'a steaming pile of witless offal'. It was too much. I had tried everything to mollify her: I had bought her a card and a biography of Jim Morrison for her birthday (she binned them in front of me); I had asked if we mightn't chat in private to sort things out ('fuck off'); I had even mailed an olive branch of a letter to her home address (she brought it into work, scrunched it up and threw it at my face). And so after the offal jibe I resolved to fight fire with fire. I'll make it to Fleet Street without Al, I told myself as I strode to Clintons. Somehow.

Upon my return to the office I was delighted to see that Thirza's hackles had begun to rise the moment she clocked the sack-like Clintons carrier bag in my hand. Big Al took one look at the card as I lifted it from the bag, clenched his teeth and shook his head, beseechingly. He knew that I was about to arm the nuclear device otherwise known as Thirza, and he even wheeled himself a few feet further back from his desk, to put some distance between himself and the blast zone. I made a big show of clearing my work station, typewriter and all, to make room for the card, which I slid lovingly from its box. Thirza was following my every move. I could almost hear the click of the countdown. I began writing in the card, verbalising sentiments that were as contrived as they were saccharine.

'Dear Dad, I hope you have a lovely birthday. This is a very special card for a very special father.'

That did it. Thirza sprang up, whipped the card from under my Biro and began pouring Olympian levels of ferocity into ripping the vintage golfing scene in two. But it had been printed on some kind of bulletproof vinyl and she couldn't tear it, however hard she tried, which served to further fuel her rage. Growling and grunting with frustration, until her face took on the hue of a ripe plum, she finally summoned up enough fury to rend the card in two, and in so doing exposed an A3-sized sheet of thin sponge that lay within.

'Who the fuck puts fucking sponge inside a fucking greetings card?' she screamed. 'And you,' she added, pointing at me, 'are a complete and utter fucking cunt.'

I gestured at the destroyed card on the floor. 'That's £11.50 you owe me.'

'Fuck you and fuck your stupid fucking card.'

The entire office was staring at us by now.

'Enough!' Big Al bellowed, slamming both fists on his desk so hard that the shockwaves upended a cup of scalding-hot coffee into his lap.

'Aaaagghhh,' he screamed, dancing a jig of pain, and tugging at the crotch of his tan corduroy trousers in a bid to lift the molten material away from his skin. 'I'm sick to death of the pair of you,' he hollered. 'You two sort out your shit right here and now or I'll sack you both. I'll get Old Man Tippex back in here, with his mayors and his fucking laminated cheques. I don't give a shit any more. And you,' he added, pointing my way, 'you can forget what we talked about. That's not happening now, not ever. Now get out of my sight, both of you, and don't show your faces 'til you've found a way to work together.'

*

She and I repaired to the basement, in a bid to broker a truce robust enough to prevent Big Al firing our arses before the day was out. I was less than hopeful.

'Look,' I said, making sure I stood outside her striking range, 'my guess is you don't want to be sacked.'

'Of course not, you fucking twat, especially not on account of you.'

I let that go. One of us had to play peacemaker, and with the fall-out from her Clintons rage still poisoning the air, it was never going to be her.

'Well, if you don't want to be sacked then we have to find a way to work together, however painful that may be. It's the least we owe Big Al, after all he's done for us.'

'For us? For you, you mean. I wasn't the one who nearly killed Fran or who ended up insulting every god botherer in the fucking Solent, was I.'

'Really? You owe him nothing? All right then, answer me this: how many editors did you send your sweary travel pieces to?'

'What? I dunno. Thirty or so. What's that got to do with the price of fucking eggs?'

'And how many got back to you, exactly? Let me guess,' I added, without waiting for a reply. 'One. Big Al. Tell me I'm wrong.'

But she couldn't.

'You owe him every bit as much as I do.'

She paced around the basement for a bit, dodging in and out of discarded office furniture and boxes of stationery and cleaning supplies.

'All right,' she conceded, 'for Big Al's sake I'll cool things. But get this straight: I might owe him but I owe you less than fuck all.'

With that she pushed past me, her face an essay in disdain.

TWENTY ONE

My truce with Thirza was excruciatingly fragile and no more sustainable than it was meaningful. It left me living on my nerves more than ever, and doubly determined to get the hell out of Portsmouth. As I saw it, I had two escape routes: quit with no job and move back home; or, shift heaven and earth to land another opportunity on one of the national tabloids, and then resign and move home, to save on rent.

Returning home with no job had the considerable advantage of being immediate and easy, but also the not inconsiderable disadvantage of having to live with the folks, who would doubtless revert to treating me like a BMX-riding schoolboy within ten minutes of me sloping through the front door. Worse, I'd be unemployed, and would wind up working on the nearby industrial estate, sticking stuff on things, or shifting stuff from here to there. I'd get sucked into some warehouse wormhole, and five years would pass before I re-emerged. It would be career suicide. That left Option Number Two.

I knew that, second time round, I'd have to impress the red tops without Big Al's help, but plenty of other regional reporters managed to land work on the nationals without a leg up, so why couldn't I? I'd just have to work my nuts off, that's all. I'd have to go into *gear* overdrive. I'd become a story machine. I'd flog so many yarns to the tabloids that one of them would have to take note.

So it was that every evening I began again to visit Pompey's dockside pubs and nightspots, trawling for stories, as I had when I first moved to the city.

By now, I knew my perfect subject: the lone mature female drinker – a rare breed indeed but worth her weight in newsprint. Why? Because there's always a story behind a woman drinking on her own, and if she's got some miles on the clock then she presents a bigger target at which to fire questions, because she's done more and so knows more people. As I moved from bar to pub to club I talked to anyone and everyone, but always kept an eye out for a lone she-wolf.

It was towards the end of an otherwise quiet and unproductive dank Tuesday night that I found Iris. She was sitting alone at the bar of the Ship & Castle, supping Guinness and smoking a roll-up. She was a big lady, so big that her expanse of backside half-engulfed the bar stool. I bought a pint of bitter, insinuated my way on to the stool next to her and we began chatting. Lone drinkers – male or female – are also nearly always amenable to conversation, which is another big plus.

Iris was a churchgoer, a Catholic, although I got the impression she attended mass out of loneliness rather than from any religious conviction because nearly everyone she had once known seemed to be dead, including her son and husband. This had to make her at least eighty, I guessed. I am but a residual Catholic, yet am fluent enough in theo-babble to establish a rapport with churchy types, if required. Rapport duly established, Iris went on to tell me about her life – or more accurately, her lost son's life.

His name had been Dominic. He'd been a dental hygienist and had perished from a cardiac arrest, aged 47, at the wheel of his Morris Minor. A passing motorist had found him slumped in his vehicle, in bushes just off the Fareham junction of the M27. He'd left a wife, Renata, 59, who was a supermarket checkout assistant. They were childless because Renata had had 'plumbing problems', as Iris described it. She showed me a picture of her son, who had been spectacularly obese. Iris seemed pencil-thin by comparison.

'Nice-looking lad,' I said, thinking it had been a miracle he had even reached forty-seven, and an even bigger one that he'd somehow managed to pour his bulk behind the wheel of a Morris Minor.

'Fifteen years my Dom's been gone,' Iris said into her Guinness. 'Beautiful service it was, at St Aloysius.'

'Here,' she added, gently placing Dominic to one side and tapping my elbow, 'talking of St Aloysius, did you hear what poor Father O'Reardon found on his altar the other morning?'

'No I didn't, Iris. What was it? A big donation?'

'Well it was big all right but it wasn't the sort of donation anybody'd want, especially not on an altar.' She pointed down at her nether regions and mimed the word 'business'.

'Business? What, you mean someone had a shi—'

She placed a hand on my arm, to prevent me from mouthing the word.

'What's the world coming to, when people see fit to do such a thing in a church?' Iris said.

She looked up at the ceiling, before adding: 'I sometimes wonder if my Dom's not the lucky one.'

*

St Aloysius was a 1960s Brutalist affair. Thirza would have loved it. 'Young' Father O'Reardon, meanwhile, turned out to be a nervous white-haired cleric who I took to be sixty but who was in fact just forty-one. Like Tony from The Clarion, something had spun the hands forward on his body clock, and my guess was it was some form of shock or trauma. I'd seen perfectly white hair like that only once before, on my cousin, Seamus, from Armagh. Seamus was arrested by the RUC on suspicion of being an IRA bomber. After a few days' incarceration, they admitted it was a case of mistaken identity, and they duly released him, but not before kicking the bejesus out of him. The first time I'd met Seamus was when he'd visited us as a nineteen-year-old, and he'd had ink-black hair. Yet when we travelled to his wedding four years later, post-arrest, I was stunned to see that his thatch had turned snowy white.

Father O'Reardon spoke in a whisper that was even breathier and more camp than David's, so that I had to lean right in to catch anything he said, and even then I had to ask him to repeat himself more than once. I was left doubting whether even Motörhead-levels of amplification would render him audible to his congregation. And he never once made eye contact, which reinforced my suspicion that here was a man with secrets. In all, he seemed to me to be utterly ill-suited and ill-equipped for the demands of parish life. He ought to have been a librarian, in a monastery.

Father O'Reardon showed me the exact spot on the altar where the stool had been discovered, 'by slack-jawed and sickened cleaner, Bridie O'Shea', as I would write it in my front-page piece for The Probe. I also penned the line 'It was an ugly deed, in an ugly church', but Big Al edited it out, saying that parishioners would be upset enough without me having a pop at their church.

'Were there footprints on the altar cloth?' I asked Father O'Reardon, pleased with my detective-like attention to detail.

'No. Why do you ask?'

'I'm just wondering if they climbed up on the altar, or if maybe they placed the faeces there.'

'I don't see that it makes much difference either way,' he whispered at the floor, his shrug suggesting that nothing about people surprised him any longer. I imagined the Vesuvius of venial- and carnal-sin stories he must be sitting on. I bet he knows enough to fill fifty red tops for a week, I found myself thinking, not without a little envy.

'Did anyone get a photo of the offending item?' I asked, as tactfully as I was able.

'No,' he said, failing to hide his growing impatience. 'We wanted it gone as quickly as possible.'

'Of course,' I said.

I knew that the last thing on anyone's mind would have been to take a picture, but I asked anyway, just in case, because I knew that the only way this story was going to get some play was with a snap.

'Of course we didn't take a picture,' said Father O'Reardon, spitting out the words, his face like that of someone trapped in a lift with someone else's cabbage fart.

'Nah, we'll pass on that one, Llew,' the duty news-editor of The Daily Ripple told me later that day, confirming my suspicions. 'There's no pic, plus it's a one-off soiling, which means it could've just been kids, playing dare or something. If it was a serial dumper then that'd be a different story, as it'd more likely be someone with an axe to grind. Tell you what,' he added, in a more promising tone, 'if it happens at least twice more, and you can land at least one pic, then we'd definitely be interested, big time. There'll probably be some reporting shifts in it for you as well.'

Them wanting a picture I totally got but why quite why someone would need to defecate at least three times on one or more altars in order for it to be a big story I still do not fully comprehend. True, during my time as a freelance reporter on The Insider I had seen tabloid hacks apply a formula-based approach to news, but that had been for disasters. For example, the formula for guestimating the number of final fatalities in train wrecks was Official Death Toll + 25 (or 50, if two trains were involved). For sinking ships it was Death Toll + 50, while for earthquakes and other large-scale natural disasters it was Death Toll x 2 + 150. Only with plane crashes were estimated fatalities not recalibrated, because everyone nearly always dies in air accidents. It came as a surprise, then, to learn that there was also a news formula of sorts for altar defecations.

Surprised or not, I simply could not shift the news editor's dangling carrot from my field of vision. As it stood, the story was going nowhere. Possibilities spooled over and over, just beneath the surface, until one night in bed I found myself working through the logistics of placing one's excrement on an altar, at least twice, without being caught.

'It's just theoretical,' I told myself repeatedly. 'Only theoretical.'

TWENTY TWO

I ATTENDED SUNDAY MASS AT St Aloysius to case the place for security cameras. There were none; security stretched no further than a lock on the front door. Part of me had been hoping that the place was bristling with CCTV, so I could draw a veil over this madness.

Perched on a pew among the sparse congregation, I was surprised to find that I rather enjoyed being back in church, that it was a quite different experience to the interminable tedium that had blighted so many childhood Sundays. I found it restful and meditative; it's not often you get to stop for an hour a week and just think about things. I somehow managed to compartmentalise this sense of serenity, so that it wasn't contaminated by the reason I was actually in the church: to find a way to get my faeces on the altar, at least twice, without being nabbed. I'm guessing that compartmentalising is the brain's way of helping us cope when we find ourselves doing terrible things. How else could death-camp Nazis enjoy cheery, chatty evening meals in the barracks, over beer and borscht, following a day of indiscriminate slaughter?

But after I spotted Iris in the congregation, my compartmentalised constructs crumbled. My subversive presence as a bogus worshiper now felt like a mortal insult to the memory of her dead son. Having spied Iris, I twitched, fidgeted and thrummed my way through the rest of the mass, begging for it to be done, just as I had as a boy.

I wasn't the only one fidgeting. I was right about Father O'Readon: a wall of Marshall amps would have struggled to make his rumour of a voice audible in such a large space. Sitting through one of his services was like watching the telly with the volume down, which probably explained the sparseness and restlessness of his congregation. And to think the poor man had to put himself through a similar ordeal at least once a day, and three times on a Sunday. Given his almost complete lack of altarcraft, his being a priest made less sense to me, even, than the notion of Thirza working in Clintons.

After I had satisfied myself there were no security cameras, I turned my attention to the timing of my Unholy Deeds. I couldn't risk someone walking in on me – I needed to find a time when the church was open, but almost certain to be empty.

'Father, nice to see you again,' I said, shaking Father O'Readon's hand at the door on my way out of mass. He could hardly have been more surprised to see me had I been Lord Lucan. 'Listen,' I continued, 'I was wondering, what's the best time for quiet, contemplative prayer, when there's no one else around? Honestly, I'm so easily distracted. I'm little better than a child really.'

He smiled. He had a warm, gentle smile, not unlike David's. 'I think you'll find that Thursday evenings, seven to ten, should suit.'

I leaned in to hear him better.

'We stay open for any late-night shoppers who may need some solace,' he added, about an eighth of a decibel louder.

'How many do you get in on Thursday nights then, on average?'

'Oh, only a handful throughout the year but that's still a few people who might otherwise have had nowhere to go, and then ... who knows? They may have been lost souls, wandering in the night.'

I imagined myself as a suicidal Thursday-night shopper, mired in debt and laden with bags of stuff I didn't need and couldn't afford, trudging towards St Aloysius to seek deliverance from the sinful excesses of our consumer society.

'Quite,' I said.

*

The night I chose for the first Unholy Deed was unseasonably warm, for May or any other month. I rummaged through the chest of drawers in my bedroom, searching for something with a hood. All I could find was an ancient white-cotton Gary Numan hooded T-shirt, whose front was filled with a stark black-and-white depiction of an android's face. It was not exactly the low-key attire best suited to the job in hand, so I turned it inside-out, but the fabric had been worn so thin over the years that the image showed through almost as strongly. No matter; it would have to do. I yanked on a baseball cap, hooked a pair of sunglasses over my ears and pulled the hood up around my face.

I made for the large, unkempt garden at the back of our house – the old pub garden. Perched by the drain was a Tesco bag. I picked it up, opened it gingerly and then recoiled at the stench from within. I didn't think it possible for faeces to go off, but it was definitely smellier than when I had laid it in there, fresh, the previous day.

I set off, bag in hand, doing my best impression of someone carrying a pint of milk. By the time St Aloysius hoved into view, in all its carbuncular glory, I had more or less resigned myself to spending an eternity in Hell, with every despot, tyrant and dictator throughout history for company. I tugged the peak of my cap further down and pulled the hood even tighter about my face.

As I placed a foot on the first of the steps feeding into the church I heard a throaty roar from behind me, followed by an almighty CRUMP, which sent a shockwave through my already overloaded nervous system. I span around, to see that a Volvo estate had been T-boned by a Ford Sierra Cosworth at high speed. I could hear screams of pain from the male Volvo driver, whose door had been spectacularly stoved in. He must have had a shattered hip and femur at the very least, I guessed. Other onlookers, who were nearer the accident than me, were shouting at a figure who was sprinting off into the distance. The driver's door of the Cosworth was flung open; he'd done a runner. This was no surprise to me. With its low-price, high-performance engine, the Sierra RS Cosworth had become the most stolen car in automotive history. Things had gotten so bad that on The Probe we even had a 'Cosworth Corner', detailing all that week's thefts.

The incident felt unequivocally like a bad omen. I should have turned around, dumped my dump in a bin, and gone home, or down the Mow. But instead I resumed my climbing of the steps.

The church was empty and silent, its heavy wooden doors shutting out even the chaos outside. I knew I must act quickly, be decisive, or I'd bottle it. I strode up the aisle as prayerfully as possible, just in case someone came in. I even bowed before the altar, and if ever there has been a more disingenuous act of devotion in the history of worship then I can't imagine what that might be. Before stepping towards the altar, I spun through 360 degrees, scanning for any worshippers I may have missed – a god-fearing midget on his or her knees, perhaps. And then I found myself standing at the altar, unfurling the Tesco bag and tipping it up, decanting my stool on to the altar's crisp white linen. One didn't need to be a believer to know that it was truly an abomination. I wanted to pick it up and put it back in the bag but my stool was so firm and cylindrical that it had careered 18 inches across the altar, leaving light-to-moderate soiling in its wake. There was no turning back. One down, one to go. I ran back up the aisle but was careful to exit the church at a pace befitting a suicidal late-night shopper.

*

I had been expecting a call from Father O'Reardon early the following day, alerting me to the latest altar soiling. I had been very clear with him after the first incident: call me straight away should any further desecrations occur and don't move anything until we've had a chance to take a photo. But the call hadn't come until three days later.

'Mr Sabler,' Father O'Reardon said, almost inaudibly down the line, 'you asked that I call you as soon as there were any more … incidents.'

'Oh no, Father,' I said. 'Don't say you've had a repeat. How dreadful.'

'Yes, I'm afraid we have.'

'When did this happen?'

'Last night,' he said.

What? It can't have taken him three days to notice an eight-inch stool festering on his altar.

'How long do you think it's been there?' I asked, as matter-of-factly as my thudding heart would permit.

'Mrs O'Shea discovered it. She's terribly distressed. It's the fourth one she's found this week.'

I dropped the receiver, which clattered on to my typewriter's keyboard.

'You clumsy twat,' spat Thirza, forgetting our truce, and holding up a hand of apology to appease Big Al, who now had zero tolerance for any unpleasantness.

I picked up the receiver. 'I'm sorry,' I said. 'I think I must've misheard you. You didn't say you've had four such incidents this week, did you?

'Yes, I did.'

Holy shit, I thought. What's going on here? But whatever weirdness was behind it, I knew that there was now no need for me to stage a repeat performance; I had my serial dumper, and soon I'd also have a photo. I was cooking with gas.

'Don't touch anything,' I ordered him, like I was senior investigating officer on his way to a crime scene. 'I'm on my way over.'

I hung up without waiting for a reply.

'Grab your lenses, Mike,' I said. 'And a peg for your nose.'

*

'I know that you asked me to call as soon as anything happened,' said Father O'Reardon, shaking my hand, 'but after the second desecration earlier this week I had reservations. I was worried that publicity might only encourage whomever is responsible.'

'I understand,' I replied, not understanding at all. 'So why did you call?'

'Because the incidents carried on happening, one after the other, on consecutive days, and I thought that maybe your paper might help us appeal for information, to catch the culprit. They clearly need help. He might even be dangerous.'

'He?'

Father O'Reardon stalled for a couple of seconds, before putting it to me that surely a woman would never do such a thing?

'You're probably right,' I conceded, the image of my monster stool rolling across his altar replaying in my mind as I spoke. 'Will you be involving the police?'

'I'll report it, but I don't see what they can do.'

'Yeah I mean, it's not like they can identify someone from their stool, is it.'

Thank god, I thought.

'Well, quite,' he said.

The sound of whimpering softly filled the church.

'Is there a dog in here?' I asked, looking around.

'No,' said Father O'Reardon. 'That's our cleaner, Mrs O'Shea. This is the fifth time the poor woman has found the altar fouled in this way, and the fourth day in a row. I don't think she can take much more.'

'Poor Mrs O'Shea,' I said, salving my conscience by telling myself that at least I was only twenty per cent responsible for all the upset.

At that moment, Mike – who'd been parking the car – clattered into the church, slamming the heavy wooden door with such ferocity that the shockwaves were like a sonic attack. He swung his heavy camera bag over one shoulder. It struck a wooden pedestal. It wobbled, perilously, almost sending the billowing flower arrangement that it held crashing to the flagstones.

'Oi, Mike,' I called out, my voice rising to the heavens in a way Father O'Reardon's almost certainly never had. 'This isn't Fratton Park. It's a church. Have some respect.'

Mike was a Portsmouth FC nut, and he lived for match days. I had seen him parade around the perimeter of the pitch in his day-glow press bib as if he were covering the World Cup final. The thing was, being a fan he'd get engrossed in the action and so he nearly always missed the money shot. Instead of capturing Pompey's striker lashing the ball home, he'd hand us a picture of the opposition keeper picking it out of the net. But surely even Mike couldn't miss a turd on an altar.

'Father, this is Mike, our snapper,' I said, taking care of introductions.

'Snapper?'

'Sorry. Paper speak. Photographer.'

'Is a photo really necessary?' Father O'Reardon asked. 'Do people really want to see such a horror?'

'I'm afraid they do, Father,' I replied. 'People can't help themselves. I pointed to the altar and gestured for the cleric to lead the way. 'C'mon Mike, let's get this over with, so we can leave these good people in peace.'

The three of us stood in front of the altar rail, studying the altar. This latest turd was more splodge than stool, appearing to have the consistency of Angel Delight. Mike began taking pictures from where we stood.

'What are you doing?' I said, aghast. 'You can't shoot from here, for chrissake. Sorry about the cursing, Father,' I added quickly. 'I forgot where I was. Mike,' I continued, 'you've gotta get a close-up.' I nudged and prodded him nearer and nearer until he was stood behind the altar, exactly where a priest would during mass. He then started shooting down at the turd from a standing position.

'You can't shoot down at it,' I said, shaking my head. 'Get on your knees and shoot across it, so you've got the interior of the church in the background.'

I pressed my palms on his shoulders and forced him to the floor, and then arranged him so that his lens was nestling on the altar, inches from the faeces.

'Right, *now* shoot.'

He fired off a dozen or so frames, then stopped, and began making odd grunting noises. He stood, clamped one hand across his mouth and was sick through his fingers, pressure-hosing vomit across the altar, and beyond.

'Jesus Christ, Mike,' I growled in his ear. 'What's wrong with you? It's just a crap.'

'You didn't have your fricking nose right in it though, did you.'

'I'm so sorry, Father,' I called out. Mike's had a funny turn, but we're done here now, aren't we, Mike? We'll get going.'

I bade Father O'Reardon farewell, and Mike and I scuttled off up the aisle as quickly as was decent. Behind us came a shuffling of feet and then a moment later, a high-pitched cry that was laden with despair. I turned, to see Mrs O'Shea standing in front of the altar, cleaning products in hand. She was unmoving for a few seconds, but then she swooned and landed on the floor with a soft thump.

*

'Well, well, well, someone's been busy, haven't they,' The Ripple's news editor said on the other end of the phone, having read a fax of my story about the St Aloysius Serial Dumper. I'd waited for Big Al and Thirza to go home before making the call because I was worried I might look so shamefaced that they would twig something was up.

'Has this priest really got no idea who's behind it?' he asked.

'None.'

'What about the fuzz? They involved?'

'They've visited but they said with no CCTV footage there's not much they can do.'

'Something's fishy here,' he said.

'You think?'

'Yeah. I mean why the same altar? Why not five dumps on five different altars?'

It hadn't even occurred to me to place my stool on an altar in another church. I had believed one altar to be as newsworthy as the next, but I could see his point.

'I reckon someone's got it in for this priest,' he added. 'My best guess is it's payback from some altar boy he rogered years ago.'

'I can't believe that,' I said. 'If you met him you'd say the same.'

'Yeah well, these priests, they spout all that holier than thou shit, while all the time they've been shagging poor little Johnny Choirboy senseless in the vestibule.'

The journalist in me wanted to correct him by pointing out that – being an entrance hall – a vestibule would make a poor choice of venue for sexual abuse, and that he probably meant presbytery or sacristy.

'Have a dig around on this priest,' he added. 'See what you come up with. And Llew, nice work. Sounds like this yarn's got the legs to make page three, maybe even the splash. Tell you what, d'you fancy coming up on Saturdays, for reporting shifts?'

I fist-pumped the air and wheeled away from my desk in triumph – literally, on my chair, receiver still in hand, so that the phone was dragged to the floor, its bells sounding in protest.

'You alright?' the news editor asked.

'Yeah, great,' I said, like none of it was any big deal. 'Cheers.'

'OK. See you Saturday then.'

I was on my way again, and this time there would be no turning back, not for anyone or anything. Certainly not for Thirza.

TWENTY THREE

WITH RIPPLE REPORTING SHIFTS NOW in the bag I no longer needed to trawl Pompey's portside watering holes for stories, and so I began again to hit the Mow of an evening. On my first night back for a good while I found Alfred in his usual spot, perched on a barstool, his back as upright as the wall he was leaning against. As ever, the creases in his trousers were a wonder of geometric precision and he was sporting a blazer with some kind of crest on the breast pocket.

'Ah, Mr Sabler,' Alfred said, saluting, before crushing my hand in welcome. 'Thought you were MIA.'

Alfred believed it a dereliction of duty not to pulverise at least one metacarpus bone in any hand offered him. 'Limp hand, limp heart,' he'd say if anyone questioned the need for making pain an integral part of his greetings protocol.

'You look even smarter than usual, Alfred. Is that some kind of Royal Navy club?' I asked, nodding at the crest on his blazer, while massaging my crumpled hand.

'No, no, dear boy,' he said. 'River Island. Gift from the daughter. She knows I love a crest. She was born when I was off fighting in the Falklands, you know.'

'Really?' I said, having heard the story only fifty times before.

A young barmaid I had never seen before asked me what I wanted to drink. After she disappeared to serve someone in the saloon bar, on the other side of the pub, I turned to Alfred. 'No Blanche tonight?'

'Been giving herself Thursdays off for a few weeks now. Bingo she says, but we think she's got a fancy man.'

'Really?'

'Listen Llew, I've got something for you. Met with an old HMS

Broadsword oppo the other day. We were shoulder to shoulder when she was hit by Argie incoming.'

I groaned inwardly. The Broadsword attack story. Again.

'Argie shell struck the flight deck, skipped off like a stone on a pond, smashed through a Lynx chopper, exploded in the briny. No casualties. Bloody miracle. If it weren't for—'

'So who's this old friend of yours?' I cut in, whisking him away from the Falklands.

'Peter Ferguson. Navy, man and boy. Went on to skipper the Ark Royal. A1 officer. A1 chap. Left the RN some years ago. Van driver now. Can't find anything else.'

'So what's the story?'

'Applied for a job piloting the Gosport ferry. Thought he'd be a shoo-in. Didn't get it. Too experienced, they said. Damned disgrace.'

The Gosport ferry was a rusting runt of a vessel that wheezed back and forth across the mouth of Portsmouth harbour, from Pompey to Gosport. That a one-time captain of the Royal Navy's mightiest aircraft carrier was snubbed for a job skippering that decrepit old tub was a great story, and would help cement my burgeoning relationship with The Ripple. Before I had time to get too excited, Bernie the Shirt walked in, with UN Mickey at his elbow.

'Arhlrhiht, Lhuh,' said Ernie.

Like Big Al, Ernie often spoke with a lit cigarette on his lip, but unlike Big Al he had not mastered the art of doing so without sending ash down his front, and a shower of it duly tumbled from the burning tip of his Silk Cut, down into his exposed shag-pile of a chest.

'Evening gents,' I said.

'Lehzhun, Lhuh, I hayuhred uht frahm deh mihsuhs dahat dehere's dihs guhruhl ahchros de sthrit woos ruhuyt cuhlehfer, ahn as whon ah rihytin cahmpuhrteshuhrn.'

I looked to Mickey, who translated: 'Bernie says that his missus knows this clever schoolgirl what lives across the street who's won some big writing competition.'

Via Mickey, I also learned that the best way to find this prize-winning young writer was to seek out her wheelchair-using father, Rollo, who ran a reclamation business from a series of nearby garages.

I knew Rollo by sight; it was impossible not to. Three of his many garages adjoined the gable end of my house, and he was forever in and out of them. I'd see him hooking them shut with a ten-foot pole that he carried in a metal scabbard that was welded to the side of his chair. Wheeling himself about with that pole sticking up, he looked like a cross between a dodgem and a one-man trolley bus. I'd glimpsed inside those garages often enough to know the real story here was Rollo, not his daughter: yes, there were some period doors and fireplaces in those garages but most of his stock was boxed household appliances.

I thanked Alfred and Ernie for their tips, bought them a couple of drinks apiece and then told the new barmaid I wanted to pop upstairs to see David.

It had been some time since I'd visited. With all the upset of Emdel and Thirza I had rather forgotten about him. I genuinely wanted to see him, and I also needed to tell him about the little chat I'd had with Skinner's wife, Daphne.

David flung himself at me like we were lovers reunited at a train station, which made me feel even worse for having neglected him.

'What a lovely surprise, Llew. I've missed our little soirées.'

'I'm sorry it's been a while. Work's been a bit crazy lately.'

He lifted my chin with a finger and studied my face.'Are you ill? You've lost that lovely colour you used to have.'

I'd not been aware I'd ever had a lovely colour, but given the complete absence of loveliness in my life at that time, I guess it was to be expected. Me caning the sauce every night for five or six weeks as part of my marathon dockside news trawl can't have helped either.

'Listen, David, I need to talk to you about Skinner. There's been a development.'

I decided to cut to the chase, just in case he harboured any hope of inflicting two hours of top-hat-and-cane misery on me. He froze momentarily at my mention of Skinner, before gathering himself and ushering me into the living room. We sat on the sofa in front of the TV, as was our custom.

'So what is it that you have to tell me, about *him*?' he said.

I walked David through everything that had happened at Skinner's executive barbecue, although I left out the part about snorting coke with

Daphne, which had been so left-field it barely seemed real to me. He listened, open-mouthed.

'She wants to destroy him? His own wife?'

'She hates his guts, almost as much as you, and there's more. She showed me how he managed to secretly film you and Max and all those other men. The bedrooms had one-way mirrored wardrobes. They're still there.'

'How could we have been so stupid,' he said, slapping his hands on his thighs.

'You weren't to know. Say, why don't we watch a film,' I added with gusto, with no prior warning to myself.

'Oh let's.' David jumped up and slid a video from his vast library. 'I bought something especially for you,' he said, smiling and waving the box at me. 'It's The Producers. I know how you like Nazis in your musicals.'

I could have kissed him. 'Thank you.'

We watched it, and I enjoyed myself so much that it reminded me of Film Nights with Thirza and Emdel. A grief-like sadness consumed me at the memory.

'Even I don't cry during The Producers, dear,' David said, patting my hand.

We laughed, and he dabbed at my tears with a tissue, just as the drink-up bell sounded downstairs

'I'd best be off,' I said, standing. 'Tonight was great. Give my best to Blanche. I was sorry to miss her.'

'Did you know she's found someone?'

'Yeah, Albert downstairs said she's got some fancy man on the go. I'm pleased for her.'

'Fancy woman, you mean.'

'You're kidding? Blanche? Fair play to her I suppose, but how d'you know it's a woman?'

'I hear them at night, on Thursdays, in Blanche's bedroom, and they're definitely not male noises. I don't know who she is because she's always gone by the time I've woken up on Friday morning. I think Blanche is building up the courage to tell me. I really don't know why on earth she'd worry about telling an old queen like me such a thing.'

A smiling David wrapped me up in another hug, and I promised I'd drop by every week from then on, like before. On my way out of the pub I tipped an imaginary hat to Alfred, Bernie and Mickey.

'Night gents. I'm off for a Chinese.'

'Can't eat that foreign muck,' Alfred said. 'Meat-and-two man. That's me.'

I headed across the road to the Sellars Chinese Take Away. Its peculiar Occidental name was explained by a blue plaque on the wall, declaring that Inspector Clouseau himself, Peter Sellars, had been born in the building. With four pubs nearby, it was always busy and I took my place at the back of a scrum of customers at the counter. It was gone midnight by the time I was served. I had the door half open when I spied Blanche, about twenty-five yards up the street, on the opposite side, walking towards the Mow. She was laughing and arm-in-arm with another women. I slipped back inside the shop and kept a bead on them, determined to get a look at Blanche's mystery woman. It was fresh outside, and Sellars' windows were fogged up, so it wasn't until they were standing almost opposite that I got a good look at her. I dropped my carrier bag of food to the floor. It was Thirza.

*

As I was walking home from work the following day, a hand grabbed a fistful of my jacket from behind and stopped me in my tracks. I swung around, to be faced with Thirza.

'What the fuck were you looking at today?'

'What?'

'You were looking at me weird all day. What's your beef now?'

'I think you're getting paranoid, Thirza.'

'And stop calling me fucking Thirza.'

'What d'you want me to call you?'

'Nothing. Now tell me, why were you looking at me all strange today?'

What was I to say? Ask whether Emdel knew she was batting for the other side? Enquire as to whether her dalliance with Blanche meant she'd split with Emdel, and if so, if there was a homeopathically small chance she and I might get together someday? Tell her that I wouldn't mind sharing her with Blanche, if that offer was ever on the table?

'I saw you last night, with Blanche,' I said, choosing the plain truth for once. 'I was just surprised, that's all. That's probably what you saw in my face today.'

'Well you can fuck right off with your surprise. And what of it anyway? I went out with Blanche. So fucking what?'

'I was with David last night,' I continued. 'He told me all about Blanche's Thursday night trysts.'

Having selected the truth, I now brandished it, with the carefully chosen tabloid noun, 'tryst', providing a cutting edge. She grabbed two fistfuls of my top and yanked me towards her, so we were nose to nose.

'That's none of your fucking business.' She threw me backwards. 'Nothing I do is any of your business.'

'You're the one who grabbed me, twice now, else I'd be walking home, minding my own business. You can't have it both ways, Thirza.'

'I told you to stop calling me that.'

'Don't worry, Thirza. Your secret's safe with me, Thirza. See you tomorrow, Thirza. Give my worst to Emdel, if you haven't already chucked him for Blanche. Thirza.'

I walked off, eyes clenched, bracing for impact – fully expecting to be chopped down from behind by some kind of street-fighting move. Instead the assault was verbal, yet no less shocking.

'I hate your fucking guts to fuck. I hope you get cancer and fucking well die.'

TWENTY FOUR

Rollo was just about the easiest man in Southsea to locate, what with him being forever in and out of his countless garages. These were located throughout the Metal Estate, so-called because its roads were named after metals, both precious and base. I lived on a podium-finish street: Silver. The estate comprised low-rise post-war flats, most of which had a garage each, which were ranged in long rows of up to a dozen. The tradition was for residents to paint their garage door a bright colour, giving them the air of giant beach huts and lending the area a strong maritime feel.

As far as I could tell, Rollo seemed to own at least half of all the Metal Estate garages and, predictably enough, I found him in the open mouth of one of them, down at the end of Steel Street. The moment he saw me approaching, he hurried to hook shut the door, leaving me to wonder how he ever achieved anything, legal or illegal, if he had to do this every time anyone happened to wander past. The door clanged shut, but not before I glimpsed a large-screen CRT TV, still in its box, perched behind a period fireplace.

'Er, excuse me. Rollo, isn't it?'

He spun his wheelchair around with practised ease. Almost in the same movement he sheathed his long wooden pole in its scabbard – a sawn-off scaffolding tube. The pole had a brass tilde-shaped hook on one end, and I recognised it as being the same as those used in my primary school, to hook shut high windows in the assembly hall. He was wearing a loose-fitting shirt, whose bagginess didn't hide his heavily muscled torso, just as sweatshirts failed to mask the scale of Thirza's breasts. His pipe-cleaner legs were incongruously thin in the context of his upper body, like Pinocchio legs on an Action Man. I thought him handsome, in a dishevelled, swarthy kind of way. Unlike most men who had a billowing moustache and shoulder-length hair, he didn't look like a 1970s German porn star, although I suspect the wheelchair might have had something to do with that.

'And you are?'

His accent sat somewhere between Cornwall and London, like Pompey itself.

'I'm from The Probe.'

'Hang on a minute, aren't you that geezer what nearly killed his work experience girl?'

'Yeah, well—'

'And what upset all those devil dodgers, by wanking in Santa's grotto?'

' What? Wanking? No, I—'

'I laughed my sodding arse off about that, I did.' He began laughing his sodding arse off all over again, slapping his Pinocchio thighs with both hands. 'Oh man,' he added, wiping his eyes, 'you're a piece of work and-a-half you are.'

I was speechless. My misdeeds that day had been all over The Tribune, for chrissake. It was a matter of public record. Maybe he'd confused me with Bob-from-Circulation's Santa, the one from Gosport, just across the water, who'd been banged up for getting over-familiar with young children. Whatever, my dignity was in shreds, and so I moved things along as quickly as possible by explaining why I had sought him out.

'Lucy's not even fifteen,' he answered, beaming, 'yet she's already twice as smart as me. D'you know, over five-hundred schoolkids from across Hampshire entered that writing competition, but she won it.'

My own folks' parental pride at my meagre achievements thus far in life was wan and feeble compared to Rollo's in Lucy; it lit up his face like an arc lamp.

'Must've got it from her mother,' he added. His expression cooled all of a sudden. 'I've seen you around,' he said, wagging a finger. 'You're always skulking about the place.'

Skulking? I lived a one-minute walk from where I stood, my place of work was a five-minute stroll and my local was two-hundred yards up the road. What was I meant to do? Fly?

'Yeah, that's me,' I answered, taking the path of least resistance. There was clearly no winning with this man.

'You live in the old pub on Silver Street, right?'

'Yeah.'

'The William the Conqueror,' he said, 'though everyone round here knew it as the Old Bill. Lovely old boozer it was. Say, is the cellar still in commission?'

I thought that an odd question, but told him that, yes, it was.

'D'you know, I was the cellarman there for a time, before this happened.' He slapped the back of a hand on one of his wheelchair tyres. 'Tell me, is it empty, the cellar?'

I thought that even odder. 'Kind of,' I said, electing not to mention the mountain of pornography I had helped Emdel lump down there. 'Getting back to your daughter,' I added, 'd'you mind if I interview her for a piece in The Probe?'

'Long as you don't dress her up as a mermaid.'

I forced myself to laugh along with him. 'We'd also need a picture of her, with you and the rest of the family.'

'No problem. Swing by about five. Lucy'll be back from school by then. D'you want her in uniform?'

His carelessly chosen words punched up images of his daughter making sexual advances, in pigtails, wearing nothing but skimpy underwear and a school blazer.

'Yes please,' I said.

'It's Flat 8a, Copper Street. See you at five.'

*

Rollo ushered Mike and me into his ground-floor flat. We had to squeeze past a pile of boxed stereo systems in the hallway. At the kitchen table sat a woman in her early sixties who had to be Rollo's mum, because they shared the same intense brown eyes. She was jaundiced and terribly drawn. I fought the temptation to winkle-out the truth of her illness.

'This is my ma, Aggie,' Rollo confirmed. 'She still keeps me in line, don't you, Ma?'

'Don't you listen to him,' Aggie said, taking my hand. 'He's always been a good boy, my Rollo.'

'So where's Lucy?' I asked.

'Putting on some war paint for the photo,' said Aggie. 'You know what girls are like. Lucy,' she called. 'They're here.'

In strode a girl-woman whose age might've been anything between fifteen and twenty-one. Like Thirza, she was a shampoo-ad brunette with fair skin, only her lips were thinner than Thirza's. Her fullest features were her eyes, which were chocolaty and deep. They must be her mother's, I guessed, for they were quite unlike those of her father and grandmother. I thought her stunning. Rollo took care of introductions.

He trundled towards Lucy and took one of her hands in his.

'Beautiful, ain't she.'

She smiled and playfully pushed his chair away.

'Stop embarrassing me, Daddy.'

'Llew,' Mike said, 'can I take my pics before you do the words? I've got that sex-swap Tory councillor to do at six.'

'It's always the bloody Tories, ain't it,' chimed Aggie, who had her back to us, pouring tea, the knobbles of her spine poking through the thin cotton top she wore. 'Bunch of bloody perverts.'

'So which way'd they go?' asked Rollo. 'Bird to bloke or the other way round?'

'Bloke to bird,' I said, mirroring his lingo. 'And for the record, his wife's standing by him.'

'Not for long, she won't,' said Aggie, 'I'd put money on it.'

(She should have because sex-swap Tory's wife would bin him a week later, days after I flogged the story to The Ripple.)

'Go on then, Mike,' I said. 'Shoot away.'

'Right, where's mum?' Mike asked, looking cheerfully from Lucy to Rollo to Aggie. Mike's bonhomie drained, as the trio fell silent and eyed the floor.

'Um, there's just the three of us, actually,' said Rollo, looking up.

Blushing, Mike finessed the trio into layout-friendly portrait and landscape compositions, as Big Al had taught him. As he was finishing up, the doorbell sounded. Rollo excused himself and trundled out. Muffled exchanges drifted in from the hall. The only words I caught were 'fridge freezer'. He returned to the kitchen, but it was just minutes before the doorbell was again chiming. This time I caught the word 'microwave'.

With photos over, Lucy led me to the living room where the walls were lined with almost as many books as David had videos. The light was much better in here than in the kitchen. Typical Mike, I thought, not doing his homework.

'You like books, I see.'

She offered an easy smile.

'How'd you guess?'

'Are they all yours?'

'Some are Dad's, the crappy ones anyway.'

Her laugh was pure, like sea air.

'Maybe you'll have your own book on these shelves one day, Lucy. So tell me about your prize-winning story.'

After fifteen minutes' Q&A I had what I needed. Except that I didn't. What I really wanted was the inside track on Rollo and his garages, but I knew I'd have to tread carefully on that one – almost as carefully as with Skinner, maybe. Rollo might be stuck in a wheelchair, with legs like pipe cleaners, but he had the air of a man who could take care of business, if needs be.

TWENTY FIVE

The front door opened, and was slammed shut so hard it rattled the sash windows in my bedroom. It was a Thursday night, around nine. Emdel was back, and I didn't need to ask why, although I knew I would; I'd been looking forward to it.

I stepped out of my bedroom and into the hall, in time to catch him before he escaped into the sanctity of his bedroom. He had on the same maroon sweater and ill-fitting jeans combo he always wore, and he was as short, plump, bald, bespectacled and professorial as ever. And yet he was somehow changed. I think it was the eyes. It's always the eyes.

I leaned against the wall, arms folded.

'Well?' I said.

'Well what?' he answered, without looking my way.

'I'm asking if you are well.'

I hadn't been, but I decided to have a little sport with him – throw him off balance, before hitting him with the Blanche curve-ball.

'No, I'm not well.'

'Hey,' I said, jocular now, 'I saw something interesting the other day.'

He had unlocked his bedroom door and was about to close it behind him, when I went all double-glazing salesman on him, and jammed a foot inside the door.

'So how are things with Thirza?' I asked through the gap. 'That bedsit of hers must be pretty cramped, as love nests go.'

Emdel lunged at the door, shoulder first, and had I not been wearing my ox-blood eleven-hole Doc Martin boots he might have broken my foot. As it was, the door bounced off the thick rubber sole. I poured all the recent hurt and anger into the kick I aimed at the door, which flew open and sent Emdel flying backwards. His feet became entangled in the maroon sweater that was still on the floor, from when he'd fled with such indecent haste, and he tumbled to the carpet. I strode in, and loomed over him.

'Come home for more clothes, Einstein, or are you back for good? My money's on back for good.'

'Get out,' he said, his face flushed with indignation.

He was half up when I gave him a shove to send him back down, and this time I leaned in close enough to smell the fabric conditioner on his clothes – the same creamy-scented brand that Thirza used, I noted, jealousy picking at my seams.

'You even smell of her.'

'Get out,' he growled, through lockjaw-tight lips. 'I won't ask again.' His face now had a similar hue to his jumpers. If it had been a cartoon, jets of steam would have been shooting from his ears.

'D'you wanna know what I saw the other night?' I said. 'I know how you love your red-hot girl-on-girl action, so you're gonna love this.'

He threw everything into getting to his feet but once more I shoved him back to the floor.

'I saw your beloved Thirza, arm-in-arm with Blanche, on their way back to the Mow, for a night of muff diving. Who'd've believed it? You wait all those years for your first-ever girlfriend, only to find out she's a dyke. It's priceless. It's funnier, even, than Glenn going to bed with a geezer.'

I forced a pantomime laugh. That did it. He became a blur of limbs, kicking and swinging punches. An explosion of pain and flashing lights filled my head as one of his blows crunched into my cheekbone. It dumped me on my backside. Emdel sprang to his feet and snapped a kick into my chest, sucking the air from me and putting me flat on the floor. His pressed a foot hard into my sternum so that the heel of his Tuf utility shoe drew a crunch from my rib gristle.

'I could kill you right now,' he hissed.

The taste of iron filled my mouth, and I spat blood on to his carpet, as much for dramatic effect as anything.

'You already killed me, when you got together with Thirza.'

'Give over. You sound like you're in some soap opera. I didn't even know you liked her,' he added after a pause, easing back the pressure on my chest a tad.

'Liked her? I loved her. I still love her.'

Did I? Really? It felt true enough as I spoke the words. Like I say: love should carry a Surgeon General's health warning.

'If you were a real friend,' I said, 'then you'd've known I loved her, but you were so wrapped up in yourself you couldn't see it.'

'It's you who's wrapped up in himself, not me,' he said, his pointing index finger aquiver. 'Thirza's right: you are pathetic.'

A primordial anger rose up in me from the swampy depths. I swept his standing leg from under him with an expansive kick. He crumpled on top of me, then rolled off, so that we wound up facing one another on the floor. In falling, an arm of his glasses had broken off, so that they sat on his face at a crazy Eric Morecambe-like angle. Our eyes met for a second, before he closed his. I studied him, watching his tears spill sideways down into the carpet. The sight of him crying, glasses askew, doused my anger, until I looking upon my old friend, vulnerable and in pain. I reached out a hand and laid it on his shoulder.

'I'm sorry,' I said, softly.

He nodded. I kept my hand on his shoulder until he had cried himself out. I thought he would never stop.

*

The newly emptied bottle of Jack Daniels lay on its side on the floor. We were sitting on his bedroom floor opposite one another, me with my back to the wall, him propped up against the chest of drawers. We'd started talking about Thirza when the bottle had been full and were still talking about her now it was empty. Eventually, I summoned the courage to ask him about Thirza's thing with Blanche.

'David said Thirza has been spending Thursday nights with Blanche for a while now. Did you know where she was?'

'No.'

'Did she not say where she'd been?'

'She didn't need to. About a month ago she told me that she wanted some space, one night a week to herself, and we agreed that on Thursdays I'd stay at Glen's.'

So he hadn't been staying at Glen's, as he'd claimed in his note. He'd been with Thirza the whole time. I let it go. 'And you didn't suspect anything?'

'You know how cramped her gaff is,' he said 'It's not really meant for two people. It seemed reasonable, so I took her at her word.'

'So how did you find out?'

'She told me.'

'What, just like that?'

'Pretty much. She sat me down a couple of nights ago and started talking about how confused she was.'

'What, you mean sexually confused?'

'Yeah. She said she'd liked Blanche for ages, back before I even arrived in Portsmouth, but that she hadn't known what to do about it. I couldn't make any sense of it. I asked her why she'd got together with me in the first place if she knew she had feelings for another woman.'

'And what did she say to that?'

'That she liked me a lot and that she'd wanted to give men one last try, in case she might be wrong about liking women.'

'What, you mean you were some kind of experiment?'

I hadn't meant it to sound unkind, like that.

'Kind of, I s'pose.'

Sadness sucked a little more from Emdel. He was wretched to his marrow.

'Jesus Christ,' I said. 'What a bitch. How could she do that to you?'

'She's not a bitch. Don't call her that. She was just very confused.'

'She didn't look confused when I saw her with Blanche.'

'How come you're angrier about this Blanche thing than me. Why is that?'

'Am I? I dunno. Anger's all her and me have left for each other. She actually hates me.'

'You're an idiot if you think that.'

'What d'you mean?'

'She doesn't hate you.'

'She wants me to die of cancer. She said that.'

'She didn't mean it. You told her your friendship with her was dead. D'you have any idea how much that broke her up?'

'She's doesn't seem very broken up.'

'She's hiding it, you fool.'

'You think?'

'I know. We talked about you all the bloody time, until I was sick of the sound of your name. Most days she'd come home from work seething at something you'd said or done, and sometimes she'd be crying.'

'Crying? Are you sure?'

'Of course I'm sure.'

'But it's like you're describing a different person. I can't imagine her crying over anything, and certainly not over me.'

'Then you don't know her anything like as well as you think, just like I don't.'

'D'you reckon it's fixable, our friendship?'

'Whose friendship?' Emdel asked. 'Yours and hers, mine and hers, or yours and mine?'

'Er, all of them, I guess.'

Emdel shrugged. 'Well, we're talking now aren't we, so that's a start. And listen, I'm sorry – you know, about Thirza. I did know you loved her.'

'You did?'

'Of course I did. Everyone did, it was impossible not to. Even Bernie the Shirt knew, and he's so pissed most of the time he can barely stand.'

'But if you knew, why did you—'

'I was a twenty-two-year-old virgin. I'd never even had one lousy kiss, for God's sake, and then along comes this beautiful girl and tells me she wants to be with me. What would you have done in my place? Turn her down? It's all right for you, you've had tons of women. You've had four since I've been down here, and they're just the ones I know about.'

It had been six, actually: two Portsmouth Polytechnic students (not at the same time, I might add); a student nurse; a naval wife, whose husband was away in the Adriatic; a foreign-exchange student; and also, ahem, Fran the Mermaid, after we bonded following her near-death experience.

'Yeah, but that was all about sex,' I said. 'That's different. With Thirza, it's love.'

'Well for me it was both. You try going twenty-two years with no leg-over.'

I could see his point.

'Okay,' I said. 'I kind of understand now. D'you think we'll be able to put this Thirza business behind us, you and me?'

We let that question linger for a moment or two, as if expecting an answer to come drifting through the ether.

'I hope so,' he said, 'but if we both still love her then it's gonna be complicated.'

I got to my feet, purposefully.

'I think what you and me need is a project,' I said, with far more conviction than I felt. 'Something we can get into together.'

'Like the sandpit?' he said. 'At school.'

'Yeah, exactly like the sandpit.'

Emdel had a faraway look in his eye, as if he were constructing imaginary motte and bailey sandcastles with me.

'Let's talk it over in the pub,' he suggested, returning to the now. 'Although not the Mow, for obvious reasons.'

'I'm pretty pissed as it is, but all right, you're on.'

In the pub, we chattered over-eagerly about nothing in particular. I think we were afraid that silence might cause the green shoots of our reconciliation to freeze, wilt and perish, and so we insulated them with layer upon layer of verbiage, as men are wont to do.

Later in bed, I lay awake half the night, thinking about what Emdel had said about Thirza being unknown to both of us. When I awoke the following morning, it was in the knowledge that I had been in love with a shadow, an echo, a stranger.

TWENTY SIX

It wasn't long before Emdel and I found a shared interest to help us re-establish our relationship: alcohol, consumed in vast qualities, mostly at home, usually with a spliff, while watching crap TV and films. Emdel didn't suffer with hangovers but I did, big time, and when the doorbell sounded one Saturday morning, I was hunched over the toilet bowl, evacuating the previous night's kofta kebab.

'It's someone for you,' Emdel said, calling through the bathroom door. 'You might wanna rinse your mouth out. She's a bit of a looker. Young, though.'

'What's her name?'

'I didn't ask.'

'Well, can you?'

'Hang on.'

'What's your name?' I heard him call down the hallway. 'Lucy,' came his reply. 'Said you interviewed her a while back, about her winning some writing prize or other.'

Lucy? What the hell did she want?

'You coming out or what?' Emdel asked. 'She's in your bedroom, waiting.'

'My bedroom? What's she doing there?'

'I showed her in.'

For a near-genius, Emdel could be pretty dumb sometimes. Why show a schoolgirl into my bedroom? For want of any mouthwash, I had a quick gargle with some water and toothpaste.

'Hello,' I said, entering my room and wiping a dribble of Aquafresh from my chops. Lucy was sitting on the bed, testing its springs. She smiled at me. 'Come into the living room,' I added, beckoning her to join me. 'It's more comfortable in there.'

She patted the mattress. 'This seems pretty comfortable to me.'

Jesus Christ, I had Lolita perched on my bed. Rollo might be in a wheelchair but if he suspected – even for a nanosecond – that there was anything going on between me and his daughter, I just knew he'd somehow rediscover the use of his Pinocchio legs and kick my arse from one side of Pompey to the other.

'Yeah, well, you haven't lived 'til you've tried our sofa,' I said, with forced levity, before making for the living room regardless. Mercifully, she followed me.

'You look terrible,' she said. 'Even worse than your mate.'

'We had a big night.' Every night was a big night.

She gave the sofa a couple of test bounces. 'This isn't as comfortable as your bed at all.'

Enough, I decided.

'What are you here, Lucy? Does your dad even know about it?'

Her coquettish nonsense fell away. She rubbed the back of her head and gave a little cough. 'I came because I need to tell you something.'

'Tell me what?'

'Who my daddy really is.'

'And why would you want to do that?'

'Because when you came over to interview me, I could see that you think he's nothing more than a common crook. You think he's scum.'

'No, hang on, that's not—

'Just listen,' she said, with one palm raised for emphasis.

So I did, and long before she had finished talking, I knew that it was the best story I'd never be able to publish – not if I wanted to carry on breathing, that is.

*

Rollo and Sheila, Lucy's mother, had both grown up on the Metal Estate. They had been school sweethearts and had wed young. Sheila and Rollo put their name down for a flat, and in the meantime lived with Rollo's mother, Aggie, following the death of Rollo's father from brain cancer some years earlier. Rollo and Sheila had Lucy in 1978, and while life in those early years was cramped and basic, the newlyweds had been happy enough.

After leaving school at sixteen, Rollo had taken a job in demolition. One thing that had surprised him about the business was just how little was recycled from the Victorian and Georgian residential and commercial properties that he helped dismantle. The only items salvaged were cast-iron radiators, for their scrap value. Everything else – fireplaces, doors, mouldings, floorboards and fixtures and fittings – ended up in landfill. Rollo, seeing value in all this other stuff, sought permission from his employer to salvage some of it on his own time, prior to demolition. He got the green light, and every few weeks he would rent a van, remove the best period features and ferry the stuff back to the Metal Estate, where he'd store it in Aggie's garage. He advertised in the Classifieds section of the local press, and was surprised at how quickly he was able to sell his stock.

Then came the property boom of the late 1980s, when house prices soared by a quarter, year-on-year. The country went renovation crazy, and as fast as Rollo could fill his mother's garage with old doors and fireplaces, people snapped them up, happy to pay ridiculous prices. So Rollo cranked things up. He invested in his own Ford Transit and set about removing tons more features. Needing more storage space, he began renting garages from neighbours, many of whom were carless. Within six months he had nine garages full of stock, and was making enough money to quit his demolition job. A year on, he had sixteen garages, and he and Sheila planned to buy their own Metal Estate flat, thanks to Thatcher's council-house sell-off scheme. They could also afford nice things for Lucy, and Rollo even took the family, including Aggie, on their first-ever foreign holiday, to Spain.

But then the accident happened. Paralytic after celebrating a friend's twenty-first birthday, Rollo toppled from the balcony of Aggie's first-floor flat. He landed back first on a low brick wall and was left paralysed from the waist down. He spent two months in Stoke Mandeville Hospital.

In his absence, Aggie kept the reclamation business ticking over and, upon his return home, helped him run it. For a little while, demand for stock held firm, but then the property bubble burst in early 1990, and house prices plummeted. The renovation craze died a death, and demand for old fireplaces and doors fell off a cliff. Almost overnight, Rollo's money dried up. He found himself not only wheelchair-bound and jobless, but also living in a country in deep recession. Rollo and Sheila's sole income was his disability benefit, so Sheila took on two cleaning jobs, and barely saw her daughter any longer. Their one stroke of fortune was that his neighbours waived their right to rent, even though their garages were rammed with Rollo's unsaleable period features

But it wasn't enough. Rollo began drinking heavily, and his relationship with his wife disintegrated. Sheila – always prone to depression – sank into a pit of despair that she was unable to escape. It had been Lucy, then aged twelve, who had found her mother, stone-cold in a bath of crimson water.

Aggie had picked up the pieces afterwards. She cared for her granddaughter and helped her son quit drinking. But even sober, and back on some kind of even keel following his wife's suicide, Rollo still faced the grim prospect of a life on benefits. It was at this point that he first considered turning to crime.

He had an old school friend, Jimmy, who had gone off the rails, and Rollo grilled him about how much money there was to be had from buying and selling stolen goods, so-called 'fencing'. Jimmy assured him that he could make a fortune – that all he needed was some 'up-front cash' to buy his first consignment of goods. If he could manage that, then Jimmy would take care of the rest.

From the outset Rollo decided he would be open with his mother, and so he talked things over with her, not believing for a moment that she would think his plans anything other than pure folly. But she hadn't. Instead, Aggie offered him her life savings of eleven thousand pounds, to buy his first consignment of stolen goods. When Rollo reminded his mother that he would be running the very real risk of imprisonment, she told him that with no hope of employment he was effectively serving a life sentence anyway, and assured him she would care for Lucy were he to be jailed.

Aggie not only bankrolled Rollo's career in crime but she also cracked his biggest problem: storage. In order to make law-breaking financially worthwhile, Rollo would need more than a single garage. But this was no reclamation business; those who agreed to store stolen goods in their garage would be accessories. They needed to tread carefully, so Aggie began by approaching a few neighbours she knew they could trust, and who also needed the money. She paid them well, to reflect the risk they'd be taking by harbouring stolen goods. Word spread, and things grew from there.

Within a year, Rollo was operating out of fifteen garages, each rammed with hooky white goods and consumer electronics. For one golden year, he was doing more business than the local branches of Currys and Comet combined.

On the risk front, Rollo had an important factor working in his favour: because of his reclamation business, he was already known to police as someone who traded out of the Metal Estate garages. Back in his reclamation heyday, he had been dogged by suspicious coppers, but because his paperwork had always been in order, they ended up leaving him in peace. Just as important, Rollo also had fifteen pairs of watchful eyes and twitching ears at his disposal; his neighbours were as keen as him to keep his operation off the police radar.

But as Rollo's star had once again been on the rise, the recession began to cut bone-deep. Unemployment and the cost of living both soared, and demand for his stolen goods fell off the same cliff as his reclaimed stock. All of his money was tied up in microwaves, fridges, freezers, cookers and stereos that he couldn't sell, and yet still he had to pay rent on the garages because the owners were running the same risk of arrest whether he sold anything or not.

And so Rollo visited his garage owners one by one, asking if they would take payment in kind, in the form of goods. They all agreed. Most were feeling the pinch and could ill-afford to replace broken or worn-out fridges, freezers and ovens.

Word soon spread around the Metal Estate that Rollo was doling out household appliances on tick, and before long a steady stream of people began calling on him. Aggie and Rollo decided they would give them whatever they needed, on trust, asking only that they pay them back whatever they could afford, whenever they could afford it. People had been as good as their word; Lucy told me that on some days, up to a dozen envelopes containing cash would drop through the letterbox of their flat – a fiver here, a tenner there.

Her story told, Lucy leaned back into the sofa, gauging my reaction to learning I had unknowingly been living slap-bang in the middle of a black-market welfare state, built on crime, trust and goodwill.

'So you see,' she said, 'he's not a criminal at all.'

Tell that to the cops, I thought, while nodding.

'And please,' she added, prayerful palms reinforcing her imploring tone, 'don't tell Daddy about any of this. He'd go mad if he knew I'd told you all his secrets.'

'Don't worry,' I said, with a wink. 'You can trust me. I'm a journalist.'

She just laughed. Can you believe that?

TWENTY SEVEN

A COUPLE OF WEEKS AFTER Lucy's visit, there was a thumping on my front door that sounded like a police raid. I opened it to find Rollo outside.

Jesus Christ, I thought, has he found out about Lucy coming over? Is he here to teach me the wronged-daddy of all lessons?

'Sorry about the noise,' he said. 'Can't reach the door knocker. Bloody thing,' he added, slapping his wheelchair.

I was relieved to see he hadn't rediscovered the use of his legs, and that he'd not be kicking my arse from one end of Pompey to the other.

'Can I come in?' he asked. 'I wanna chat to you about something.'

He spun his chair around and asked me to haul him up the doorstep. It seemed I had little choice. Once inside the house, he wheeled himself into my bedroom, without so much as a by your leave.

'Well, well, well,' he said, shaking his head. 'The Old Bill saloon bar. It's like stepping back in time. My old man used to bring me here on Sundays when Ma was cooking the roast. That was before he got sick, mind. I'd sit over there in the corner, between your bed and that dirty big cactus. Me and my old schoolmate Jimmy'd play shove ha'penny, while our old men got tanked.'

He wheeled himself towards my cylindropuntia bigelovii, a member of the cholla family of cacti, which stood in a pot near my bed. It was about the same height as the seated Rollo. I'd been growing it for nine years, and it went everywhere with me. (I didn't trust Mum not to kill it with over-watering. This was a woman who could over-water a pond lily.)

Rollo wheeled himself towards the cactus and reached out a hand to touch it.

'Easy,' I warned him.

'It looks harmless enough,' he said, shrugging. 'It's covered in fur.'

'That's not fur, those are thousands of tiny spines. Watch this.'

I picked up a T-shirt from the pile of unwashed clothes I was saving up for my Sunday afternoon trip to the Wash 'N Go Launderette. I brushed the T-shirt against the cactus and an offshoot came away, stuck fast to the cotton. I held it up for Rollo's inspection.

'This cactus is nicknamed the Teddy Bear Cholla because it's furry and seems harmless, but you don't want to be cuddling this sucker, believe me, not unless you want half a pound of it stuck to your face. It's got spines that hook into skin, and they hurt like hell.'

'How d'you get into cactuses, then?'

I fought the urge to correct him, by saying 'cacti'. Not everyone appreciates having their conversations sub-edited.

'Spaghetti westerns. Me and my dad watched them all. It was the first time I'd ever seen cacti. I thought they were incredible. Still do. So what was it you wanted to talk to me about?'

'Your cellar.'

'My cellar?'

'If memory serves, the cellar hatch is in this room some place, right?'

What was it with him and my cellar? He'd mentioned it a couple of times when I'd first approached him about interviewing Lucy. 'You're parked on it,' I said, pointing. 'It's under the rug.'

'Would you rent it to me?'

'The rug?'

'No, you muppet. The cellar.'

The old ones are the best.

'What d'you want my cellar for?'

'Storage.'

'Storage? If people round here know just one thing about you it's that you're not short of storage space, so why on earth would you want to rent my cellar?'

'I'm looking to take delivery of something that can't go in the garages.'

'Which is?'

'You're a journalist,' he said, inching his chair towards me. 'So tell me, Mr Reporter, what d'you think I use those garages for?'

What the hell's his game here? Best play a straight bat. 'That's none of my business.'

'I ain't buying that, son. I saw the way you eyeballed me when you came round to talk to my Lucy. You were like some dog slavering over a big juicy bone.'

He was pointing at me now, and he rolled himself another quarter wheel-turn closer.

'Hang on a goddamn second,' I said, backing away. 'You invite yourself into my house and then start threatening me?'

'Who's threatening you?'

I walked to the door and opened it wider. 'You can leave.'

'All right, all right, calm down will you. Maybe I got off on the wrong foot.'

The part of me that has security clearance to press the self-destruct button dared me to quip, 'The wrong wheel, you mean,' but happily I ignored it.

'Look, what I came round here to say was that although you work for the papers, I trust you.'

'You do?'

Somehow, I had managed to sound surprised at his declaration of trust, rather than confused, which was what I actually was.

'Yeah. You've an honest face.'

'Look, this is all very nice, about you trusting me and all, but where's this leading?'

'Down your cellar, hopefully.'

'All right, out with it. What d'you want my cellar for?'

'Well, here's the thing, Llew …'

So it's Llew now, is it?

'… the recession's killing me. I need to branch out into something that's slump proof, just to tide me over, like, just 'til things pick up.'

'Slump proof,' I parroted.

'Yeah. Like funeral homes,' Rollo offered. 'The worse things get for us, the better things get for them.'

'You want to stash stolen coffins down my cellar?'

'No, you dope, that was just an example. Porn, that's what I'm talking about. The wanking sector. Porn's about as slump-proof as it gets. In fact, the shittier life is, the more us fellas wanna buff the old helmet, 'cos it's an escape, like, ain't it.'

I scratched my head. 'Er, yeah, well here's the thing, and you're not gonna believe this, but you know our cellar, well it's sort of already half full of porn.'

'What? You're fucking kidding me. Whose?'

'It's my housemate's.'

'Can I take a butcher's?'

I asked him to wheel himself off the rug, then I peeled it back to reveal the cellar hatch. I unlatched it and swung it back, then climbed in, to turn on the lights.

'D'you need a hand getting down?' I called up to him.

'Fuck off do I.'

With impressive upper-body strength, Rollo lowered himself backwards down the steps, his Cuban-heeled boots clopping uselessly on each one. At the bottom he plonked himself on the concrete floor and cast an eye about the place.

'Holy fucking schmoley,' he said, prefacing this with a whistle. 'All this belongs to your little mate?'

'Yeah, but he wants rid.'

'You mean he's selling?'

I nodded. 'He was thinking of advertising it as a job lot but isn't sure how to go about it.'

'Is he in, your mate?'

'Yeah.'

'Go tell him he's got a buyer.'

I fetched Emdel, first briefing him about everything Rollo had said.

After some too-ing and fro-ing, Emdel agreed to sell his porn to Rollo for £1,900, a rate of £100 per crate. He had wanted double that sum but Rollo said that his sweaty mitts had been all over it and that half the magazines were probably glued together and loads of the videos likely worn out, and that he could take it or leave it.

'Right,' Rollo said, rubbing his hands together after sealing the deal, 'let's get down to business. I'll pay you fifty nicker a month for your cellar, apiece.'

'Yeah, see, we had a word about this upstairs,' said Emdel. 'Before we agree to anything, we wanna know where this porn of yours is coming from.'

'You don't ask them sort of questions, son,' Rollo said, wagging a finger.

'We do if it's going down our cellar,' we chorused.

Rollo sighed. 'Oh for fuck's sake, all right then. It's coming from down Bristol way, some private shop what's been knocked off. I wouldn't touch it if it was local. The only porn shop I know of round here's owned by John Skinner, and I don't want nothin' to do with him. Happy now?'

'You know Skinner?' I said.

'Course I know Skinner. He's a bigger crook than me. He offered me a load of hardcore years ago, nasty stuff, the sort that's illegal here. I turned him down. He's some kind of psycho, that bloke. So, are you in?'

'I still don't get why you can't store the porn in your garages,' I said. 'Why does it have to come down here? What aren't you telling us?'

Rollo shook his head. 'You're a right skittish pair of fuckers, aren't yer?

He went on to explain that the reason he couldn't use the garages was that they were baking hot in summer and freezing cold in winter, and that the magazines and videos would spoil. He also revealed that many of the people he rented garages off were OAPs, and that they probably 'wouldn't approve of me selling that sort of thing'. Quite why law-breaking senior citizens would draw a moral distinction between harbouring stolen electrical appliances and stolen porn was lost on me. Must be a generational thing, I reasoned.

'Well?' Rollo said. 'What's your answer?'

Emdel and I exchanged glances, turned to Rollo, and nodded. Fifty sovs a month each for doing nothing very much was money for old rope.

'Great, but I'll need more from you herberts than just storage. I'm going into the mail-order business. I'll need a full suite of services.'

'Hang on a minute,' I said 'you didn't say anything about—'

'Just hear me out, will ya. Hear me out.'

We listened as Rollo outlined how he wanted us to line the walls with shelves and then catalogue the porn, including Emdel's. He then wanted to produce a 'pukka mail-order catalogue', so that punters could place orders by post. 'You're in the print game,' he said, nodding my way. 'It'd be a doddle for yer.' He also said we'd need to turn the cellar into a mailroom, for when orders started flooding in.

'That's a hell of a lot of work,' I said. 'What's in it for us?'

'Three big ones. Each.'

And just like that, Emdel and I became pornographers, although technically he had been one for the best part of a decade already. We didn't even give Rollo's offer pause for thought, because here was a shared endeavour *par excellence.*

'Right,' said Rollo. 'Time to get serious. The stuff'll be arriving in two nights. You two'll have to help load it into the garages.'

'I thought it was coming down here,' Emdel said.

'Only once the driver's gone. He's an old mate but he's a recovering smackhead and I ain't taking no chances. Once a junkie, always a junkie, so I want him thinking it's going in my lock-ups. And remember,' he added, pointing to each of us in turn, and switching into full-on threat mode, 'I'm paying you to keep your mouths shut, so I want you to cut down on the booze, capiche? You stink of it, the pair of ya. You'll need clear heads and tight tongues for this work. Deal?'

We shook on it, although I had no intention of cutting back on anything, and I was pretty sure the same was true of Emdel.

*

The following Monday the porn arrived in a white long wheel-base Transit at 2.40 a.m.

'Alright, Jimmy?' said Rollo, shaking the driver's hand.

'How's your Ma?' Jimmy asked.

'Not great.'

'Sorry to hear that. Give her my best.'

'Hang on a second,' Rollo said, pointing at Jimmy. 'Come here, you.'

'What?' Jimmy said. 'Why?'

'Just fucking come here.'

Jimmy walked across to Rollo – fearfully, I thought.

'Bend down. Give me a good look at your face.'

'What's this all about?' Jimmy said.

'Just fucking bend down.'

Jimmy did as he was told. Rollo cupped Jimmy's chin in a spade-like palm and squeezed his cheeks hard so that Jimmy's lips became comically pursed.

'You're clammy as fuck. Are you using again?' Rollo pushed Jimmy's face away.

'No, Rollo, I swear. I've just got a touch of the 'flu, that's all. There's a lot of it about.'

'If you're lying to me about this porn, I'll do you. I don't give a fuck about us being friends. I'm going to ask you one more time: where's this lot from?'

'It's from Bristol way, like I said. I swear on your Ma's life.'

That seemed to satisfy Rollo because he ordered Jimmy to open the rear of the van. Taped-up rubble sacks were heaped from floor to ceiling, front to back – a veritable mountain of porn. The four of us formed a chain, from van to garage: Jimmy in the van, Rollo sitting at its open doors, then me, then Emdel, who placed the sacks in one of the garages. That part was quick and easy. What nearly killed us, though, was shifting the sacks from garage to cellar once Jimmy had gone. Rollo sat sentinel in front of the garage as we traipsed to and fro, back and forth to the cellar, lumping them one at a time.

'Is that all you can carry,' Rollo complained.

'They're bloody heavy,' I said, panting.

'Right pair of saps you are. If it wasn't for these damn legs I'd be carrying them three at a time.'

I didn't doubt him.

By the time we were done, the sun was beginning to cast feeble light on our beaded brows. I collapsed into bed, aching and sodden, to grab a couple of hours' kip before work. I dropped off to sleep in a heartbeat, above a Matterhorn of pornography.

TWENTY EIGHT

EMDEL 'BORROWED' A COMPUTER FROM work, so that he could catalogue the porn on a spreadsheet in the cellar, which had a couple of wall sockets for power. I drove my shit-brown Allegro into the JCN loading bay at a previously agreed time. Emdel was there, ready and waiting with the hardware. He hoiked it in the boot, and I was gone. When I'd asked him if he was worried he might be caught, Emdel had shaken his head.

'If we behave like nothing's wrong then that's how it'll look,' he'd said. 'Just act normal.' And he'd been right because no one in the loading bay batted an eyelid.

I also 'borrowed' a chair from work and, using an old trestle table in the cellar, Emdel's subterranean work-station was complete. We spent a week of evenings lining the walls with shelves, and after that we were faced with the herculean task of sorting through the porn. What surprised me – and horrified Emdel – was the amount of hard-core gay material we found.

'I'm not going near the fag stuff,' Emdel said, shuddering. 'Not with all this AIDS.'

'Oh for chrissake,' I said. 'D'you seriously think you can catch HIV from a magazine or a video?'

But there was no shifting him, and I was left to handle the gay stuff on my own. I would call out titles – Seven in a Barn, Back Passage to India, Black Inches – and Emdel would enter then into his spreadsheet, muttering under his breath as he did so.

Night after night, sorting through those sacks, it became clear that Emdel's thirst for porn had never really gone anywhere; ditching his collection had simply been an expedience, so as not to jeopardise what he'd had going with Thirza. I suppose one can't spend ten years laying down semen-soldered neural pathways and expect them to vanish overnight.

Sometimes, as we toiled in the cellar, his barely suppressed passion for porn would surface spectacularly, like a dolphin corkscrewing through the air.

'Aaaaggghhh,' he howled one evening, as we were unbagging yet more stuff. 'These mags are rare German imports – Rodox, Backdoor, Color Climax, New Cunts.'

'Rare? What, you mean like Penny Blacks?'

'More like Penny Reds.'

He handled them as a museum curator might ancient artefacts, with such care that white cotton gloves would not have seemed out of place.

Another time, when we were cataloguing films, he reeled across the cellar, cradling a video like it was a holy relic.

'Jesus, cock,' he said, at top volume.

This was a profanity Emdel reserved for use only when febrile with excitement, so I knew it must be something big, in his universe at least

'It's Honey Throat!' he announced, reverentially.

'What the hell's Honey Throat?'

He eyed me like I was the dumb kid in class.

'It's only a John Holmes classic.'

Jesus. He'd watched so much porn he was actually star-struck by the performers.

'John who?'

'Come on! John Holmes, a.k.a Johnny Wadd. His knob was insured by Lloyd's of London for $1 million an inch.'

I had to ask. 'So what was it insured for?'

'$14 million,' revealed Emdel, heading up the steps with Honey Throat.

'Oi, where are you going?'

'Where d'you think I'm going? To watch it.'

'I thought you were done with all that.'

'Nah, this is a classic. I've been on the look-out for this for years.'

If sorting through Rollo's stolen porn took over my life, it absolutely consumed Emdel's. The truth was that never in the history of employment has one man been better suited to a single task than Emdel was to cataloguing one of the largest collections of pornography ever assembled in Hampshire, possibly even the Northern Hemisphere. The task consumed him, and he, it. My role was confined to filling shelves according to Emdel's instructions, and sorting the gay material he refused to touch, some of which was at the extreme end of hard-core. For weeks, the pair of us burned the midnight oil, but however late I clocked-off, Emdel would work on, hunched over his spreadsheet, light from the purloined computer reflected in his glasses, behind which his eyes glowed just as brightly. He spent waaaaay too long in that cellar, even taking a week off work, so he could go full-time for a spell.

'It's the final push,' he explained.

At the end of that week, in the murk of one horribly early morning, the cellar door crashed open, ripping me from slumber.

'It's finished,' Emdel announced. 'It's done. Come, see.'

He beckoned me down.

'For the love of God, I'm not getting out of bed to look at a bloody spreadsheet. Show me in the morning.'

'It is the morning.'

'I'm tired. I'm hungover. I'm going back to sleep.'

'No, you gotta see this.'

Clearly, there was no winning here and so, clumsy with sleep, I followed him down. He eased himself back in front of the glowing screen.

'Right,' he said, with the air of one who's omni-competent. 'Ask me for something, anything.'

'Okay. I'd like ... you to go to bed and leave me alone.'

'No, come on, ask me for some porn. Any genre, any magazine, any video. Go on, ask me.'

'Oh, for chrissake, I don't know. Big dicks.'

'Easy. A few taps later, and he was urging me to study the screen. 'See, I've crossed-referenced all films featuring outsized penises. So here, we have all titles starring Johnny Wadd, Long Dong Silver, Ron Jeremy and a few others.'

'Fantastic.'

'Ask me another.'

I sighed. 'I dunno. Cumshots.'

'Be more specific. Facials, tits, or cream pies?'

'What's a cream pie?'

'A load of spunk coming out of a fanny or arse.'

'Lovely, but no thanks. Facials.'

'White or black?'

'White or black what?'

'White or black faces, of course.

'Of course. Black.'

'Solo, group or bukkake?'

'What the hell's bukkake?'

'It's a Jap thing,' Emdel explained. 'Dozens of men queue up to shoot their wads on a woman's face.'

'What? Who on earth'd want to see that?'

Emdel coughed nervously.

'So?' he added, a little too quickly. 'Solo cumshots, or group cumshots?'

'I don't know. Solo.'

He tapped a couple of keys. 'And there you are,' he announced, gesturing at the screen, beckoning me closer.

'What am I supposed to be looking at? It's just a list.'

He smacked the keyboard and threw his weight back in the chair so that it almost toppled over and he had to windmill his arms to stay upright.

'This is wasted on you,' he said. 'Look, we've got 287 items in this cellar that have a concentration of solo black facials. You can ask for anything, it doesn't matter what, and I can tell you exactly what we have, how many we've got of them and where they are on the shelves.'

'Alright, Einstein. Find me some gay black solo facials.'

'You can look for the fag stuff yourself,' he said, his features crumpling in disgust. 'There's still a massive pile of it over there you've yet to sort,' he added, pointing to a large mound of bags in the corner.

I was beginning to suspect that Emdel was a card-carrying homophobe, and that some re-education might be overdue.

'Emdel. Can I ask you a question?'

'Sure. What d'you want me to find? Big tits? Anal? Spit roasts?'

'No, it's not about your spreadsheet, wonderful though that is. I'd like you to answer me this: does the sight of the erect male penis excite you?'

He sprang from his seat and jabbed the air in front of me. 'I'm no fucking fag.'

'No one's calling you gay. Look, let me put it another way. Think about all the porn you've ever watched in your life. How many erect penises d'you think you've seen in that time?

'Dunno.'

On the back foot. Great.

'A million. Let's say a million.'

His bunched brow told me he was running an all-the-erect-penises-I've-ever-seen calculation.

'More like 400,000.'

'Okay, and of those 400,000 erections how many would you say have involved ejaculation?'

'About half,' he replied without hesitation.

'So you've watched 200,000 ejaculating penises over the years? Correct?'

'More. probably, as I've watched some of my vids four or five times and I've looked at each mag, I dunno, maybe ten times.' He ran another calculation. 'About 2.5 million, roughly.'

'And how did they make you feel, would you say, each of those 2.5 million ejaculating penises?'

'What d'you mean?'

We were on to emotion now – not an Emdel strong suit, especially not emotions that concerned ejaculating gay penises.

'Well, did you feel disgust 2.5 million times?'

'What're you getting at?'

'Stay with me. Let me ask you another. What do you enjoy more – porn with cumshots or porn without?'

'With, obviously.'

'So you've enjoyed watching ejaculating penises roughly 2.5 million times and yet you're repulsed by gay porn?'

'Are you saying I'm some kind of closet queer?'

'Oh for chrissake. No, what I'm saying is that an individual penis's theatre of operation is neither here nor there. An ejaculating penis is an ejaculating penis.'

'Not if it's shooting over my fucking face, it's not.'

Well, at least I tried.

TWENTY NINE

'UNBELIEVABLE,' SAID ROLLO, AS HE sat at his kitchen table thumbing through the 120-page mail-order porn catalogue I'd just handed him. 'Now this is what I call a labour of love. I reckon your mate'd've paid me just so he could do this. I mean look at this section here, with porn stars listed by cock size. That's a stroke of genius.'

I allowed his unintentional play on words to pass, as unsavoury images of Emdel – hard at work and play – skulked through my head.

'Always keep your reader in mind,' I said, basking in the halo effect of Emdel's warped genius. 'That's the first rule of publishing.'

Rollo shifted across his kitchen to a Welsh dresser and rustled about in a drawer.

'Here's an extra two-ton for a job well done,' he said, peeling off twenty tenners from a fat roll of cash. Rollo's idea of being broke was clearly different from mine.

'Cheers.'

I decided on the spot to levy a fifty-quid Homophobia Tax on Emdel, because he had resolutely refused to process any of the gay material, in the end declining even to input gay titles into his spreadsheet. 'Are you now suggesting,' I'd asked him, 'that you can contract AIDs just by typing the word 'gay'?'

Rollo slapped the table. 'Now to make some proper cash,' he said. 'Listen, I need to get some bunce together to pay for an ad in a bunch of the jazz mags. Once I've done that, orders for the catalogue'll start coming in, and when you've mailed out the catalogues, it won't be long till orders proper flood in. D'you know where everything is in that cellar of yours?'

'There's a pile of gay stuff we've still to process, but other than that it's like the British Library of Porn down there. We could issue membership cards.'

'Good, 'cos if punters are ordering by things like cock size then you'll need to be able to lay your hand on every single fricking item down there.'

*

British Library of Porn. Membership cards. The harder I tried to not think about it, the more brain real estate it ended up hogging. I mulled over every conceivable aspect of establishing and running such a venture, but two questions above all others spooled in my head, like a mantra on a rotating Buddhist prayer drum: Who would join such a library? Where might one find such people? It's just theoretical, I kept telling myself.

The answers came to me at work, from nowhere, when I was typing up a story about a gardener who read Agatha Christie novels to his prize-winning amaryllis. Men like Emdel – that's who'd want to join a porn library! It was so bloody obvious. And where might one find such people? JCN, of course.

'What are you grinning at, Bandit?' Big Al asked.

'Nothing,' I said, shrugging.

'Dreaming of blowing Gary Numan, probably,' said Thirza.

My God, I thought, ignoring her cheap shot. There's enough backed-up semen in JCN to send a tsunami of it crashing down through Portsea Island.

*

'So let me get this straight,' Emdel said when I laid the porn library idea on him. 'You'd expect me to drum up members from my place of work?'

'Kind of, yeah, but the whole thing's just theoretical.'

'What you're suggesting is illegal, right?'

'Theoretically, yes.'

'And it'd be me running the risk of getting sacked, not you?'

'In theory, yeah, but how much risk is there, really? I mean members won't want to get caught any more than you, because their jobs'll be on the line as much as yours. It's got in-built risk limitation. Theoretically.'

'So what d'you want me to do? Place an ad on the canteen noticeboard? Wanted: members for illegal hard-core porn library?'

'Word of mouth, genius. Start with Glen and let it grow organically.'

Emdel began running risk and profit calculations, scribbling busily on scraps of paper.

'It's a runner,' he announced, looking up from his jumble of numbers, 'Let's do it.'

'Hang on a sec,' I said. 'What d'you mean it's a runner? Are you mad?'

Emdel eyed me quizzically, tilting his head, like a dog baffled by the ways of the human world. 'It's your bloody idea. D'you wanna do it or not?'

*

We agreed that Glen would be key to the operation's success. Emdel would invite him to be member #1. We could think of no man in Christendom who'd be keener to join a porn library. I did trust Glen, yet I could never fathom him. I'd say he was almost as bright as Emdel, but unlike Emdel there was an intangible disconnect between him and the world, which was bridged only when he sang and played the guitar. It was like a geneticist had attempted to clone Emdel, in the dark and on the cheap, and come up with Glen.

Before offering Glen the chance to join our library we had to first show him the stock, and so Emdel invited him round one night and we took him down the cellar. As Glen surveyed the cellar's labia-strewn and glans-packed contents, I'm pretty certain he had some form of out-of-body experience.

'It's ... it's ... amazing,' he spluttered. He explored the fleshy stock ranged before him with an acute sense of purpose and deliberation, and I do believe that had we left him to his own devices, then one-hundred years hence someone would have stumbled across his leather-clad and cobwebbed bones, propped up against one of the cellar walls, a dust-frosted copy of Strictly Anal aflutter in his skeletal lap.

So it was that Glen became the cornerstone of our clandestine business venture. We agreed Jason was a suitable candidate as member #2. Over the coming weeks, Emdel would seed membership by mentioning, in passing, to a select band of trusted colleagues, that he and Glen happened to have access to a house full of porn. Things would either take off from there or they wouldn't, but just in case they did we jotted down a few house rules, as well as some logistical and strategic points. These were:

1. Move Emdel's TV and video from his bedroom into the cellar, so films could be screened simultaneously in the cellar and living room.

2. Offer two-tier membership: Regular and Premium. Regular members to pay five pounds per visit, with access only to videos, which they watch in the living room. Premium members to pay seven-pounds-fifty for access-all-areas, including the magazines in the cellar. Plus, they get a choice of films. Members block-booking five or more visits in advance to enjoy a 15% discount.

3. All members to receive a screening itinerary, drawn up by Emdel.

4. Don't invite. Be asked. This was Emdel's rule, and while not quite pivotal enough to warrant a capitalised 'r' for 'rule', it was nonetheless crucial for operational security, the principle being that Glen and Emdel would accept as members only those colleagues who approached them about joining. (We decided to ignore anyone who approached Jason because, well, he's Jason.)

5. No uninvited guests on the door. Any infraction and the library closes with immediate effect, with no refunds.

6. No masturbating on the premises. (Difficult to enforce without cameras, we realised. We did consider taking the toilet door off its hinges but then we'd have to take dumps in public, so in the end we set a two-minute limit on toilet use. Not even a sexual desperado could knock one out that quickly, we reasoned.)

7. Don't tell Rollo. Ever. About any of it. Ever.

*

For the grand opening of our porn library, Emdel chose a screening of Throbbin' Hood, the contemporary tale of a libidinous and well-endowed employee who sets out to teach his greedy and mean-spirited boss a lesson, one shag at a time. I thought it was a fitting choice, given that Rollo was not only a Robin Hood-type figure but that he was also the library's patron, sort of.

As the film ran through its gusset-soaked paces, Glen and Jason stared almost unblinkingly at the screen, neither moving nor talking, and this is pretty much how they remained for the entirety of the library's six-week existence. For if they weren't at work then they were at our place, consuming porn. Jason even took time off, and talked Emdel into lending him the house keys. He then spent two days straight in our cellar, doubtless breaking Rule 6 with gay abandon.

For two weeks it seemed our library would get no further than members #1 & #2, but then one evening Jason and Glen arrived with member #3. Mani.

'Good day Mr Loo,' said Mani, shaking my hand. He introduced himself as a son of Bombay, who was on a placement at JCN, as part of his computing degree.

'I am having a present for you,' Mani added, fishing into an unbranded and diaphanous royal-blue plastic bag, the kind beloved of charity shops and market traders. It was a T-shirt. I eyed it with feigned delight, as a towerblock-dwelling gameshow contestant might a speedboat. The T-shirt bore one of those meaningless slogans that follow the same formula the world over: place + number + random club + year. The one Mani gave me said 'St Louis 6198 Members Club 1990'. Mani himself was sporting a similar top, bearing a similarly random slogan, as he did every time I was to see him. It made me wonder whether in India such apparel was aspirational.

I warmed to Mani, more so than to Jason and Glen; he was sweet-natured, plus his mannered-but-mangled English made him sound like one half of a music-hall double act.

Straight guy: D'you give Christmas presents in India?

Mani: Oh, yes, we are loving Farmer Christmas.

Straight guy: Did you see the game last night?

Mani: Yes, I didn't.

Straight guy: Imagine being able to suck your own dick, like Johnny Wadd.

Mani: That's unpossible.

It was through Mani that members #4 and #5 joined – JCN's very own Brothers Grimm, Bryan and Darryl, a brace of leather-clad hairballs, both of whom were head-banging chess freaks. Before I met them I didn't know it was even possible to play chess while watching porn.

Their first visit was memorable for all the wrong reasons.

'Glen in?' Bryan asked on the doorstep.

'Actually,' I said, 'this isn't Glen's house. This is my house.'

'Who are you?'

'No, no, no. You've got it back to front,' I said. 'It's me who asks, 'Who are you?' So, who are you?'

'Bryan, with a Y,' said Bryan. 'And he's Darryl, with a Y.'

Bryan always spoke for the pair of them, what little speaking there was.

'And what do you want, Bryan and Darryl with Ys?'

'Er, well, Mani said, sort of, you know, that we could ...'

'Oh for chrissake come in. Mani mentioned you. D'you want Premium or Regular membership?'

'Premium, with two months upfront,' said Bryan. 'That's over fifteen per cent discount, correct?'

'Er, no, cor-wrong. It is fifteen per cent.'

'But one month is fifteen per cent, correct?'

'Yes. And?'

'If you are adopting a system of compound discount, which would appear to be the case here, then two months' discount should be greater than the fifteen per cent that accrues from a single month booked in advance.'

Great. More cybermen. I was in frigging Dr Who.

'It's 15 per cent. Take it or leave it.'

They took it, in cash, on the spot.

'Do you have much by the way of anal?' asked Bryan. 'We both like anal.'

At last, a question I understood.

'Yes we do. It's all clearly labelled, but please put everything back where you find it.'

After Bryan and Darryl joined, things seemed to take off exponentially, just as Emdel's scribbled probability formulae had predicted it would. By week six we were up to twenty-one members, all of whom had approached either Glen or Emdel at work, requesting membership.

The money rolled in so fast we couldn't drink it all, although we did try. As for the library, it more or less ran itself. The JCN androids might not have made for great company in any other context but they were porn library members par excellence, never causing any trouble and always abiding by the rules. Occasionally Emdel or I might pop into the living room or down the cellar to check that their motherboards weren't overheating, but that was about it.

There was only one real headache: the cellar could only be accessed through my bedroom, which meant I was forever being disturbed by members pulling all-nighters, and so I introduced a weekday curfew of midnight, and 2 a.m. at weekends. But no matter how smoothly things ran, lurking at the backs of our minds was our darkest fear: what if Rollo finds out.

*

'Oi Sabler,' came the call from behind me as I neared home, having just left work.

Rollo wheeled towards me with what looked like real intent.

He knows about the library. He's gonna kill me.

'Listen, I've placed an ad for the catalogue in all the jazz mags. Do us a favour will you – here.' He proffered a wad of banknotes and a scrap of paper. 'Go buy all the mags for us. I've written down the titles here. I wanna check they've run my ad right.'

I studied his list. The relief I felt upon realising Rollo hadn't rumbled our porn library – and wasn't about to kill me, painfully and slowly – was supplanted by dread, at the prospect of having to buy a dozen top-shelf publications, including one gay title, Honcho. I pictured myself standing red-faced at some newsagent counter, thudding a pile of wank mags down in front of the proprietor. They'd be sure to think me gay, and that I was trying to disguise that fact by hiding a gay mag in a pile of heterosexual ones I didn't really want. There would be disapproving glances for sure. Worse, maybe even a knowing wink.

'And another thing,' Rollo added, with a trace of menace, 'what's the script with that Roller what's been parked outside your gaff recently?'

Stay calm. He doesn't know anything. He's just seen a car, that's all.

'Oh that.' I said, dismissing it as a mere trifle, while struggling to ignore my spastic sphincter. 'That's Jason's. He's a workmate of Emdel's.'

'Well some copper was eyeballing it the other day. It's drawing attention. It's a fucking clown's car; it belongs in a circus. Tell the cunt to park it some place else.'

I nodded and smiled, and waited until Rollo was out of earshot before sucking in a series of deep breaths, to still my thumping heart.

That evening, the moment I heard Jason pull up outside our front door, I was up and out and tapping on his window. As ever, Glen was in the front passenger seat. He got out of the car and waltzed through the open front door of the house, neither waiting for Jason nor offering any kind of greeting to me. It was pure Glen.

'Wotcher Llew,' Jason said, grinning and rubbing his hands together. 'It's lesbo action all the way tonight.'

'T'rrific. Listen, Jason, you can't park your motor here any more. It's drawing attention. You gotta park it somewhere else.'

He bristled. 'What d'you mean I can't park her here? She might get stolen.'

Her? She?

'This little lady stays right under my nose,' he added, shutting the driver's door and caressing the roof, as one might the cheek of a girlfriend. 'What if someone stole her? What'd I do then?'

Little lady? The stroking? My god, it suddenly all made sense: Maureen wasn't flesh and blood, but rust and algae. Jason was in love with his car. I wondered if we oughtn't to add a few motoring titles to the library.

'I don't care, you've gotta move her – I mean, *it*. You do know this porn library isn't exactly legal, don't you? If we get rumbled then all of us are in the mire, and you'll probably lose your job.'

With that, Jason taxied Maureen around the corner and parked just down from Rollo's garages, which was every bit as bad. Over the coming days I repeatedly asked him to park it well away from the house, but he refused. In the end I got so frustrated I threatened to take away his library membership unless he did so, but when that left him on the verge of tears I took pity and relented, and so Maureen remained where she was.

*

I got up extra early on Saturday morning to buy Rollo's magazines, so that when I reached the nearest WH Smith it had yet to open. I wanted to be the first customer inside. Having to pay for all those porno mags would be traumatic enough, without also having a queue of rubberneckers behind me. A security guy opened up the shop, and as I walked in I glanced across to the tills to see who would be running their eye over my purchases. It was a middle-aged woman, stout and with a homely air about her. She might have been anyone's mum. It couldn't have been worse.

I ventured across to the magazines stand, and following a couple of minutes' faux browsing of sports titles to get my nerve up, I plucked a copy of Razzle from the top shelf. I found Rollo's ad on page seven: Huge collection of red-hot Dutch, German and Scandinavian hard-core mags and videos. Straight, Bi and extreme Gay. For a catalogue write to Portsmouth PO Box 69. I grabbed the other eleven magazines on Rollo's list and hastened to the checkout. With each title that Mrs Mum rang through, she eyed me more suspiciously, and then she got to Honcho. She snorted and muttered something about 'gay plague'. She bagged-up my purchases and handed them to me, before folding her arms and sucking-in her cheeks. When I proffered my money she nodded at the counter.

'Put it down there,' she ordered.

She placed one hand inside a paper bag and picked up my cash like it was dog shit. She tipped the money into the open register so that, pinball-style, the coins ricocheted into random compartments. The notes she manoeuvred into the till using two biros, like chopsticks.

It was too much. I retrieved Honcho from the carrier bag and riffled through it, making a big show of gurning and licking my lips. In that particular issue there happened to be a concertina-fold centre-spread. I shook it free from the body of the magazine, so that three-and-a-half feet of muscle-bound construction worker – nursing a hard-on as big as the claw hammer in his other hand – wallpapered the air. I turned the poster around, so she could see him in all his glory.

'Would you just look at that,' I said. 'He'd split me clean in two, and d'you know what? I'd love every second of it.'

THIRTY

It was a Tuesday morning. I looked up at the clock: 9.30am – police-call time. One of the least popular chores in local newspaper journalism is the police call, the weekly trip to the local station to jot down that week's roll call of shoplifters, burglars, drink-drivers and Sierra Cosworth thieves. The job nearly always gets dumped on the most junior reporter, which on The Probe meant Thirza. But after just one visit to the cop shop it became clear that putting Thirza in a building full of sexist and misogynist coppers was a spectacularly bad idea.

'I'm telling you, Al,' she said, having returned from her first police call, 'if one of those fucking pigs wolf-whistles me next week I'll swing for one of those pricks.'

And so police calls were handed back to me, on the spot.

That Tuesday morning I had hoped to tell Big Al that I was quitting my job. The plan was to move back home temporarily and continue working Saturday reporting shifts on The Insider, which were going well. I'd probably have to take a crappy job during the week to make ends meet but I could live with that; I was confident The Insider would offer me something more substantial before too long. But I couldn't tell Big Al any of this because he had a dental appointment, and wouldn't be in until later. Thirza saw his absence as an opportunity to take a free hit.

'What the hell are you wearing, you twat,' she said, as I prepared to head off to the police station.

'Don't start.'

'Who's ever heard of a T-shirt with a fucking hood? And I'll bet it's some Numan shite too. Dumb, dumb, dumb,' she added, with derisory shakes of the head.

*

'I'll buzz you through,' the duty sergeant said. 'Someone'll be with you in a minute.'

I eased through the steel-reinforced door and made my way down a bleak corridor. The entire station was decorated in the same two-tone green-gloss colour scheme beloved of all institutions. I was making for the press room when a plain-clothes officer I'd not seen before pushed through a set of double doors and was headed towards me. He glanced my way and then stopped dead in front of me, as if taken aback by something.

I offered him my hand, thinking he must be the officer they'd sent to meet me. 'Llew Sabler, reporter on the Probe. Don't think we've met before.'

He took my hand, surprise still on his face. 'DI Simmons. I'll see you in the press room presently. Can I get you a tea or a coffee?'

'Tea'd be nice, thanks. White without, please.'

DI Simmons kept me waiting long enough for my buttocks to begin sweating on the wooden seat. Strange, I thought. I was never normally kept waiting. I also found it odd they'd sent a detective to meet me. Low-level media stuff was way beneath his pay grade. Usually they sent a lowly PC to do the police call, or sometimes even a back-office civilian. When the door finally opened, DI Simmons stepped in with another plain-clothesman I didn't recognise. He was carrying a portable tape recorder. Neither of them had any tea, I noted. They sat opposite me. DI Simmons placed a folder on the table. Even upside down I could read 'St Aloysius' printed on a white label on its front. It was like a punch in the guts, and I had to focus everything on keeping all emotion off my face. The other officer placed the tape recorder on the table, while DI Simmons slid a few sheets of paper from the folder and set them before me. They were grainy CCTV images of a traffic accident. I recognized the Volvo and the Sierra Cosworth. The other officer clicked the recorder into action and spoke our names aloud, adding their job titles. The other one was called DI Bull.

'Mr Sabler,' said DI Simmons, we would like to interview you, under caution.'

'I don't understand. What about?'

'It's in connection with a series of recent incidents at St Aloysius Catholic Church,' said DI Bull. 'Please know that you're entitled to a solicitor but you are not under arrest at this time, and you are also free to leave, should you so choose.'

DI Simmons read me my rights.

Why I didn't walk out right then I shall never fully understand. Something inexplicable compelled me to stay. It was as if I had a ringside seat for someone else's gripping drama, someone who just happened to look and sound exactly like me.

'I'm not saying anything,' I said.

They exchanged a glance. I bet they couldn't believe their luck – that of all people, a journalist had waived his rights.

'Recognize these?' DI Simmons said, nodding at the photos.

I stared blankly at him.

'These are images taken from CCTV cameras mounted opposite St Aloysius Catholic Church.' He gave me the date and the exact timings the images had been captured. 'There was a hit and run that night,' he continued. 'A man was badly injured and we're still looking for the person responsible. But something else happened at around the same time. Someone defecated on the altar in the church.'

He replaced the images with three more, all of which showed me leaving the church. They had been blown-up and were grainy. My features were almost completely obscured by cap, hood and glasses, but the distinctive android face on my white hooded top was clearly visible.

'The cameras also happened to pick up these images,' said Di Simmons. 'These show a male figure leaving the church moments after the accident. He is wearing a very distinctive top. The same design of top that you are wearing right now, in fact. And he is also about your height and weight. Mr Sabler, you have written a series of stories about the desecrations in St Aloysius for your paper, have you not?'

I nodded.

'And I also happen to read The Insider newspaper. They also published a story about the desecrations. On their front page no less. Were you aware of that?'

Again, I nodded.

'I would expect you to be aware because the Insider story had your name on it. You must have turned a tidy profit from the publication of that story.'

I stared at him blankly.

'Note for the record that Mr Sabler declined to answer that question,' DI Bull said into the tape recorder.

'Can you account for your movements on the night in question?' DI Simmons asked.

In my head, I asked him if he meant movements with legs or movements with sweetcorn.

'Note for the record that Mr Sabler declined to answer that question,' DI Bull repeated.

Only at this point did I come to my senses and ask for the interview to be terminated.

'That is your right,' said DI Simmons. 'But we'll be in touch soon. Until then you remain under caution. And Mr Sabler?' DI Simmons picked a transparent plastic bag off the table. 'Please remove that top and place it in this bag. It's evidence.'

'But I've only got a vest on underneath.'

'It's a nice day. You won't freeze.'

I removed it and dropped it in the bag. Having bought it in 1981, it was like saying goodbye to an old friend.

Upon returning to the office – after first nipping home to get another top – I dragged Big Al down to the basement and told him what had gone down at the station. I didn't mention anything about quitting my job; those plans had been scattered to the winds. He listened, slack-jawed – too shocked even to pull on his smouldering Marlboro.

'So they think it was you that shat on the altar?' he said when I'd finished.

'Yes.'

And was it?'

I sighed. 'It's complicated, Al.'

'For fuck's sake Bandit – you shat on a frigging altar? Why?'

'I didn't shit on it, technically. I placed my crap on it. I had it in a Tesco bag. It was just the once.'

'Tesco bag? Just the once? Well that's all right then, ain't it. You're scott free. What the hell were you thinking?'

'I needed to get away from here – away from Thirza.'

'So you shat on an altar? Genius.'

'Well if it hadn't been for that car crash it would've worked. It got me my shifts on The Insider.'

'And why the hell didn't you walk straight out of that station the second they read you your rights? You're a bloody reporter. You should know the drill better than anyone.'

'I wasn't thinking straight.'

'No shit. This is bad news, Bandit. That mermaid and Santa crap'll be nothing compared to this. Ad sales'll probably go through the floor. People could lose their jobs, you dope.'

I slumped against a decrepit and dusty photocopier. 'I'm sorry. I've let you down. Again.'

'Yes you have.'

I slid down the photocopier to the floor and sank my head between my knees. After allowing me to mumble despairingly for a moment or two, Big Al patted my shoulder.

'It's done now, Bandit. We've gotta focus on what we can control, but before we do that I want you to tell me everything – and I mean everything. Start at the beginning, with that old bird you met in the boozer.'

I ran Big Al through the whole sordid affair.

'So,' he said, after I'd wrapped up my account, 'let me get this straight. The first shit wasn't yours, the second one was, but the third, fourth and fifth ones weren't?'

I nodded. 'Yeah. I'm only twenty per cent guilty.'

'And one-hundred per cent deluded because they'll do you for the lot. 'They've got you bang to rights. You need a solicitor, my old son.'

'I can't afford a solicitor on my wages.'

I kept to myself the fact I could easily have afforded one on the cash I was making from Rollo's porn.

'Apply for legal aid. Things should be straightforward enough on a guilty plea.'

'Guilty plea?

'You've got no alibi, they've got you on film wearing that top, you profited from the story and to cap it all, thanks to that mermaid nonsense you've also got previous for fake news. Plus, you bloody well did it.' Big Al counted the points off on the fingers of one hand. 'So yeah, guilty,' he added, with a look to suggest that even to consider pleading not guilty meant I must be mentally enfeebled.

'But if I'm convicted then no editor in the land'll ever hire me again,' I protested. 'I'll forever be that reporter who shat on an altar on a slow news day.'

I saw a lifetime of crap jobs stretching out before me, and sank my face into my hands.

Big Al ground a cigarette into the floor, pulled another from the box and jabbed it at down at me. 'You should've thought of that before you set off with your turd in a Tesco bag.'

THIRTY ONE

My solicitor was a stern-faced woman with short dark hair and a penchant for utility clothing. She reminded me of Colonel Rosa Klebb, the Bond baddie who had a poisoned-tipped retractable knife in her shoe. The first words she spoke were to tell me that what I really needed was a time machine, so that I could go back to the original police interview and leave before saying anything. Real helpful. Next, she asked me if I was guilty. I had agreed with Big Al that I would plead guilty, to avoid jail time, but there was a sneering quality to her question; her dark, hard eyes hinted at contempt, and so I changed my mind. At my protestations of innocence, she did a double-take of Oliver Hardy proportions.

'Innocent?' she parroted.

'Well, that's just great isn't it. My own solicitor thinks I'm guilty.'

I found myself feeling righteously indignant. I was responsible for just one of the five desecrations, for chrissake. Why should I carry the can for whoever was eighty per cent guilty of this crime?

'Mr Sabler, as far as the Crown Prosecution Service is concerned the evidence points incontrovertibly to your guilt. This case is not winnable, under any circumstances, and if you are innocent then I am sorry about that.'

She didn't look sorry. She looked as if someone had asked her to imagine drinking a pint of greenies.

'The evidence is all circumstantial,' I said defiantly, really getting my shoulder behind the righteous indignation.

'Yes, but it is about as compelling as it's possible for circumstantial evidence to be. And then there's motive. They can show that you profited from this offence.'

'I know it doesn't look good,' I said. 'Yes, I was in the church that night, but I was praying. It was not me who did those terrible things.'

From somewhere, I conjured a reality distortion field in which eighty percent innocence became one-hundred percent. I was wronged, dammit. I was some kind of martyr.

'They can throw me in jail,' I told her, standing, so that I could loom over her as I set out my noble case. 'I don't care. I'm not pleading guilty to something I didn't do.'

*

During the second police interview I was charged under Section 2 of the Ecclesiastical Courts Jurisdiction Act 1860, which forbids 'riotous, violent or indecent behaviour in any place of worship'. I was told that, if convicted, I'd likely face two months inside, the maximum term for such an offence. I was bailed and informed that because mine was a summary offence it would be heard at Portsmouth Magistrates Court, where a panel of three magistrates would decide my fate (rather than a jury, as at Crown court). DI Simmons said I would receive notification of my trial date through the post. Seeing how they had dredged up a 133-year-old law to nail me, I wondered if I oughtn't attend court wearing a stovepipe hat, pantaloons and cravat.

Ms Klebb might as well have kicked me under the table with one of her toxic blades for all the good she did me in that second interview. She just sat there, mute, as DI Simmons piled even more circumstantial evidence on top of the K2 of it they already had. He said the mermaid fiasco showed I was not averse to writing fake news, as Big Al had warned they might. But he also said the Santa debacle demonstrated my contempt for the Christian faith. At his mention of the grotto incident, an ectoplasm of disgust issued from Ms Klebb, and I knew then that I would fire her bony Russian lesbian counter-intelligence arse.

'You're meant to be my lawyer, and yet you've sat in judgment on me right from the off,' I said the second we stepped outside of the station, jabbing a finger at a point about five millimetres from her breastbone. 'You're a disgrace. Get lost.'

*

'It's prejudicial,' said Big Al, reading that day's Portsmouth Tribune, his voice muted by all the old office equipment and furniture crammed into the basement. It was getting to feel like we were spending half of our time down there. 'There's no doubt about it,' he added, slapping the paper with the back of his hand.

Skinner had once again splashed me across his paper's front page. He must have come in his pants when he learned I'd been charged. 'Pompey hack on church-outrage charge' was the headline. There wasn't much meat to the story because of pre-trial constraints on what they could say, but that hadn't stopped them using the grotto picture again – of me in my Santa-nailed-to-a-crucifix T-shirt.

'It's trial by newspaper,' Big Al continued. 'That picture makes you look like a god-hater. It's prejudicial,' he repeated. 'You need to give that solicitor of yours a ring.'

'Yeah, about her.'

Big Al looked at me over his glasses. 'What about her?'

'I kind of sacked her, yesterday.'

'What? Why?'

'She doesn't believe I'm innocent.'

'That's because you're not bloody innocent.'

'I'm mostly innocent. She despises me, I could tell.'

'So what's the great master plan now? Plead not guilty? Defend yourself?'

I shuffled from foot to foot, looking at the ground.

'Ted Bundy defended himself,' I said, as if that were QED.

Big Al choked on a lungful of smoke and coughed until his eyes were watering.

'Ted Bundy got the bloody chair,' he said, once he'd recovered his poise. He dabbed at his eyes with a Paisley silk-kerchief that he plucked form his breast pocket. 'Please tell me you're not serious.'

'I'll do my legal homework. I've a gift for research, you know that. And like you say, this Tribune front page is contempt of court, so that's grist for the mill, right there. I can't give up on my career just like that, Al. I can't. I'm gonna fight to the last second.'

'You can fight all you want, you fool, but you'll end up doing time, and your career will be shot anyway.'

THIRTY TWO

After a night of trying – and failing miserably – to blot out my troubles with a bottle of Jack, my head felt like someone had taken a lump hammer to it in the dead of the night. The pain was so intense it prompted a wave of nausea. I stopped by a bus shelter bin and threw up into it, apologising to an elderly lady who was waiting there with a tartan shopping trolley.

'Here,' she said, 'aren't you that reporter, the one who did those disgusting things in that church? You ought to be ashamed of yourself.'

'Er, I'm innocent actually, thank you very much,' I said, feeling far too ill to counter her accusation with much conviction.

'Well *they* don't think you're innocent,' she said, pointing up the road towards The Probe offices.

I squinted up ahead but my eyes were still watering from being sick, so that everything was distorted by tears.

'I can't see that far. What's going on?'

'Protesters.' She folded her arms. 'And it's not the first time, is it. Just what is it you've got against the church, exactly? What's God ever done to you, apart from love your sinful soul?'

I threw up again, missing the bin this time but not apologising. I walked off, feeling that my actions had spoken louder than any words ever could.

After another hundred yards my tears had dried sufficiently to reveal the throng of people gathered outside the entrance of The Probe. In my peripheral vision, I saw a figure cross the road just behind me, and a few seconds later Bob from Circulation was at my elbow.

'I see the devil dodgers are back, Sabler,' he said with a snide little grin that exposed his wooden-looking teeth. Seeing them made me feel ill again. 'Nice work,' he added. 'This ain't gonna sit well with advertisers. You're a selfish bastard.'

'What'd you brush your teeth with this morning, Bob?" I asked. 'Dog shit?'

'Yeah, yeah – real funny, laughing boy, but you won't be wisecracking when you're in those prison showers. Your sphincter'll end up looking like the top of a duffel bag. I tell you something, I'm glad I'm not you, Sabler.'

His mention of prison intensified the throbbing in my head, and I darted over to a low wall skirting a block of flats and dry-retched over it. In that moment I felt so wretched I might even have swapped places with loathsome Bob, had someone offered me the chance.

I grabbed a few deep lungfuls of air in a bid to calm my spinning head, and with palms on knees I watched Bob walk on up ahead. He stopped in front of the protesters and started speaking to them. Then the bastard was pointing down the street, at me. At that, the crowd launched into some dirge of a hymn, one of those whose current note telegraphs the next three. I wiped my mouth, took a deep breath, and walked towards them.

The group – about fifty-strong – were ranged behind a banner that someone had fashioned from a bedsheet. 'Your day of judgment will come', it said. The message had been crudely daubed-on with what looked like creosote, which had leached into the weave of the fabric, making the lettering appear out of focus.

As I reached the group, some of them broke off from singing, to boo and catcall me. 'Shame' seemed to be their noun of choice. Most of the protesters were women, as they had been before, in the wake of the Santa affair. At the back of the group I caught the eye of a large-but-short lady. It took my addled senses a moment or two to recognise her as Iris. I looked away immediately, such was the intensity of her hurt and disappointment. It left me feeling far from eighty per cent innocent. My eye then caught another familiar female face. She was singing with venomous glee and had one end of the banner clutched in both hands. It was Rosa Klebb, my so-called solicitor. Looking straight at me, she stopped singing and joined in the others who were shouting 'Shame!'

It was too much.

'You've spelled judgement wrong,' I told her, pointing at the bedsheet. 'Judgment without an 'e' is for legal use only. That's you all over though isn't it, rushing to judgement.'

I stood tall in front of the group, sweeping an outstretched arm from side to side, aiming an index finger at each of them, including Iris.

'Who are you to judge me?' I shouted above their din. 'What happened to innocent until proven guilty? Call yourself Christians? It's you lot who should be ashamed, not me.'

A flashbulb fired. I looked in the direction it had come from and recognised one of The Tribune's photographers. Skinner. He would keep putting in the boot until I couldn't get up, but I wasn't down and out just yet.

'Screw the lot of you,' I shouted.

The Tribune's front page later that day was dominated by a large photograph of me, pointing accusatorily at the protesters, below which was the headline, 'Screw you all'.

'What is it with you, Bandit?' Big Al said, shaking his head as he scanned the Tribune's latest piece on me. 'Are you trying to outdo Fred West in the popularity stakes?'

'I haven't killed anyone,' I reminded him.

I looked across at Thirza. She was typing up a story, and didn't look up. She'd been impassive like this ever since I'd been charged with the St. Aloysius desecrations. It was unnerving. I'd have preferred her to pour record levels of scorn and abuse down upon me. At least I knew where I stood with that.

*

The protesters proved relentless. They were outside the office by 8.30am every morning and didn't leave until I did. One of them even created a placard to encourage passing motorists to beep, to indicate that they supported their cause, whatever that cause was. Having me cast down into the eternal flames of Hell, probably. Every day for nearly a week I endured cries of 'Shame' and 'Repent' as I arrived at work, and then again as I left.

When regional TV got wind of the story I knew it was only a question of time before The Insider found out too. Naively, I thought they might actually stand by me, and allow me to continue working Saturday reporting shifts, at least until I was convicted.

'What the hell are you doing here?' the news editor said, almost choking on his coffee as I rocked up for my latest Saturday shift. 'I left a message for you yesterday, with someone called Bob, saying for you not to come in any more.'

That bastard. I'll knock his wooden teeth down his throat.

'You made us look like a right bunch of tossers with that altar-stunt of yours,' he continued. 'We ran it as a splash, for fuck's sake. Go on, get out of here, before the editor clocks you. He wants to drape your bollocks from his rear-view mirror.'

'But I'm innocent,' I protested, looking around the newsroom for support. All eyes were on me, and none suggested sympathy for my cause.

I glanced across at the editor's glass-fronted office. He was on the phone, thumping the desk. He was always hitting something, or screaming at someone. I thought it a miracle he'd not had a stroke or heart attack already. He looked out into the newsroom, and his eye caught mine. He leapt from his chair like a thousand volts had passed through it. His door crashed open. I winced, shut my eyes, and braced for impact.

'Oi, cant,' he screamed,' somehow making the ultimate term of abuse even more abusive by substituting an A for a U. Slowly, I turned to face him. Only those who were some distance from the drama were looking our way, I noticed. Those nearest the blast zone were typing furiously, eyes down.

'You facking stitched us up, you miserable little wanker. Shitting in a facking church? Get your ragged hole outta my newsroom, or I'll tear off your facking head and shit down your scrawny facking neck, you cant.'

Even Thirza's tirades were less eviscerating, and yet as he fixed me with his maniacal stare I found myself in a state of preternatural calm.

'No actually, you can fuck off,' I said, pointing at him. Even those closest to us stopped tapping and looked up.

'What'd you say?' His words were slow and soft, as if he was unsure what he'd heard.

I pointed at him.

'You're worse than those Christians outside my office,' I said, 'judging me guilty before I've even stepped near a courtroom. And another thing. You're banned.'

His lips moved but no words came out.

'Banned?' he said eventually. 'Banned from what?'

But I didn't know; it just seemed like a good thing to say.

'Just banned.'

He shook his head and pointed to the door. A faint smirk played across his face. 'Hop it,' he said.

'Good luck, son,' the news editor called out.

*

The Insider wasn't the only newspaper to be spooked both by the Christian protesters and my upcoming trial.

'You'll still be on full pay, Bandit,' Big Al said, his body language one big apology.

'But suspended? That makes me look guiltier than ever.'

'Things've gone beyond guilt or innocence – this is about people's jobs now. I warned you this'd get serious. The protests have dragged the paper's numbers through the floor, and that mob is clearly going nowhere while you're still here, so you can't come to work any more. It's as simple as that. I've drafted a press statement, explaining everything. It won't make you look guilty, Bandit, I promise – at least no more guilty than you actually are.'

'But what'll I do?'

He sighed through his nose and cast his eyes to the ceiling.

'You still planning to go ahead with this madness of yours, of representing yourself in court?'

'Yeah.'

'Then I'd say you've got plenty to bloody well get on with, wouldn't you? And go home, Bandit. Go see those lovely folks of yours. How have they taken it?'

'Um, well...'

'Oh, for the love of god, don't tell me you've said nothing. They're your parents, they've a right to know. So when *are* you planning to tell them, exactly?'

'Well, I was kind of hoping, you know, that I might get off, maybe, and that they'd, well, never need to find out about any of it, hopefully.'

'Son, what world are you living in? When are you gonna stop with this eighty per cent innocent crap?' He jabbed a finger at his own chest. 'It's partly my fault – I should've shopped you to the publisher the moment you told me you were guilty. Wake up, Bandit. You're in a world of shit and pain. Take responsibility. There's no running away from this. Tell your folks. Plead guilty. Pay your fine, do your community service and then rebuild your life. People've come back from worse. You just need a bit of courage, that's all.'

I nodded, but it was the nod of someone who wants the talking to stop because their head is hurting.

'Am I talking to myself here?' he said.

'No, I'm listening.'

'And Bandit.'

'Yeah?'

'Stay out of trouble while you're on suspension. D'you think you can manage that?'

'Course, Al.'

THIRTY THREE

Post suspension, I dedicated myself to Rollo's mail-order porn business. We'd already mailed out over one thousand catalogues, and now orders for magazines and videos were starring to flood in. My habit was to rise around midday, invariably hungover, and watch crap telly for an hour, before heading to the post office to pick up that day's PO Box mail-orders. I'd then make for the cellar to fulfill the orders. Emdel's spectacular spreadsheet made processing most orders a relatively straightforward process, although I found using the spreadsheet a little discomfiting. It was like stepping inside his semen theme-park of a mind.

The problems arose when trying to fulfill orders for gay material. While three-quarters of Rollo's stock had been catalogued to within an inch of its seamy life, the gay stuff was a disaster zone, with videos and magazines strewn knee-deep across one end of the cellar, because Emdel flat-refused to have anything to do with it, and I had refused on principle to do the work on my own. This meant that for gay orders, I was reduced to rummaging through piles of random material, cursing Emdel as I did so. Despite this, I liked being down the cellar. It was like a dark, dank womb that protected me from the vicissitude of my upstairs life.

One mid-afternoon, when I was digging frantically through gay mags and videos, like a rescue worker looking for earthquake survivors, the phone rang. It's probably Big Al, I thought. He was helping me build my contempt of court argument against The Tribune, for re-publishing the Santa photo.

'Llew here,' I said into the receiver.

'It's Daphne Skinner,' came the reply. She was breathless, like she'd been running. Or was she scared? 'I called your office but they said you'd be at home. I'm in a phone box. Take down this number and call me right back.'

She gave me the number and hung up. I rang it.

'Llew,' she said without pause. 'Something big's gone down. John's been doing his absolute nut. Someone knocked off his private shop in the Leigh Park Estate.'

'When was this?'

'About six weeks ago.'

'Six weeks ago! Why are you only telling me now?'

'I only found out about it yesterday,' she said, with a hint of irritation. 'I knew something big was up because he had his men rip out all the wardrobes, and we've since had new ones fitted. But I didn't know what was going down, exactly. Then last night he was screaming down the phone, and I listened at the door.'

'And?'

'He was going mental about the robbery.'

'Because he wants his porn back?'

'No, not the porn. A bit of stolen porn's nothing to him in the great scheme of things.'

'What, then?'

'You remember what we talked about when you came to the barbecue, about the blackmail tapes?'

'Yeah, course.'

'Well, whoever turned over the shop stole more than they bargained for.'

'The tapes?'

'Yeah. That's what this is about. He's spooked, big time.'

'Christ almighty. Who was he shouting at? D'you know?'

'Freddie, his security guy. Ex-navy. Big bloke, blond, some kind of special forces bod. You know, the sort who can kill you with his thumb. It was Freddie and some other meathead who ripped out the wardrobes.'

'What d'you know about this Freddie?'

'Not much, only that he lives down Poole way. That's where John keeps his yacht. Freddie skippers it when John takes his cronies out sailing.'

'What was he shouting about down the phone?'

'I can tell you exactly what he said: "It's been six fucking weeks since the shop was robbed so why the fuck haven't you found those tapes yet? I pay you to crack skulls and get results, not to play about on boats."'

'Did he say anything else?'

'He told Freddie to step up the hunt, to throw more men at it. That's all I heard. And Llew.'

'Yeah?'

'Can I ask you something?'

'Sure.'

'Did you really shit on that altar?'

'No, Daphne, I didn't.' At least not the first, third, fourth nor fifth times I told myself, yet again.

'I didn't think so. Good luck with the trial. He was a bastard for running that piece on you. Take care, honey. I'll be in touch if I hear anything else. Bye.'

I called Big Al immediately.

'Those tapes could be anywhere by now,' he said, after I'd run Daphne's call past him. 'Chances are, they'll be lost forever. Shame,' he added, 'but at least Skinner's suffering. That's something.'

'It's probably a local job,' I said. 'Those tapes might still turn up somewhere, mightn't they?'

Before the sentence had left my lips, my guts were turning cartwheels.

I replayed events from the night Jimmy rocked up with the porn, Rollo had given him the third degree – about whether Jimmy was using again, and about whether the porn really was from down Bristol way. Jimmy hadn't had the 'flu at all, I realised. He had relapsed, and had been so desperate for cash that he'd knocked off Skinner's shop, and lied to Rollo about it.

'Hello? You still there, Bandit?'

*

I pushed through the door to the Mow's saloon bar. I was after Alfred, and was never more pleased to see him in his usual position, although in truth the odds of him not being there were short; Blanche had bar stools that spent less time in the place than he did.

'Thank god you're here, Alfred.'

'You're out of breath, old chap.'

'I ran here.'

After putting the phone down on Big Al, I'd sprinted from the house. If we really did have Skinner's porn in our cellar then we also had his blackmail tapes, and the shadow of Skinner's goon, Freddie, loomed large over me. It would surely be just a question of time before Freddie got round to scoping out Rollo, and once he had Rollo in his sights then I'd be next, given my history with Skinner. So my first port of call was Alfred, that one-man Royal Navy archive.

'I'll be the first to admit that I like my drink,' said Alfred, 'but not enough to run here.'

'It's not that … I need to speak to you … about something. Urgently.'

I gave him a reworked version of what Daphne had told me, omitting names and all mention of porn.

Alfred swirled his triple cognac around his bowl of a glass before he spoke. 'Poole, you say? Special forces, you say? That'll be the SBS.'

'The what?'

'SBS. Special Boat Service. Based in Poole. Recon specialists. Elite marines. First men to step foot on the Falklands. Helped secure South Georgia. Led the assault on Port Stanley. SAS of the navy. Absolute top drawer.'

'So they're tough then, these SBS guys?'

Alfred readjusted his tie, which was covered in small, indeterminate crests. 'Lethal. Kill you with a look. Why the panic?'

'Er, I might have pissed off the wrong person.'

'Then best watch your back,' Alfred said, patting my hand. 'Hate to see you get hurt, old boy.'

THIRTY FOUR

If Skinner's blackmail tapes really were somewhere in our cellar then we needed to find them, and fast. Freddie had been hunting them down for six weeks already; he must be closing in on us. There was only one place the tapes could possibly be: amid the carnage of the unsorted gay porn. It wasn't just a case of having to rummage through it all either. If we were to find those blackmail tapes then we would need to put every single unsorted gay video into a VCR and speed-scroll through.

'There's no way I'm watching that fag stuff,' Emdel had protested.

'Oh, for chrissake,' I'd said. 'Can't you give your gay-bashing alter-ego the week off? This is life and death. Or maybe you want Skinner's man to snap our necks like twigs, is that it?'

My outburst had prompted Emdel to suggest enlisting the help of our porn-library membership. His plan was to get a message to them at work, for them to come over to ours that night, because we had 'a big announcement' to make.

Bryan and Darryl arrived dressed as warlock and druid respectively. The Brothers Grimm had by now progressed to watching porn, playing chess *and* partaking in Dungeons & Dragons – in character. And who says men can't multi-task? Mani, as usual, was wearing one of his random and meaningless sports club T-shirts. Jason, meanwhile, pulled up bang outside the front door in Maureen, with Glen on board. Over recent weeks Maureen had been creeping nearer and nearer to the house, and I had conceded defeat. Even the threat of Rollo kicking my arse was insufficient motivation for me to again face-down Jason's frankly disturbing separation anxiety over Maureen.

'Gentlemen,' I said, when everyone was gathered, 'I am afraid that tonight is the last night of the Silver Street Pornography Reference Library.'

A collective groan went up. I thought Jason might cry.

'Thank you for your loyal custom. Naturally, we'll refund any of you who've paid in advance up to the end of the month.'

'Excusing me, please Mr Loo,' said Mani, with his hand in the air, like it was primary school. 'Can we be taking anything with us, as a mammary of our time here?'

'You mean like a souvenir?' I said, smiling at his latest music-hall verbal blunder.

He nodded, sideways, in that way people from the Indian sub-continent do – on telly, at least.

'This isn't a gift shop, Mani,' I said, 'and anyway, I don't think your mother would appreciate a copy of One in the Pink, One in the Stink, do you? Why don't you buy her a snow globe instead.'

Everyone laughed, including Mani, even though he later asked me what a snow globe was.

'But why are you closing?' Glen asked, when things had calmed down.

'Because we're tired,' I lied. 'We want our lives back.'

Emdel nodded his staged-managed agreement.

I looked from one android to the next. 'Gentlemen,' I continued, 'we have a favour to ask of you tonight. The owner of all the lovely merchandise that you've been enjoying so much these past six weeks has asked us to locate a number of, um, specialist videos that are extremely collectible and quite valuable. His need is quite urgent and we'd appreciate it if you could help us locate them.'

'What's in it for us?' asked warlock Bryan. 'We're still paying for tonight, don't forget.'

'Yeah,' chimed Darryl. It was the only occasion I ever heard him speak.

A murmour of agreement rose from the others. I looked at Emdel. We'd foreseen this.

I beckoned for silence. 'Okay, fair enough. As a thank you for your work, everyone can take a few items home with them, free of charge. How's that?'

As one, they surged towards the door.

'Hang on, hang on,' I said. 'Hold your horses. I meant at the end of the night, after you've helped us.'

'So what do you want us to do?' Glen asked.

'You've probably noticed that at one end of the cellar, the floor is buried under a mass of unsorted magazines and videos. We need you to work your way through all that stuff, sampling every video, until we have what we want.'

'But what are we looking for?' asked Jason.

This was the tricky part. From what I knew, the androids were barely any less homophobic than Emdel, and here I was about to ask them to spend an evening watching some of the vilest gay porn ever committed to magnetic tape. There was nothing for it, so I just came out with it.

'It's hard-core gay material. Highly collectible,' I reminded them, as if this would somehow soften the blow.

'No way,' Glen said.

'Forget it,' said Bryan.

'What is being wrong with gay?' asked Mani. 'I am very gay fellow.'

'It's not that kind of gay, Mani.' I explained. 'It's the kind of gay where two men, um, you know ...' I made a fist and slid my index finger in and out of it.

'Oh, no, no, no, no, no,' he said, joining the chorus of disgust.

We'd anticipated this, too.

'Okay,' I said. 'If you help us then you can take home as much free porn as you can carry. How does that sound?'

After some prevarication they agreed, but as they made for the cellar their body language was that of conscripts, ordered to charge across open ground towards enemy guns. Down in the cellar, I stood beside the chaotic mound of gay videos and magazines, waiting for them to gather around.

'We have to watch all of the videos in this huge pile because the tapes we're looking for could be any of them.'

'How will we know when we've found them?' asked Glen.

'Good question,' I said. 'What you're looking for is any film that's been shot from a single fixed-position camera, and that shows two men on a bed ... doing stuff. There'll be no editing or plot-lines and the lighting will also likely be rubbish. Home videos, basically. And old, dating back to the 1970s.'

'They don't sound very valuable,' said Bryan.

'One man's pig is another's man's pork,' I said, not knowing where the idiom had come from or what it might mean. 'Isn't that right, Emdel?'

But Emdel was nowhere to be seen. He'd sloped off, as far away from this subterranean gayathon as possible.

'Right,' I said, shaking my head at his latest dereliction of duty. 'Get to it lads. You'll see that we've set up two work stations, each with a TV and VCR. Take it in turns to watch and to sort.'

THUMP, THUMP, THUMP. Even from down in the cellar I could hear the front door being hammered by a fist. It could only be Rollo. I raced up the steps to intercept Emdel, to stop him answering the door, but I was too late.

'What the fuck is that clown car doing parked outside your gaff again?' Rollo yelled at me, as I appeared at Emdel's shoulder. 'Where's the berk what owns it? I wanna speak to him.'

Breath, Llew. Nice and steady.

'He's inside,' I said, acting all light-hearted. 'Playing Dungeons & Dragons.'

I heard feet thudding up the cellar steps, like echoes of my pounding heart.

'What the fuck?' said Rollo, looking from me to Emdel. 'Who's down your cellar, you motherfuckers?'

The pair of us swapped looks of alarm, which only intensified at the sight of Darryl and Bryan heading down the hall towards us. They joined us at the door.

'Who... who are they?' Rollo asked, momentarily too stunned to shout or curse. 'Who the *fuck* are they?'

'Bryan,' said Bryan. 'With a y.'

Bryan stuck out a hand, as if he expected Rollo to rise from his chair, climb the two steps into the hall, and shake it.

'Fuck you, Merlin. This isn't a social call, you cunt. Sabler, get me in the house – now!'

I hauled his chair backwards up the steps.

'Llew, that stuff you want us to watch is disgusting,' said Bryan, tugging at my elbow. I motioned for him to button it, but he pressed on. 'There were men and dogs doing stuff in the very first film I watched. Me and Darryl have had enough. You can keep your free porn.'

Rollo pivoted his chair on a sixpence. 'What'd he say about free porn?'

'Bryan,' I said, 'take Darryl and go back downstairs with the others.'

'What others?' Rollo hissed.

'We don't have to stay if we don't want to,' Bryan said, addressing me but glancing at Rollo.

Sensing Rollo was about to erupt, Darryl and Bryan thought better of attempting to leave, and made for the cellar.

'Emdel, go with them,' I said. 'I need to speak with Rollo.'

'Too fucking right you do, Sabler,' Rollo said.

I was alone with him in the hallway for mere seconds when he wheeled himself at me with such speed I had no time to react. His steel footrests clattered my shins, and as I doubled up, howling, he grabbed two fistfuls of my thick hair and jerked my head around so that I was facing him, and with such violence that my vertebrae popped like firecrackers. He leaned into me, close enough for me to smell fish on his breath.

'Talk. What the fuck were Merlin and Gandalf doing in the cellar, and who else is down there?'

Half bewildered with pain and panic, I struggled to think straight.

'Let go of me and I'll tell you.'

He released my hair and shoved me backwards, so that I landed on my backside. I didn't even try to stand; pain was gunning in my shins like a brace of performance engines. So I sat there, massaging away some of the agony, and told him about Skinner's porn empire, his blackmail racket, Daphne's phone call – about her husband's shop being robbed, blackmail tapes and all.

'And how the fuck does any of that explain why a bunch of freaks are pawing through my porn?'

'Because they're helping us look for Skinner's blackmail tapes. See Rollo, your porn isn't from Bristol. Jimmy lied to you. It's Skinner's, and he wants it back. More specifically, he wants those tapes back, because in the wrong hands they could get him sent down, and I'm very much the wrong hands.'

He sat there wordlessly. Just seconds earlier he'd been all bunched muscle and straining sinew but now he was slumped and flaccid, all the air sucked from him. If I had any hope of hiding our library venture from him, now was the time.

'Merlin and his mates came round to play Dungeons & Dragons,' I said, appealing for reason. 'They're only in the cellar because they're helping us sift through the unsorted gay stuff for Skinner's tapes. I told them they could take a few magazines and videos each as payment. They're helping you, Rollo. That's the truth.'

'Hang on,' he said. 'Did you say unsorted? Are you telling me there's stuff down there you haven't catalogued?'

'Yeah, well, we had a labour relations issue, but don't worry – the gay stuff's still being mailed out. It just takes a bit longer, that's all.'

'I paid you to catalogue all of that porn, not some of it. You're a bigger fucking crook than me, and that altar stunt of yours proves it.'

Rollo was trying to summon anger, rather than actually being angry, as he'd been before. He had a faraway look in his eye.

'Lucy warned me to stay away from that porn,' he said. 'I should've listened to her.'

'Lucy knows about the porn?'

'Course. We do everything as a family – me, Lucy and Ma. She came over here to butter you up with that Robin Hood story. Without your cellar, the mail-order thing wouldn't've been a runner.'

It was my turn to have the air sucked from me.

'That was all lies then, what she told me?'

'No. Everything happened exactly like she said.' Rollo sat in silence, looking into the mid-distance. He was someplace else.

'I'll go check on progress downstairs and report back,' I said quickly, desperate to grab a few moments alone with the androids, to make sure none of them mentioned anything about a porn library. If they did so, then Rollo would not have to summon anger; a pyroclastic flow of it would explode from him.

I flung myself down the cellar stairs.

'Right, gather round,' I said, only a shade above a whisper, in case Rollo had rolled himself anywhere near the hatch. I laid the Dungeons & Dragons cover story on them, then lifted my trouser legs to show them my swollen, bleeding shins. 'He did this without even knowing about the library. He attacked me just for you lot being down here, so just imagine what he'll do if any of you lot mention the library. So mum's the word, okay.'

The androids nodded, but I could see the evening was beginning to take its toll on their circuitry. Their eyes were glazed and their heads lolling. I could only pray that none of them would blow a resistor, and then go on to blow our cover story. Seconds after I'd finished speaking, a soft thud issued from above, and I guessed Rollo had levered himself from his chair to my bedroom floor. Almost immediately, he was levering himself down the cellar steps on his arms.

I offered him a chair, and he hoisted himself into it with practised ease. He sat for a few moments, casting his eye over the core membership of the Silver Street Pornography Reference Library.

'Dungeons & fucking Dragons,' he said, with a shake of the head and a suck of the teeth. 'And which of you losers owns the Roller?'

'She's mine,' Jason said, beaming. 'Beauty, isn't she.'

'No she fucking ain't. She's a dog, and if you park it anywhere round here again I'll do the fucking tyres. Capiche?'

Jason nodded, and whimpered, like a pup having its nose rubbed in its mess.

'Get back to work,' he ordered them. 'No one's leaving 'til you've found what we're looking for. You two,' he added, pointing at me and Emdel 'Stay down here and supervise. I'm going upstairs for a bite to eat and to watch some telly. Come get me when there's anything to know. You got any peanut butter?'

*

We worked in silence. I sat at one work station and Jason at the other. The rest of them had refused to watch any videos, and were instead sifting through the pile of porn on the floor, along with a grimacing Emdel. Jason – being malleable and compliant – had been lumbered with the video-watching brief.

After three hours' gazing at every gay sex act imaginable – some involving objects and beasts that had no earthly business being anywhere near a human orifice – I was fit to collapse. Surprisingly, Jason was bearing up far better than me, whipping through tapes at a fair lick, seemingly detached from the sordid action playing out on his screen. He clearly had a facility for this kind of work, although how he might apply it to the wider job market, I'm unsure.

'Hey, Llew,' Jason said, giving me a prod, after I'd nodded off momentarily. 'What about this one?' He was pointing at his monitor, which showed two men on a bed. 'A single fixed camera, no frills,' he added. 'Just like you said.'

At that, the others crowded around Jason's screen.

'It's pretty tame compared to most of the other stuff,' said Jason. 'No animals, fisting, shitting, or nothing. Just a bit of anal and oral and lots of kissing.'

'Eject it,' I said. 'Show me the casing.'

He gave me the tape, and I turned it over in my hand. On the spine was a hand-written date: 5/5/78, and two pairs of initials in the same loopy script: EW & HG.

'Right,' I said, holding up the tape for everyone's inspection. 'See this writing on the spine? That's the kind of thing you need to look out for.'

Within an hour they had trawled through everything, and I had thirteen similar tapes piled at my feet.

'Right lads, your work's done here. Thanks for your help, and for your membership. Good luck.'

'Are we having gifts now, like you did say?' Mani asked, hand in air.

The others chorused Mani's question, with slightly more serviceable English.

I lifted my trouser legs, to reacquaint them with my battered shins. 'If you wanna try to sneak past him with an armful of his porn, be my guest. Just don't expect me to visit you in hospital.'

They shuffled about, muttering to themselves.

'I think we'll come back,' said Glen, speaking for them all.

'A wise choice. Emdel will let you know when's good,' I said, after which they filed upstairs.'

'Where are you freaks off to?' I heard Rollo shout. 'Middle fucking Earth?'

A moment later, Rollo appeared at the mouth of the cellar.

'We've got the tapes,' I called up to him.

'Bring 'em up here,' he barked. 'They're mine. I want 'em as insurance, in case Skinner tries anything.'

'You can have them when I've made copies,' I replied. 'You're not the only one who wants some insurance. Don't forget whose house Skinner's porn's in.'

'All right, but make sure them tapes are with me in two days. Don't make me come knocking. Now get me the fuck out of this house, Sabler, you cunt.'

THIRTY FIVE

It was Bernie the Shirt who told me that Rollo's mother, Aggie, had died from stomach cancer. He'd heard the news from his wife, who was a dinner lady at Lucy's school. I'd bumped into Bernie at a local convenience store near the Mow, and with no UN Mickey to translate, he'd had to repeat himself multiple times, during which most of his Silk Cut ended up as ash in his exposed chest hair. In the end, a cursing Bernie had grabbed my notebook and scrawled his news in there, shoving it back at me and muttering under his breath as he left the shop. His writing was almost as indecipherable as his voice was impenetrable, but I just about made it out.

Even though Rollo and his duplicitous daughter were the last people I wanted to visit, I felt honour-bound to pay my respects.

*

Rollo was slumped in his chair outisde his flat, greeting mourners. I was in a thirty-yard queue that grew no shorter in the time it took for me to reach Rollo's front door. Most of the mourners were carrying envelopes, and I wondered if these contained sympathy cards or repayments – or perhaps both? As I stood in front of Rollo, he gave me a blank look that could have meant anything, from numb grief to the promise of more violence against my person. At least he took my proffered hand, which was a good sign I felt. I told him that we needed to talk, and then headed inside the flat.

Aggie was lying in state in the living room in an open coffin. She was skeletal and appeared not just dead, but mummified. Everything about her was desiccated and sunken. Her skin was the colour of Dijon mustard.

As I filed back out of the flat I cast about for Lucy, but there was no sign of her. She must be at school, I thought. I'd heard people say that in times of grief it's important for people to stick to routines, especially if young. Maybe that was it.

'Excuse me everyone,' Rollo said in a booming voice when I emerged from the flat. 'I've got some important funeral business to discuss with this fella here,' he added, grabbing a fistful of my trouser leg. 'I'll be back shortly. Thank you all for coming to pay your respects. It's greatly appreciated.'

Rollo wheeled himself down the queue of people, all of whom lowered their heads as he passed, with some of the older ones even clutching imaginary hats to their chests. When clear of the flats, Rollo took a couple of lefts and rights and stopped in a Metal Estate cul de sac I'd not seen before.

'You done my copies of those tapes yet?'

'Yeah. I'll drop them off tonight.'

'I want the originals,' he said, jabbing a finger my way.

'S'fine. Here.'

I reached inside my jacket and slid out a fat wad of postal orders, bound by an elastic band. Rollo's mail-order punters paid by postal order because it meant he didn't have to put anything through a bank account.

'The money's rolling in,' I said. 'Every day seems to bring more than the last.'

'Yeah,' he said, flat, as if I'd handed him a damp dishcloth.

'So what will you do with the tapes?' I asked him.

'Depends how this plays out. Hopefully I won't need 'em at all. How much of the porn's left.'

'Just under half, but we want rid, now,' I told him, my heart shifting into top gear. I knew he'd not take kindly my demand. 'You can't expect us to keep selling it while Skinner's man out there, hunting us down,' I added, with as much conviction as my racing heart would allow.

He aimed a finger at me. 'Fuck off. You'll keep going for another two weeks. Whatever's left after that, we'll ditch.'

'Two weeks?' I said, aghast. 'No way. What if in that time Skinner finds Jimmy, and makes him talk?'

'He'd've picked him up already if that was gonna happen,' Rollo said, sounding pretty sure of himself, from which I drew a little comfort. 'Besides,' he added, 'you let me worry about that toe-rag Jimmy.'

It was hard to know who was worse news for Jimmy – Rollo or Skinner. And I didn't want to know.

'Two weeks is too long,' I insisted. 'It's all right for you. The porn's not down your cellar, is it.'

'Oh, for fuck's sake Sabler, all right then. Give it another week, then ditch whatever's left.'

I nodded my thanks.

'Listen,' he said, running his tongue over his teeth. 'Before you go, I've gotta ask: did you really wank over that altar?'

'What? I didn't wa—' I stopped myself from correcting him, the moral distinction between defecating on an altar and masturbating over one being something of a grey area. 'No, I didn't.'

'Okay, just curious. And Sabler?'

'Yeah?'

'Thanks for coming today.'

THIRTY SIX

AGGIE'S FUNERAL CORTÈGE BROUGHT SOUTHSEA to a standstill, such were the numbers following her coffin on foot. The Metal Estate had turned out en masse to honour their de facto matriarch. One frustrated motorist, tailing the cortège in first gear, beeped his horn in frustration, prompting those mourners closest to him to engulf his car. They pounded on its windows and coachwork with their fists, screaming the kind of abuse more often heard on a football terrace. There was no more beeping after that, from anyone.

There was neither hearse nor carriage. Instead, Aggie's coffin was borne upon the shoulders of her friends and neighbours, who took it in turns to share that privilege. Leading the cortège was Rollo and Lucy. Both looked hollowed out, and I felt for them. It had been Aggie who had held their worlds together when life had threatened to destroy them.

I shadowed the cortège from the pavement. Having met Aggie just the once I was more onlooker than mourner. Mike was with me, shooting away. I wasn't sure about the protocol of taking photos at a funeral. Mike did get some funny looks but I thought Rollo and Lucy might welcome some pictures later on – that they might look at them and take comfort from being reminded just how many lives Aggie had touched.

There was to be no service, only a committal because Aggie had been an atheist. Rollo would deliver a eulogy, and that would be it. I already knew what he was planning to say because he had asked me to go over his words a few days earlier. I feared for him, and how he would cope; what he was planning to say was shocking.

I took up position at the back of the huge crowd that gathered in the cemetery. I was around twenty-five yards from the graveside. Silence settled upon us, until the only sounds were birdsong and the rustle of the breeze through the canopies of the large yew trees that were dotted about the place.

'Thank you all for coming here today,' came Rollo's voice through a loudspeaker. 'I just wish Ma could have seen these amazing scenes for herself. She would have been overwhelmed. Ma,' he continued, after a pause, 'was a one-off. She cared about others more than she cared about herself. You only need to look around you today to see the truth of that.

'Today isn't about me or Lucy, and how broken up we are at Ma's passing. Today isn't about how any of us feel. Today is about Ma. We're here to celebrate this amazing woman and her amazing life.'

There was a ripple of applause.

'I'd like to share with you just one story about Ma. It won't be an easy one for me to tell and neither will it be an easy one for you to listen to, but it sums up what this incredible woman was all about.

'I think most of you know my history – about the reclamation business, the accident, the drinking ... and Sheila. I was in a very bad place back then, and so was our Lucy. Things got pretty dark. In fact they got so dark that one day, in tears, I told Ma I couldn't go on, that I'd had enough, that I wanted to end it all.

'What d'you think she did? D'you think she showered me with motherly love, telling me that everything would be all right? No. She left the room, and I heard her rummaging about in the cupboard under the stairs. When she came back in she was holding a length of yellow washing line, still in its packet. She tossed it into my lap.

'D'you know what she said to me? She said that if I was going to kill myself then I'd better bloody well do it in one of my garages because Lucy had already found one parent dead by their own hand.

'Ma left the room after that, and I heard her go out. So I was left there, staring at that cord in my lap. I didn't move from that spot for hours, thinking about what she'd said. I sat there for as long as it took me to understand what she'd really meant by it. I came to understand she'd meant that life is not about us as individuals, it's about us as people, as families, as friends, as colleagues, and as communities. She made me see that none of us is answerable only to ourselves. Have you ever wondered why selfish bastards are so fucking miserable? That's why. And what's more selfish than doing yourself in. That's what Ma taught me that day, when she saved my life. Thank you all again.'

Someone near me began clapping and the sound of birdsong and rustling trees was quickly drowned out by the thunder of applause, which rolled on and on because no one wanted to be the first to stop.

Some minutes later Rollo came past, being pushed by Lucy. He was sobbing. Crying is a function of physical pain and emotional upset. But sobbing? This issues from the soul, and finds best expression through the shoulders. Piston-like, Rollo's were pumping wave upon wave of grief through him, until he was paralysed by it. Lucy was impassive as she pushed her father, looking up ahead with eyes that were dry and unseeing. Her pain would surface later, I knew – but for now she was being strong for her dad.

THIRTY SEVEN

The initials on the spine of the videotape were 'DH & MO'. It was the only blackmail video whose pairs of initials started with a D and an M. It had to be David and Max. I slipped the cassette into the caddy, rewound it to the start and pressed 'play'. I sat back, chewing my lip until the screen flickered into life. I recognised the backdrop immediately: Daphne's bedroom. As with the other tapes, the room was empty to begin with. I fast-forwarded, until two figures entered at high speed, like a pair of randy Keystone Cops. Then I hit 'play'.

Max had his back to the camera but David was facing it. He was impossibly youthful and handsome, and seemingly happy. They began undressing one another, and then lay on the bed, Max still with his back to the lens. They kissed, as passionately as I've ever seen any couple kiss. David took control, not something I had imagined him ever doing. He rose to his knees, straddling Max, whose face was now in profile, but partially obscured by crumpled bedding. David slid down Max's body, and took Max into his mouth. His lover groaned, and in his ecstasy turned his head to the side, so that he was now facing the hidden camera.

'Jesus Christ almighty,' I announced to the empty cellar. It's bloody Father O'Reardon.'

*

'So let me get this straight,' said Big Al, swilling the remnants of his tea around the mug, as he eased back into my living room sofa. 'The priest whose altar you shat on was cavorting with your man David in one of those tapes?'

'That's right.'

'Are you sure it's him? That film was shot a long time ago.'

'It's definitely him.'

He took a thoughtful draw on his cigarette. 'I'm still trying to get my head round how you got hold of those tapes in the first place.'

I'd told Big Al that someone had rung my bell late one night and had left them in a gaffer-taped sack on the doorstep. It was the best I could come up with. He seemed to buy it, in as much as he bought anything I said any more.

'I swear, Bandit,' he added, 'your life's like something from a frigging Marvel comic.'

'So what's my superpower?'

'Idiocy,' he replied without pause. 'You're Twat Man.'

'This is gonna sound weird,' I said, aware I might be about to cement my new super-antihero status, 'but I've got this funny feeling Max O'Reardon will end up talking to me, about the blackmail.'

Big Al spluttered, sending a plume of smoke across the room. He spent the next half-minute wracked by a coughing fit.

'You've gotta quit those things,' I said, once his beleaguered lungs had settled back down.

'I've changed brands, to Consulate,' he said, as if inhaling menthol on top of seven thousand other chemicals amounted to a health kick. 'Anyway, it's not these things that're killing me – it's you. What planet are you on, exactly? That priest isn't talking to you in a million years.'

'Yeah, but he's not your average priest. He's got no business being a cleric. It feels all wrong.'

'So now you're a judge of what's right and wrong? This, the man who crimped one off up at the holy end of a church.'

'I mean it, Al. Something about him doesn't add up.'

'What, because he's gay? Half the world's Catholic clergy bat for the other side.'

'No, not that. Think about it. He's been a priest for a good while, which means he must've entered seminary not long after he was blackmailed. That's no coincidence. The two things are linked somehow, I just know it.'

'So what if they are? The fact remains that you took a dump on his altar, so forget about the bloody priest, and focus on your man David. We need him to go on the record. He's our only hope. Without him on board then all we've got is a pile of old videos showing a bunch of blokes going at it. It'll be a glancing blow, not a knockout punch.'

'Maybe,' I said. 'But what about Thirza?'

'What about her?'

'Does she know about any of this? The tapes? Us tapping-up David?'

'No,' he said, wagging a finger. 'Things're complicated enough without John being involved. I'll tell her once we've got what we need from your man.'

'And if I get nothing from him?'

'Then there's nothing to tell. The story's dead.'

'But David might still tell Blanche I tried to get him to talk, and word's bound to get back to Thirza. She'll do her nut if she finds out we went behind her back.'

'I'll handle John,' Big Al said, with the air of a man who had faced far bigger workplace problems, not least of which was writing tomorrow's news alongside someone who liked to mainline vodka. 'Besides,' he added, 'She's a changed woman these days. That lady of hers seems to have calmed her right down. So don't worry about John,. Just concentrate on David. You'll need a clear mind if you're to get him to open up.'

'It won't be easy,' I said, 'even if I do say all the right things. It's gonna be a massive shock to him when he finds out I've got those tapes.'

'Then you need to ease those nerves of his.'

'But how?'

I picked up a beermat from off the coffee table and rubbed it up and down against my bristly chops, losing myself in thought as it rasped pleasingly.

'Hang on,' I said, holding the beer mat aloft in my inspiration, like a referee carding a player. 'Why don't I tell him that now I've got the blackmail tapes, Skinner's got no hold over him any more. I can remind him that he's finally free.'

'But what if Skinner's made copies of those tapes?'

'He only removed the one-way mirrors in his house a few weeks ago, after his shop was turned over. I think he got complacent. I think the tapes I've got are the only copies.'

'Go with that then, Bandit. Remind your man he's finally free of all this Skinner crap, and hopefully that'll loosen him up enough to talk.'

'Okay, but I'm not gonna push it,' I warned him. 'If David wants to talk, he'll talk.'

'Fair enough, but if he does open up then you be ready with that shit shorthand of yours and be sure to get everything down. Don't give him a chance to change his mind.'

'There's something else I'm gonna have to have to tell him before I get that far, Al.'

'What's that?'

'That if the cops end up charging Skinner on the strength of our story, then David'll be subpoenaed, and'll have to repeat in court whatever he's told us. He'll also be cross-examined, brutally, and the whole sordid affair'll be pored over by the nationals – and all with Skinner looking on. He needs to know all that.'

'You've got to be shitting me, Bandit. This is a man who's not been out of the house since 1984. One mention of courtrooms and you'll have him diving behind the sofa. It'll be game over.'

'But it's only right he knows what he's getting himself into. I think of him as a friend.'

'Don't. Mention. Subpoenas. I'm telling you. Concentrate on getting him to talk. We can deal with all that legal stuff further down the line. We'll look after him when the time comes, I promise you that.'

'I don't know, Al. I'm not comfortable with it.'

'You were comfortable enough shitting on that altar.'

He had a point.

'And need I remind you,' he added, 'this might be the last story you ever write. You're up before the beak in a fortnight. This is your chance to go out with a bang, and who knows? If you help put Skinner away then it might be a redemption thing for you. It's a fickle old world, Bandit. One minute you're the hack who crapped in a church, and the next you're the hero who helped jail a scumbag newspaper boss. People've got very short memories.'

'But not mentioning subpoenas. Wouldn't that be like using David, kind of?'

'Listen, my old son, life's not all black and white; there's a world of grey out there. If you mention subpoenas, there's no more David for sure, and Skinner's in the clear. Then no one gets justice do they – not David nor any of those other poor sods Skinner blackmailed. The bastard gets clean away with it. That's what's at stake here, Bandit. I'll leave that one with you.'

*

As ever, David enveloped me in a hug.

'And to what do I owe this pleasure?' he said, looking at his watch. 'It's a bit early in the day for musicals, even for me.' He leaned back and studied my face. 'How are you bearing up under the strain of that awful court case and everything?'

'It's not that,' I said. 'I've something to tell you. Can we sit down?'

Perched next to him on the sofa, I ran through everything – starting with Daphne's phone call about the burglary and ending with how I'd watched the tape of him and Max. As I spoke, David closed in on himself.

'Don't look so worried,' I said, patting his knee. 'This is good news. You know what it means, don't you? It means Skinner no longer has the tapes, which means he can't use them against you or any of the others. It means that you're finally free.'

He looked up, and faced me, stonily.

'Am I? Really?' All this stuff has been hanging over me for so long I barely know anything else. I doubt I shall ever be free again.'

'But what's not true. You *are* free, you just don't know it yet because you're in shock. Just give it a little time. This is a positive thing. It's definitely a positive thing.'

'You think?'

'I know.'

He gave me a watery smile.

'Listen, David, there's something else. I need to ask something of you.'

He frowned, and signalled for me to continue .

'Would you consider speaking to me about all of this, on the record?'

'All of what?'

'Your Skinner nightmare. The parties, the blackmail, how it's ruined your life and the lives of all those other men. Everything.'

He shuddered.

'B ... b ...but then the whole world would know about the awful things he made me do,' he said, standing. He started pacing about the living room.

'Why would I do the very thing that he threatened me with all those years ago? It makes no sense.'

'It makes perfect sense. You can make Skinner pay for what he's done. If you speak out then those tapes become hard evidence. Without you, they're just some old blue movies.'

He was still pacing, only more frantically now. 'I don't know, Llew. This is all so sudden. I think I need to lie down. Actually, I think I'd like you to go now, please.'

'Of course,' I said. 'Can I come see you another time?'

He didn't answer. He left the room and I heard his bedroom door click shut. I had planned to tell him about Max. It was just as well I didn't, else Blanche would have been left scraping his whimpering frame off the living room carpet.

*

'Bandit, you've got to get him to go on the record, and soon,' Big Al urged, down the phone. 'You'll be in stir in a fortnight, and that'll be game over for you.'

'Thanks for reminding me.'

'You say you'll plead guilty and then I'll stop reminding you. How's that?'

'David's not gonna talk,' I replied, sidestepping his offer; I had no idea how I would plead. I was doing everything in my power not to think about the trial. 'He's gone right back into his shell.'

'Are you sure didn't mention subpoenas?'

'Of course I'm sure. We didn't get that far. He fell to pieces at the mere thought of talking to us.'

I sighed, long and deep.

'Is Skinner really off the hook if David doesn't talk?' I asked.

'Yeah, he is, barring a miracle.'

THIRTY EIGHT

THE DOORBELL SOUNDED. I ROLLED over in bed to look at my clock: it was almost midday. What day was it, though? With no work to go to, there was nothing to delineate weekdays from weekends. I settled on Thursday.

I was expecting it to be Big Al. He'd said he'd drop by to thrash out strategies to get David to open up. I loped to the door, securing my dressing gown as I went, steeling myself for an earful about still being in bed at such an hour. Big Al felt I lacked self-discipline, and that prison might even be good for me in that regard. I could always rely on him to mention prison at least once every time we talked.

But it wasn't Big Al – it was David, and he pushed past me into the house.

'That bastard, that bastard, that bastard,' he repeated over and over, pointing at me as if I were the bastard in question. 'I want revenge,' he added, through clenched teeth.

I was too stunned to reply. His presence made no sense in any context other than Blanche's flat. It was as if he were an alien that had been teleported into my house. I wondered if I might not still be dreaming.

'I'm going to tell you everything,' he said, arms outstretched, like a holy man administering absolution. 'The parties, the blackmail, those vile films he made us do – everything. Get your notebook. I'm ready to talk. Have you got any gin?'

'Er, no. Only Jack Daniels.'

'That'll do. Make it a large one.'

*

I phoned Big Al the moment I had shown a drunken David from the house, some two hours later. He had indeed told me everything – too much, in fact. I could have done without the detailed descriptions of canine sex acts.

'And he didn't baulk when you mentioned subpoenas?' Big Al asked.

'No, if anything it spurred him on. D'you know what he said?'

'Go on.'

'That he feels he needs justice the same way he needs air. By the end he was so pissed and angry I thought he might trash the joint. I had to wrest a reading lamp from his hand at one point.'

'Well, he's got a lot to be angry about. When'll you have it written up, Bandit?'

'First thing Monday, latest.'

'You lovely boy. We'll run it in the next issue. This is big league. This time next week Skinner'll be history.' I heard him take a long draw on a cigarette, presumably a Consulate – unless he was done with his health kick and was back on Marlboros. 'It's just a shame that you won't be able to enjoy your moment of glory for a little longer than a few days, because you'll be banged up.'

Prison. Again. He would not give up until he had persuaded me to plead guilty.

'If you keep your head buried in the sand for much longer, then you'll get reamed from behind by everyone,' he added. 'The magistrates, the press ... not to mention your cell mate.'

'Give me a break, Al.'

Deep down I knew he was right, but regardless, I wanted my world to remain normal for as long as possible, if only in my head. I was a bit like a suicide jumper, mid-flight, trying to convince himself there is no such thing as the ground.

THIRTY NINE

BY THE TIME ROLLO PULLED the plug on his mail-order venture, Emdel and I had mailed out enough Jiffy Bags of porn to do what an Argie missile couldn't: sink HMS Broadsword. Rollo demanded that we dump whatever stock was left.

'And no funny business,' he warned, pointing a loaded finger at each of us in turn. 'Just bag the stuff up and take it down the tip. Capiche?'

Just minutes after I'd helped Rollo from the house, Emdel was left scratching his head.

'So let me get this straight,' he said. 'We're going to let Glen, Jason, Mani, Bryan and Darryl have all the porn that's left over, but only if they take the gay stuff as well?'

'Yeah,' I confirmed. 'That way they get the free stuff we promised them for helping us find the blackmail tapes, and also we don't have to worry about dumping any of it.'

'And what if Rollo finds out? You heard him. That bloke scares me.'

'He scares me too, but he's not gonna find out, is he. We'll have the androids come round late at night, when Rollo's safely tucked up in bed. With five of them on the job they'll be in and out in no time. No one'll see anything. It'll run like clockwork.'

*

The androids arrived en masse at one in the morning, as agreed. They poured out of a white Transit van so battered and decayed it made Maureen look like something from the Royal Garage. They filed into the house, and towards the cellar.

'Hey, where's your bags?' I asked as they passed by.

'Here,' Jason said, holding up a thin roll of bin liners.

'Bin liners?' I said, grabbing the roll from him, and tearing off a bag. 'They're not even decent ones,' I added, holding it up to the light. 'These're too flimsy for kitchen waste, let alone a half-ton of porn. The videos have got sharp corners – they'll cut these bags to shreds. I told you to get rubble sacks.'

'I couldn't find any. It'll be fine,' Jason said. 'We're only carrying them from yours to the van, and from the van into Glen's.'

'And where the hell did you get that van?' I asked, shoving the bag and the roll into Jason's chest.

'It's a mate's – a little favour that I called in.' He winked, as if he were some kind of big-shot wheeler-dealer.

'Little? Bloody microscopic, you mean. That thing's cruddier than your Roller. Is it even roadworthy?'

'No it isn't,' Glen called from my bedroom, as he and the others made their way to the cellar. 'We kangarooed all the way here. I've still got a headache.'

'S'not my fault,' Jason said. 'I'm used to Maureen. Her gear change is as sweet as honey.'

Shaking my head in despair, I repaired to the living room to work on my Skinner exposé for The Probe. It would almost certainly destroy him, of that I was sure, especially now that David's thirst for justice was unquenchable and his resolve unshakable. I would relish having my muddied professional reputation restored, however briefly, before my trial flushed it down the toilet for good.

Three sides of typed A4 later, Glen popped his head around the living room door.

'We're done.' he said. 'It's all bagged up.'

'Including the gay stuff, like we agreed?'

'Yeah, but we've no idea what we're going to do with all that crap.'

'Take it down the dump,' I said, 'but not in that ridiculous Transit. Use Maureen.'

Jesus Christ, I thought. Jason's got me at it now. It's a bloody car, I reminded myself. It's got an exhaust, not an anus.

'And for chrissake,' I added, 'make sure you re-bag the gay stuff in rubble sacks before you dump it. If that lot splits open up the tip you'll be lucky to get out of there alive.'

I'd been to the municipal dump just once during my time in Pompey. Most of the staff looked like they didn't welcome much colour in their lives, especially not pink or black.

'Okay, okay' Glen said, with a hint of irritation. 'I get it.'

They traipsed back and forth from cellar to van until everything was loaded.

'See you around, ladies,' I said from the doorstep, as I watched Glen and Mani clamber up into in the cab alongside Jason, and Bryan and Darryl hop into the back with the bags. Bryan was struggling to secure the doors from inside the van, and so I stepped outside in my bare feet to help him. My hand was reaching for the van door when Jason fired up the engine, and then crunched the van it into gear. I winced: a washing machine full of ball bearings would have made less noise. The Transit lurched forward, violently. Both rear doors swung open, and Bryan and Darryl were catapulted to the tarmac, landing at my feet, along with four sacks of porn – all of which split open and disgorged their sordid contents across the road. On and on the vehicle lurched, distributing porn like some kind of demented muck spreader. I looked on, frozen, as if in a nightmare, before snapping out of it and sprinting after the van.

'Stop, you idiot,' I called. 'STOP.'

By the time Jason heard me, Silver Street had kerb-to-kerb porn carpeting. Bryan and Daryl, meanwhile, were sitting in the road, nursing bruised limbs.

'What happened?' Jason said, as he stepped from the van and surveyed the carnage ranged before him.

I clenched and unclenched my fists.

'*You* happened. Clear it up, now,' I hissed. 'All of you.'

I helped them scoop up the porn, each of us scuttling about frantically, hurling armfuls of videos and magazines into the van. A neighbour from across the street watched on in a dressing gown, leaning on the door jamb – arms crossed and shaking his head. A few doors up, another man peered down at us from a window. I kept an eye out for Rollo, expecting him to come wheeling around the corner, in a blur of fury.

While on the look-out for Rollo, I spotted a man in an expensive-looking saloon car at the end of the road. His engine wasn't running, and he was looking on at us, impassively. I thought it odd, but in all the android madness he slipped from my mind. When we were done reloading, I climbed up into the driver's seat.

'Keys,' I demanded, looking at Jason and holding out a hand. 'Now. If you want something done,' I added, 'bloody well do it yourself.'

The pedals had no rubber sleeves, and their cold metal was soothing on my bare feet, which were smarting from the gritty road. I started the engine. Going from neutral to first was fine but shifting from first to second sent the van into drugs-crazed kangaroo mode, so I shifted back down, and we drove the two miles to Glen's place at 10mph, via the back streets so we'd not be pulled over by cops. Jason tried to make small talk but I told him to shut up. Even if I had wanted to listen, the Transit's engine – screaming in first – would've drowned him out.

'Shoes,' I said, when we reached Glen's place. 'I need someone's shoes. I leaned down and starting yanking at Jason's trainers. 'These'll do.'

'Oi,' he protested. 'You can't have those. They're my lucky pair.'

'Well thank Christ you didn't wear your unlucky pair.'

I pulled them off his feet and on to mine. They were unpleasantly warm and tight but would have to do. I set off. At the end of Glen's road, as I crossed the main drag, the same man I had seen earlier – sitting in the posh car, watching us – drove slowly past. He didn't look my way. I watched him disappear from sight, and the pinching trainers were such a distraction I forgot all about him.

*

By the time I got back to Silver Street, Jason's trainers were utter torture, and I was waddling from blister pain, looking like I'd shat myself.

The house was quiet; Emdel had gone home to visit his mother, who'd been hospitalised with an asthma attack, I went into the kitchen, grabbed a half-empty bottle of Jack, and then headed into my room. The androids had left the cellar hatch open. I took a long draft of Jack, and stared down into the darkness. That cellar had become the epicentre of my life, yet now it was just an empty space once again. I climbed down, bottle in hand.

The androids had done a thorough job; the porn was completely gone. All that was left to suggest the place had been anything other than an old beer cellar was some mailing equipment – scales, franking machine, mail sacks, pre-paid postage ink-stamps and a stack of Jiffy Bags. With the place shorn of porn, the sound of my footsteps was no longer muted, but harsh and scratchy. The natural damp odour of the place had also reasserted itself, having been eclipsed for a time by the smell of paper and ink.

I took a deep draft of bourbon, before setting the bottle down, and stuffing the postal equipment into a couple of mail sacks. I took one last look around, and smiled. Over the previous couple of months, Emdel and I had toiled deep into many a night, first cataloguing the porn and then mailing it out, for the self-pleasure of punters from Aberdeen to Truro, and pretty much everywhere in between. I wondered if, for Emdel, Project Porn had been personal in a way that it hadn't for me. I mean, his DNA had been all over the endeavour, both figuratively and literally. In mailing the pornography to the four corners of the UK, I wondered if Emdel had not felt that part of him, too, was being dissembled, packaged and posted far and wide.

With exhaustion clouding that thought, I climbed back up into my bedroom, closed the cellar hatch, slid the rug back into position and collapsed into bed. I slugged some more Jack, and was asleep before it was done burning my gullet.

FORTY

I WAS PINNED TO THE railway track by some invisible force. It was night-time, and silent. The rails started singing, soft at first, like a lament, but louder with each passing second. There was a distant train whistle that all too soon became an ear-shredding shriek. A steam locomotive roared my way. The engine's wheels locked, sending out twin showers of sparks that filled the air with foundry smells. My screams were lost in that of the wheels. I clamped shut my eyes, ready to be sliced into thirds, but then I awoke – to find I was in bed, able to move only my head and ankles; everything else was trapped under the quilt. My senses cleared, and a figure – looming and shadowy – revealed itself to me. The creeping warmth of puddling urine caressed my buttocks. I think I might have yelped, like a distressed puppy.

The light was turned on. The figure above me was shadowy no longer, but more looming than ever. He was astride me, his knees pinning me tight. He had a full head of dark hair that had been butchered into a mullet, and he was sporting a moustache that had annexed half of his face. Unlike Rollo, who had similarly ambitious facial hair, this man absolutely resembled a Seventies German porn star. The Hai Karate aftershave that Herr Porn was wearing transported me, portal-like, into the folks' living room on Christmas morning 1980, to Dad unwrapping the grooming kit I had gifted him. My eyes met Herr Porno's. They were impassive, like this was just another job for him, one that was keeping him from being in his rightful place, snuggled up next to Fraulein Porno.

'Do we have your attention, Mr Sabler?'

The voice came from somewhere behind Herr Porno. A second later its owner appeared at the side of my bed. He was tall, lean and muscled, mid-fortyish and with blond hair that was little more than a cap of stubble. He was handsome, in an Action Man kind of way. In one large hand he held a roll of clingfilm that was thrice the diameter of any I'd ever seen in the shops. The sight of it took me beyond fear to an other-worldly place where time moved so slowly that I was able to glimpse the true nature of things. In that roll of clingfilm, I saw death, and yet I had never felt more alive. Inexplicably, I bristled with confidence and a spectacularly misplaced sense of indomitability.

'Let me guess,' I said, eyeing the man with the clingfilm. 'It's Freddie, isn't it? SBS Freddie, from Poole. How the mighty have fallen. From Falklands hero to pornographer's henchman. That's some career path. What's next? Working the door at Secrets Nightclub, opposite the pier?'

Freddie blinked rapidly. His jaw muscles bunched.

'And who's this?' I said, looking up at Herr Porno. 'You look like something from one of Skinner's gay flicks. Which one was it? Arse Bandits Ride Again?'

Herr Porno wound back a fist and was about to crunch it into my face, but Freddie grabbed his arm and put him in some kind of hold – one Thirza doubtless knew, I thought. Herr Porno gave a grunt of pain.

'You're not to leave a mark on him, you cretin,' Freddie hissed. 'We talked about that. Right, you,' he added, pointing at me with the clingfilm. 'Let's get down to business.'

'Business?' I said. 'By that I take it you mean you want me tell you where the blackmail tapes are, so that you can get on with trussing me up in that clingfilm and hanging me by the neck 'til I'm dead, then unwrapping me and clearing off, so it'll look like I've topped myself – because of the stress of my trial next week. Tell me I'm wrong.'

I had no idea where any of that had come from; the story had just unfolded before my eyes.

'How the fuck did you know th—'

'Shut up,' Freddie told Herr Porno, 'and stay shut up. And you,' he added, tapping my head with the heavy roll, 'can be as clever as you like. It'll make no difference.'

'If you think I'm gonna talk when you're going to kill me anyway, you're an idiot.'

Freddie smirked. 'Me? An idiot? I wasn't the one driving across town in a bouncing van full of porn and morons.'

It was a fair point, well made.

'We followed you,' he continued. 'It wasn't exactly difficult. We know where to find your moron mates, if we need to, but we're not interested in them, or the porn. We just want the tapes – the originals, that is, not the copies we found in your cellar, while you were off hopping across town. You left your front door on the latch, by the way.'

Freddie tutted and shook his head.

'We've had eyes on that Rollo Baer for a while.' he continued. 'We picked the locks of all his garages but found nothing to link him to any of this business. We were about to call it quits, but then you and your mates went hopping by in that van, spewing porn across the street. D'you know, you might just about be the stupidest person I've ever met. I think we might actually be doing you a favour here, by putting you out of your misery.'

I vowed that – should I somehow escape the clutches of Freddie and Herr Porno – I would truss Jason up in clingfilm, and force him to watch me torch Maureen.

'Once we clocked your cellar,' Freddie went on, 'it all fell into place. Baer used it to store the porn, and you helped him flog it by mail order. Then you chanced across those tapes, and you knew exactly what they were, and whose porn you had. The gaffer told me how you were poking about his gaff during the barbecue. Then you told Baer that he had Skinner's porn. He demanded you hand over those tapes as insurance, in case we ever caught up with him. But you made copies first, for that rag of yours. Tell me I'm wrong.'

Again, he smirked, then perched on the side of the bed, pulling the bedclothes python-tight about my shoulders. 'So you see, Mr Sabler, all we need from you is your silence. Nothing else.'

'You're too late. I said,' dredging defiance from somewhere. 'The story's already written. We've got one of Skinner's blackmail victims to go on the record.'

'So?' Freddie said, shrugging. 'Without those tapes, whatever you write will just be words.'

The truth of it was sickening. Before, we had the tapes but no David, and now it was the other way round. I had to sow at least some doubt in that scumbag Skinner's twisted mind.

'We don't need the tapes,' I lied. 'Skinner blackmailed dozens of men. When we publish, others'll come forwards. We've already tracked down another of his victims. It'll end up in court, with Skinner in the dock.'

Freddie and Herr Porno looked at one another, and laughed.

'We know where all of them live,' Freddie said,'those who aren't already in the boneyard, that is. Once we've had a quiet word, none of them fags'll be going to court, you can be sure of that.'

Jesus Christ, I thought, with a shiver. They know where David lives.

Freddie patted my cheek.'Enough of this crap.'

He picked at the clingfilm with his nails, peeling off a length that he unwound to the carpet. Herr Porno winked at me, and groomed his moustache with a thumb.

As death crept closer a deep gloom engulfed me. I shuddered under Herr Porno's weight, to shake it off. Laser-guided fear took over; all systems switched to War mode. Time slowed to a standstill. Each breath became a lifetime. Think, Llew, think.

I had to find a way to force a struggle, so that at the very least I might scupper Skinner's plans to have my death look like suicide. If my corpse carried marks of violence then Skinner would have no choice but to dispose of me. I would then forever be a crack in his defences, and Big Al would launch fusillade upon fusillade of facts at that crack, until he brought Skinner's walls tumbling down. Maybe Thirza would help him, I thought, buoyed by that prospect. Perhaps she'll even grieve for me? I might get closer to her love in death than I ever managed in life.

I shook off all thought of Thirza, and closed my eyes – seeing my room in more detail than ever before. I explored every square millimetre of it, seeking something, anything, that might help me change the narrative. The cactus! I opened my eyes and turned my head to the left. The teddy bear cholla was three-to-four feet away. Between it and the bed lay a pile of dirty laundry. I looked from Herr Porno to Freddie, who was now unspooling length upon length of clingfilm.

'I'd like to say a prayer,' I said.'Before … you know.'

'Pray all you like,' Freddie said.'It won't do you much good.'

'I want to kneel. A man should be allowed to kneel for his final prayer.'

Freddie shrugged. He stood, and gestured for Herr Porno to follow suit.

I eased myself upright in the bed, and massaged some life back into my deadened arms. I pivoted and let my feet drop to the carpet. On top of the laundry pile was the nonsensical 'St Louis 6198 Members Club 1990' T-shirt Mani had given me. Herr Porno was to my left, Freddie to the right, neither more than a couple of feet away. Shaping to kneel, I snapped out my left arm and snatched the T-shirt. Almost in a single movement I cast it over the cactus and yanked it back, feeling the blessed weight of offshoots clinging to the cloth. I sprung to my feet and shoved the T-shirt into Herr Porno's face, the spines stinging my palm through the cloth. He sank to his knees, clawing at his eyes. I had never heard screaming like it. I switched the T-shirt to my right hand. Instinctively, Freddie lunged at me. I whipped out my arm, elbow locked, and Freddie's face sunk into the T-shirt with sufficient force to drive dozens of spines deep into my palm. I welcomed the pain; it honed my already razor-like senses. Freddie dropped to the floor alongside Herr Porno, where they howled and writhed in unison.

Naked, I swiped my house keys from a nail in the wall beside the bedroom door. I stumbled from the house and out into the street, chubbing the front door behind me. Even outside I could hear their agony. I pounded on my neighbour's front door. She was a widow in her sixties. We'd chatted at Aggie's funeral; she'd been at school with her. The door opened. She looked me down and up, and then down again. Her mouth was open, but she said nothing.

'Call the police,' I said. 'Some men've just tried to kill me.'

Mouth still agape, she gestured for me to come in. After closing the door behind us she removed her dressing gown and handed it to me.

'You got Rollo's number?' I asked.

She nodded.

'Call him, before you call the police. Tell him he's in danger. Tell him to get the hell out.'

I vomited at her feet, spattering her slippers and the hem of her nightie. I could smell the sickly sweet Jack. It was the last thing I remembered, before coming-to in hospital.

FORTY ONE

Big Al picked me up from Portsmouth General. I was still foggy from the sedation they'd given me. My hands were lightly bandaged and they throbbed in syncopation, each an echo of the other. I could not imagine the pain that an eyeball full of cholla spines would cause, but then I didn't have to imagine, because Freddie and Herr Porno's screams were still echoing around my skull.

By the time Big Al reached Silver Street I was panting like an abandoned dog in a sun-baked car. My heart was galloping and I was able to catch mere sips of breath. That the car was foggy with mentholated smoke didn't help matters. I sank down into the brace position, as if we were about to crash land.

'No, no, not here,' I whimpered into the passenger footwell. 'Don't make me go back in there.'

'All right, Bandit, all right,' Big Al said, pulling over. 'No one's going to make you go anywhere. Listen, why don't I drive you to Wycombe, home to your parents? That's where you need to be right now. You need proper rest, proper care.'

But I couldn't go home. It would be too complicated. The folks still knew nothing of my impending court appearance, which was now less than a week away. I looked across at Big Al.

I shook my head. 'Can I come back to yours, Al? Please. I can't be alone.'

He sighed. 'Mine? I've got five nippers. You'd get more rest at a bus shelter than you would at my place.'

We sat in silence. Big Al sucked hard on his cigarette. He did some of his best thinking when smoking.

'Tell you what, give us your house keys. I'll nip inside and get your stuff, and then we'll take you to a B&B. You can stay there until your trial. The publisher can bleeding well pick up the tab, after everything you've been through for the cause,' he added, opening the car door. 'This story's big league, Bandit. Proper big league. We've got Skinner by the goolies.'

'Don't forget my typewriter,' I called after him, as he made for my house. 'I've got changes to make to the story.'

He stopped and turned. 'You lovely boy,' he said, a glowing Consulate punctuating his toothy grin.

*

Seaview Bed & Breakfast provided blessed sanctuary in a very post-war English kind of way. I was able to read the daily papers in a communal sitting room, half-consumed by a wing-backed easy chair. For company, I had couples with names such as Des and Joan, and Ken and Mary, whose exquisitely crafted small-talk had the welcome effect of swaddling me against the outside world. Having a cooked breakfast every morning was also comforting, even if the landlady's bacon was covered in white flecky bits, and her toast was burnt. And then there was my room, with its swirling carpet and patterned wallpaper and curtains. It was an essay in oranges and browns, the palette of my childhood.

Following breakfast, it became my habit to spend the rest of the day in my room, lying on a bed that was lumpen with industrially sprung steel. I kept the windows open, day and night, so that the sea's back-and-forth swooshing might wash me to sleep. Sleep was the only respite I had from the resident terror that Freddie and Herr Porno's social call had left me. Even then, I would sometimes wake up panting and sweating, and frantically trying to wriggle out from under Herr Porno's bulk.

By late afternoon I'd be getting hungry and would look forward to Emdel's post-work visit. He always brought cod, chips and mushy peas, and the smell of vinegar would linger long after he'd left. Thirza didn't visit. Her absence left me feeling abandoned and hurt, and yet also relieved because I didn't have the wherewithal to cope with something that messy.

Emdel had no qualms whatsoever about continuing to live in Silver Street, and he dismissed my concerns for his safety with cold logic.

'Who's going to attack me?' he asked. 'The men who came after you are in custody, as is Skinner – and anyway, only you and Rollo even know I was involved at all. The cops didn't even bother interviewing me.'

But they wanted to interview me all right. I'd been on my way to the station, to give a witness statement, but had had another panic attack in Big Al's car, and he'd had to take me back to my B&B. After some debate, the police agreed to take a statement from me at Seaview.

*

DI Simmons and a colleague duly announced themselves one morning, shortly after breakfast. The landlady showed them to my room. She didn't know what to make of it: was I victim or crook? I think in the end she decided I was trouble either way, because after the police visit, she would cross her arms and suck her teeth at the sight of me, and I swear that my bacon grew fleckier and my toast more burnt.

'Well, here we are again, Mr Sabler,' DI Simmons said, as he closed my bedroom door. 'It seems that you can't stay away from us.'

'I'm the victim here,' I said, way too quickly.

'Of course,' he said, with a look that was a little too knowing for comfort. 'We've watched some of those tapes you chanced across, and your editor has given us an advance copy of your story. Nice work, by the way.'

'Cheers. It'll be hitting the streets this Thursday,'

'Thanks to you, we've got a strong case against John Skinner, and that's before we take into account the attempt on your life. How are you, by the way?'

'Every time I leave this place it feels like I'm having a heart attack.'

'That's the trauma,' said DI Simmons. 'We see a lot of that in our line of work. Don't worry, it'll pass in time. Maybe you should see a doctor. You might be able to request a deferral on your trial, if you're mentally unfit to stand.'

'Thanks, but no. I'm pushing ahead with it. I want to clear my name.'

I had never believed it more. I was a hero, for chrissake, wounded and broken in the line of duty. My stock had never been higher. I would fight the noble fight.

DI Simmons shrugged.

'Back to this Skinner business,' he said, nodding at the other detective, who was sat at the ancient vanity table that dominated the bay window. He picked up his pen and readied himself to take down my statement.

Over the next few hours, DI Simmons had me recount my brush with death in microscopic detail. Discussing the attack was not at all distressing; it sounded like something that had happened to another person. The attack became a problem for me only when setting foot outside the B&B, because then I saw Herr Porno and Freddie everywhere.

My statement about events that led up to the night I was attacked was almost entirely true. I lied only about how I had come by Skinner's tapes. (I said someone had dropped them on my doorstep one night.) Naturally, I made no mention of Rollo, Jimmy, Emdel, or the androids, and of course said nothing of the mail-order venture, the library or the kangarooing Transit. And when asked why I thought Skinner suspected I had his tapes, I told them it must have been dumb luck – that I was a sworn enemy of Skinner's, and he'd had his men search my place on spec, just in case. But apart from that, the way I told it was the way it happened.

'Thank you,' DI Simmons said at the end of it all. 'That can't have been easy for you.'

He's let me off lightly, I thought. Too lightly. I chewed the inside of my mouth.

'If it makes you feel any better,' said the second detective, slipping my statement into a zipped wallet, 'the men who attacked you are still in hospital, under guard. You blinded the pair of them, maybe for keeps. They're still on morphine, for the pain.'

It didn't make me feel any better, because the moment I left the safety of Seaview, I knew that I'd see the pair of them everywhere anyway, lurking, ready to pounce.

'There's just one more thing,' DI Simmons said. His demeanour put me in mind of Colombo, the dishevelled American telly detective, who always got his man with one last insouciant question, invariably asked just as he was about to leave the room. Had DI Simmons' life been shaped by Colombo the way mine had been by Lou Grant? I wondered. 'When we were going over the crime scene,' he continued, 'we found a deal of mailing equipment in your cellar. I wonder, what's the story with that, Mr Sabler?'

'Is this part of my statement?'

'No, I'm just curious.'

'Well, unless you interview me under caution, you can stay curious.'

I wasn't about to let my mouth start flapping, as I had so foolishly in the station, when quizzed about altar business.

He stiffened.

'Oh, I'm curious about a whole lot more than just that mailing equipment. I'm curious about how those tapes happened to end up in your possession. I mean, come on. Someone just happens to drop them on your doorstep, not long after Skinner's shop is burgled? Really? So tell me, how did this source of yours know the significance of those tapes, when they were just a handful of porn films among thousands of others? No, the only people who knew about those tapes were Skinner, his crew, the men he blackmailed … and you. I think you robbed Skinner's shop, to get hold of those tapes.'

He'd got it so wrong, and yet so nearly right. I didn't know whether to laugh or cry.

'Look,' I said, 'I'm saying nothing, apart from that you're wrong, because someone else did know about those tapes: my source. So either interview me under caution, or don't.'

DI Simmons took a step towards me, and pointed an index finger between my eyes. 'Be under no illusion, Mr Sabler. Under different circumstances we would absolutely interview you under caution – not only about how you really came by those tapes, but also why you had all that mailing equipment in your cellar. My best guess is that after you stole Skinner's porn you decided to cash in, by selling it through mail-order.'

I could have sworn I heard the ice cracking beneath my skates, like gun reports.

'Different circumstances?' I said, fighting to keep my breathing under control. 'What different circumstances?'

'I mean if you hadn't given us Skinner's head on a plate, at considerable risk to yourself,' he said, still pointing.

He stood like that for a few seconds, before folding his arms.

'Do you mind a word of advice?' he continued, a little more softly. 'Whether or not you are convicted next week, I think it's time that you found a different career. Your job is corrupting you, Mr Sabler. I've seen it happen to men on the force, and I see it happening with you. Get out, before it's too late.'

His words left me with too much to process. I had some kind of neurological kernel panic, and froze.

'We'll see ourselves out,' he said. 'Think about what I said.'

FORTY TWO

I GRIPPED THE SIDES OF the passenger seat in Big Al's car as if there was a thirty-foot drop on either side. I battled to get my breathing under some semblance of control.

'You want your head looking at,' Big Al said. 'Why didn't you take that copper's advice, and seek a deferral? There's no way you're fit to face trial.'

'I'm going for ... the sympathy vote,' I said, squeezing the words out between breaths that may as well have been drawn through a soggy straw. 'I'm a ... hero, remember.'

'A hero? A fool more like, and a deluded fool at that. This time tomorrow you'll be in stir, and still your poor old parents don't have the first idea about any of it. Are you leaving it for me to tell them? Is that it?'

I reached inside my suit jacket and slipped out an envelope, which I placed on the dash.

'This is for ... my folks. I didn't ... want it to be on ... prison notepaper.'

'A letter? Are you serious?'

'It's easier to ... explain things in ... a letter.'

'For you maybe. I've been living your crap for months and I still can't get my head around half of it, so how are your parents gonna make head or tail of it from a letter? You should've told them long ago. That,' he added, tapping the envelope with a finger, 'is the coward's way out.'

We let his words hang in the air, until he turned into the magistrate court car park.

'Right,' he said, manoeuvring into a space, 'we've only got an hour to play with. We need to get you calmed down.'

He stubbed out a Consulate in the dash ashtray and wound down his window, telling me to follow suit.

'Breathe with me, Bandit,' he said, wafting his hands like an orchestra conductor. 'Like this. Nice and deep, nice and slow. That's it, you got it. Good lad.'

It took three Consulates for our synchronised breathing to tame my unruly heart.

'Al,' I said, once I was calm enough to talk properly again, 'that copper said something that I just can't stop thinking about. He said that the job had corrupted me. D'you think I'm corrupt?'

He twisted around to face me, and draped his arm across the back of my seat, like he was reversing. His cigarette burned inches from my left ear.

'You shat on an altar to drum up some news, that much I know. I also know for a fact you're not telling me everything about the Skinner business. There's no way that those tapes just turned up on your doorstep, and I bet that copper didn't buy it either, did he?'

I shook my head, and cleared my perfectly clear throat.

'You remember that fence I told you about?' I said. 'Rollo? Well, it all started when he asked if he could stash a load of porn down our cellar, and then—'

He slapped an open palm on the steering wheel. 'I knew it! I bloody knew it. So have they charged you with anything else?' He pointed through the windshield at the court building. 'On top of all this?'

I told him what DI Simmons had said, about them cutting me some slack because I had delivered Skinner, and had nearly died in the process.

'Let me ask you a question,' he said, sliding his Michael Caine specs up his nose. 'Do you *feel* corrupt?'

I sighed and rubbed the back of my head.

'A bit, I s'pose. Yeah.'

'Then there's your answer.'

He drew back his outstretched arm and took a draw on his Consulate.

'All this has gotta stop, Bandit, or you'll be dead before you're thirty. You're a journalist – you're meant to be writing the frigging news, not making it. It stops here, today, in that courtroom. You're going in there and you're gonna plead guilty, because you *are* bloody guilty. And whether they jail you or not, you're gonna have a long hard think about your life, and where you're headed. For the love of god, you've got to start being honest, with yourself and with others. Agreed?'

I nodded, without looking at him.

'Right, time to get going. You've got a date with a judge. And Bandit?'

'Yeah?'

'Don't worry if they send you down – it'll be to some cushy open prison. Think of it as Butlins, with a dirty big fence. I'll come visit. Promise.'

'You're not coming in with me?'

I couldn't keep the surprise – and slight hurt – from my tone. I had assumed he'd be lending moral support in the courtroom.

'Best if I don't. I know one of the magistrates. It might look like I was trying to swing something for you.'

I nodded, closed the car door, and made for the courthouse. At the top of the steps, outside the entrance, was the same photographer who had been in the crowd of protesters. Skinner may have had his chips but clearly he was intent on making sure that everyone knew I'd also had mine. The photographer hoisted his camera to his eye and fired off a series of shots, his motor winder whirring.

'Sorry,' he said, lowering the camera. 'I'm under orders.'

'It's okay,' I said. 'You're just doing your job.'

'Fuck it,' he said, opening the back of his camera and yanking the film out. 'I'll tell them my rig jammed. I'm sick of that place, the shit they have me doing. I'd much rather work for you guys.'

'Thanks,' I said, offering him my hand. 'I appreciate it.'

I entered the building, and cast about reception for somewhere to sit. Airport style, the seating was in welded-and-bolted rows. I sat opposite a respectable-looking woman in her mid-forties, a professional type, judging by her impeccably tailored trouser suit. I wondered what she might be up for. Speeding? Drink driving, perhaps? Two seats away from her was a young black guy – quite possibly Portsmouth's *only* black guy. The woman kept sneaking looks at me.

'That photographer outside,' she said, pointing at me. 'He's there for you, isn't he? You're that reporter, the one who did unspeakable things in that church.'

'Hey, lady,' the young guy said, before I had a chance to react. 'Maybe your man here's innocent, like I. Say – is you innocent, lady?'

'That's none of your business,' she answered, blowing air through her nose in indignation.

He pointed at me, while still looking at her 'Yet you's making him *your* business.'

She muttered something, while sliding a seat further away from him. He returned my nod of thanks.

My Timex wristwatch told me it was Tee minus fifteen. I closed my eyes, and began the process of planning the rest of my life. I would plead guilty. Big Al was right: it had to start there. But where would pleading guilty lead me? I tried to imagine my life, five years hence, but gave up on that when I was unable to picture myself being anywhere other than in some warehouse, working in a boredom-induced fugue state, as execrable pop played in the background. Maybe I should go back to school – do A-levels, and maybe even a degree? I could become a teacher, perhaps. It wouldn't be newspapers; nothing would ever replace journalism. But it wouldn't be the worst thing in the world. I could help shape young, impressionable minds. Surely knowing what *not* to do in life is every bit as valuable as knowing what *to* do?

A familiar voice punctured my plan-making.

'Mr Sabler?'

I opened my eyes. DI Simmons stood before me.

'Would you come with me please,' he said. 'And don't worry,' he added quickly. 'It's good news, or else I'd not be speaking to you right now, seeing as I was due to give evidence against you.'

'See lady,' the young guy said, slapping his knee. 'Him's innocent, like I.'

Bewildered, I followed DI Simmons across reception to a closed door. He knocked gently on it, and when there was no reply he opened it and beckoned me inside, flicking the lock behind us. It was little more than a box room, with a table that had two chairs either side. We sat.

'You no longer have a case to answer.'

'Excuse me?'

'Last night a forty-two-year-old man came forward, and claimed responsibility for the church desecrations. His story holds water and he has been duly charged. You are free to go.'

I sat back in my seat, staring blankly ahead.

'It was the priest. Maximilian O'Reardon. I'm not at liberty to discuss details, because of sub judice, but his story will come out soon enough – I'm sure that you and your colleagues will see to that. There's something else.

Mr O'Reardon also told us that he is another of John Skinner's blackmail victims. It was your story that made him come forward, on both counts. Mr O'Reardon is willing to testify in court against John Skinner. You're speechless,' he added, after waiting for a response. 'Well, you don't have to say anything. Just go home. Get some rest. How are you feeling, by the way?'

'Um, better than I was five minutes ago, thanks.'

'Listen, Mr Sabler, I was only doing my job. All the evidence pointed strongly at your guilt, so strongly in fact that when O'Reardon came forward to confess, we didn't believe him at first.'

'It's okay.'

'And before you go, there's one more thing. John Skinner's wife has also come forward. She's given us a statement, about the blackmail plot and plenty else besides. It seems I owe you an apology.'

I had told so many half-truths and outright lies that I wasn't sure what he might be about to apologise for, and so I said nothing.

'She was your source, wasn't she,' he said. Someone really did dump those tapes on your doorstep. It was her, wasn't it, Mrs Skinner.'

'I couldn't possibly say.'

He smiled.

'Protecting your source. I get it. I'm tempted to say that she was your Deep Throat, but that would be a terrible joke. And don't worry by the way, we're not interested in how she came by the tapes. Our best guess is that she arranged to have her husband's shop knocked off, but we really don't care. Mr Sabler?'

'Yes.'

'I know now that you didn't have Skinner's porn in your cellar, but can I ask – what was the mailing equipment for? It's bugging me. You don't have to tell me if you don't want to.'

'You were half right, actually,' I said. 'My flat mate had a life-long porn addiction. He spent so much on it down the years that he had enough to open a library. But then he got a girlfriend, and rather than chuck it all out we decided to sell it. Being in the print game, I knocked up a catalogue, and then we advertised in all the jazz mags, and we sold it all by mail order.'

How easily lying comes to me, I thought. I've just riffed on reality without skipping a beat. Is this how corruption works? Are these the cogs and wheels that allow it to function?

'Huh, fancy that,' DI Simmons said, standing and showing me to the door. 'D'you know something?' He paused in the doorway. 'I've not met anyone who has seemed more guilty than you, and yet here you stand, innocent of it all. I've never been more wrong about anyone.'

He offered me his hand, and we shook.

'I'm sorry for what I said, about you being corrupt.'

I wanted to thank him, for having jolted me to my senses, but instead I told him that it was okay, that he had called as he'd seen it.

'I saw it wrong though, didn't I,' he said. 'Anyway, best of luck, Llew. And keep up the good work.'

Jesus H Christ, I thought, that's the last thing any of us needs.

FORTY THREE

My acquittal sparked a tabloid feeding frenzy. My story had it all: intrigue, squalor, scandal, public outrage, blackmail, attempted murder, and redemption. And to cap it all, the serial altar-dumper turns out to be the very priest whose altar it was. All that was missing was sex. The press were desperate to interview me, but because they couldn't find me they went after my parents, who knew only the little I'd belatedly told them. (I had phoned, to reassure them that I was safe, and had given them a broad-brushstrokes version of everything else.)

After things calmed down, a couple of weeks after my acquittal, they came to visit me at Seaview, staying a few nights. It was the only way they could get to see me. I was fearful of returning home, even for a short time, in case I got sucked into a vortex of motherly devotion and wound up never leaving. It was lovely to see them. Having so nearly lost me, they smothered me in love, although they were unable to mask their hurt at my having kept them in the dark about so much, for so long. It wasn't just that altar I had shat all over.

The coverage I received in the national press was little more than a re-hash of Big Al's brilliant seven-page Probe exclusive, which he'd written following my acquittal. 'Innocent!' trumpeted his front-page headline. I wondered if he'd been tempted to prefix this with '80 percent'. Under the head was a photo of me, sat at my typewriter. It had been taken in my first week on the paper, a lifetime ago, to introduce me to readers. Big Al made the same photo available to the nationals. It was strange, having my face stare back at me from the morning papers. I enjoyed it for a few days, until I read a breathless editorial in The Insider, declaring me to be 'the brave new face of journalism'. I almost choked on my breakfast at the hypocrisy of it. After that, I stopped looking at the papers altogether.

All the media attention left my landlady a little star-struck, and it became her habit to curtsy before me, like I was royalty. My bacon also became fleck-free, and my toast a golden brown.

'Mr Sabler,' she said with a curtsy, as I was finishing off my breakfast one morning, 'I'm sorry to interrupt, but there's a call for you.'

I ate a few last forkfuls, and followed her to the little reception desk in the entrance hall.

'I'll give you some privacy,' she said, walking off as I picked up the receiver from the counter top.

'Sabler?' came a voice I hoped I'd not hear again. 'It's Rollo Baer.'

'How'd you find me?'

'Forget that, and answer me this, you cunt: what the hell were you playing at? I heard there was porn all over the street. Are you suicidal, or just plain fucking stupid?'

I said nothing, thought nothing. I didn't care about him any more, or what he thought.

'Can you talk?' he asked, angry still.

'No.'

'Stick to one-word answers then. Listen, did you mention me to the cops?

'No.'

What if I'd said 'Yes,' I wondered. Would I be forever be looking over my shoulder, for Rollo?

'That's good, for me and you.'

And there is my answer.

'Do they suspect anything, about you having Skinner's porn?'

'No, not now.'

'Because his missus came forward? Is that what threw 'em off the scent?'

'Yes.'

'So they *were* on to you then, about the porn, before she went to the cops?'

'Yes.'

'Let me guess: they thought you knocked off Skinner's shop, to get at them tapes, so you could write a red-hot exclusive.'

'Yes.'

'S'fucking lucky she ratted him out then, ain't it. Saved your sorry arse. And another thing, how did you know that neighbour of yours – the one you who got to warn me – wouldn't blab to the cops about it?'

I was beginning to wish I hadn't bothered warning Rollo at all. 'I spoke to her at your mum's funeral. I knew she was a family friend.'

'Fair enough. Listen,' he added, softer now. 'I cleared nearly twenty-five big ones on that porn. I must want my fucking head looked at, but I'm gonna pop a bonus through your letter box, for you and your little mate, even though you're a right pair 'o cunts. Oughta pay for that B&B of yours for a bit.'

'Thank you.'

'And Sabler?'

'Yeah?'

'Stay out of trouble. No more wanking in grottos or on altars.'

There was a click, and the line went dead.

FORTY FOUR

I WAS LEANING OUT OF my bedroom window, staring across Clarence Esplanade to the Solent. In the late February dusk, its waters were solemn and brooding. The lights of Ryde, on the Isle of Wight, twinkled, like a constellation that had dropped from the sky. My mind was empty of thought. Some might call that meditation, but in truth it was exhaustion. Trying to think with a marshmallow for a brain is difficult. My stomach growled. At least my intestinal tract remained in good working order. I thought of the fish supper that Emdel would soon be delivering to my door. Eating, sleeping and staring out of the window. This was my routine. Thanks to Rollo's cash bonus – supplemented by the statutory sick pay I was receiving from The Probe – I had the funds to stay at Seaview for a further four or five weeks. After that, I had no idea what would happen. Knowing would require thinking, and like I say, thinking was a problem. There was a knock at the door, and I started to slaver, like one of Pavlov's dogs.

'For you,' said Thirza, proffering a fat bundle of newspaper. Wafts of fish and vinegar met my nostrils. 'I made sure they wrapped it in a copy of The Tribune.'

'I wasn't expec—'

'I know. I spoke to Emdel. I told him I'd bring your food across tonight. It's high time you and me talked, don't you think.'

'Um ... I ... I find it difficult, talking. It's like, I don't know, I can only think in 2D or something.'

'Then I'll talk, and you listen. You can still nod and shake your head can't you?'

I nodded.

'Then we'll be fine.'

I took the aromatic bundle from her, and sat at the dresser. I ate from the newspaper, with a knife and fork I'd purloined from downstairs. Thirza looked on from the bed. I offered her a chip.

'I've eaten, thanks.'

When I was done, I wiped my mouth on a page from The Tribune. It was the Classifieds section, I noted.

'You've got newsprint all over your face,' Thirza said, shaking her head.

I waited for her to add 'you twat', but it didn't come.

'You can't stay here forever, Llew. Life's passing you by.'

I shrugged.

'The phone's stopped ringing at work for you, did you know that? In those first few weeks after you were acquitted, the nationals were clamouring after you, offering you stuff. Even the BBC called, about you working on some investigative programme. Big Al gave you all the numbers, but you didn't call any of them, did you? And now you're yesterday's news; they've all forgotten about you. So tell me, what's the big plan? Stew in this place with a load of pensioners, indefinitely, like something from Cocoon?'

'I ... I couldn't speak to those media people,' I said. 'Just the thought of it left me shaking.'

'That's because you've been cooped up in here for too long.'

She bounced on the mattress.

'And how on earth do you sleep on this bed? What's it stuffed with? Stones from the beach?'

'Something's different,' I said, wagging a finger at her. 'About you.'

'I'm not here to talk about me.'

'I've got it. You're not swearing. "How on earth?" Since when did you ever say stuff like that?'

I took a closer look at her, and the truth of it was revealed: there was a serenity about her I'd not seen before. It was in her every movement and expression, and was even in her clothes. She was still dressed like a builder – boots, jeans and sweatshirt, and still she wore no make-up – but her clothes now hugged her curves rather than hid them. In the subdued yellow light of my room I thought her beauty soft, warm and gentle, like a kiss. I felt that for the first time, I was seeing the real Thirza.

'I'm not angry like I used to be,' she explained, matter of factly. 'And d'you know why that is? Because I took time to figure out who I am and what I want. It was painful, and not just for me, as you know. And that's exactly what you need to do – figure out who you are and what you want, and you can't do that stuck in a room that looks like something from a museum.'

'But I can't leave this place. I'll end up freaking out.'

'And when's the last time you had a shave, or a bath? I can smell you over the fish and chips.'

'I ... I ...'

'You're vegetating is what you're doing. Of course you're freaking out. Your brain's turning to sludge.'

She stood, as if to attention.

'Right, you, up,' she barked, with more than a hint of the old Thirza. 'Get your coat. You're coming with me.'

She grabbed both my hands with hers, and hauled me upright.

'What d'you mean?'

'We're going outside, for a little walk, and no arguing. If you won't go through the door then I'll push you out of the window. Either way, you're leaving this room with me. Now.'

*

'Well, it's a start,' she said, closing my bedroom door behind us. 'At least we got you outside. Next time we might even make it all the way to the pavement. Breathe, Llew, breathe.'

She steered me to the bed, sat me down and bookended my shoulders in her hands.

'Nice and easy. Slow and deep. In through the nose, out through the mouth, that's it. Calm down. You're perfectly safe.'

I don't know how long it took her to help me apply the brakes to my racing heart. When things got like that, I lost all sense of time.

'Those men who tried to kill me,' I said, once I'd marshalled my senses. 'I see them everywhere.'

'I know you do. Al told me. Look Llew, you need help – professional help. That's another reason we've got to get you out of this place. You've got to see your GP.'

'I know. I'll try my best to get little further every day, like you said.'

Arms folded, she looked me hard in the eye, and nodded her head.

'Yeah, you will. I'll make sure of it. I won't allow you to end up like David.'

*

It took me a fortnight to reach the first of the benches that were set fifty metres apart along a mile of promenade. Thirza came every night, with fish and chips. After I'd eaten, she'd lead me from Seaview. Her fist was as iron as ever, but she had acquired the softest of velvet gloves. She kept my hyperventilation largely in check, with constant encouragement and gentle support, but a few times we'd had to turn back because I'd had a full-blown panic attack. On one occasion she'd practically had to carry me back into the B&B.

'See,' she said, when we reached the first bench. 'I knew you could do it.'

We sat looking out to sea, huddled in our winter coats. The tide was out, and the sea was invisible in the murk. The sibilance of the waves was carried to us on a kelpy breeze.

'It may've taken us two weeks to get here but the next bench will take half that time, and the one after that, half again. We'll keep going until we've reached Southsea Common, at the other end of the esplanade.'

'I don't know, Thirza. It seems like a long way.'

'You've just got to keep showing yourself that you're safe from those men who attacked you. They're in custody, awaiting trial. Bit by bit you've got to teach your brain that the fear it's producing is irrational.'

'You know something? You sound just like Emdel.'

She chuckled, and brushed away a lock of air that was dancing across her face in the wind.

'Actually, this was his idea – getting you to go from bench to bench.'

'So you two are talking again?'

I felt a spasm of jealousy, and pushed it down, some place way deep.

'Yeah, we're talking. We're good. I've been spending a little time with him in the Mow. You know I live there now, right? With Blanche.'

'Yeah, so Emdel said. I'm happy for you both. And how's David?'

'You're not gonna believe this, but he's moved out.'

'Moved out? Where? It was only a few weeks ago that he'd not venture further than the Mow saloon bar.'

'Well he's a totally different person now. You'd barely recognise him.'

'Where's he moved to?'

'You'll never guess, not in a million years.'

'I don't know. Edinburgh?'

'No,' she said, half-laughing, half scoffing. 'Why Edinburgh?'

'He mentioned once how he desperately wanted to go to the Festival. I could see him in Edinburgh. He'd fit right in there. I mean, the entertainment world's one big gay chorus line, isn't it? John Inman. Kenneth Williams. Frankie Howerd. Larry Grayson. Lionel Blair. The list's endless.'

'Is Lionel Blair gay?'

'Course he is.'

'Huh. Anyway, no, not Edinburgh. Somewhere much closer to home.'

'I dunno. Give up.'

'Wait for it: he's moved in with Max, the priest. He's living with him and Max's mother up the coast, in Emsworth.'

'What? You're kidding me.'

'Nope. Moved in last week. The two of them've been inseparable since Max came forward. Actually, he asked if it would be okay to meet with you. I think he probably wants to apologise – you know, about not coming forward sooner. D'you mind if I give him the phone number at Seaview?'

My guts gave a humpback-bridge heave. I knew I must summon the courage to tell her the truth, and soon, if our born-again friendship was to mean anything. I had told so many lies to so many people that I barely knew any longer what the truth was. I had become trapped in a hall-of-mirrors maze of my own making. But there was one truth that was crystal clear: being with Thirza made me feel whole again, for the first time in an age. But how long would that loveliness survive once she knew the truth about me? If I told her now would it last to the next bench, even?

'Earth calling Llew, hello.'

'Sorry. What were you saying?'

'I was asking if you minded if I give Max your B&B phone number. He wants to meet with you.'

'Er ... yeah, sure.'

She took my chin in the palm of one hand. 'You look a little pale, even in this light. Are you okay?'

'My heart's racing a little.'

'C'mon then, we'd better get you home.'

FORTY FIVE

IN THE END, I HELD off telling Thirza the truth until we reached Southsea Common, more than one month worth of benches further down the esplanade.

'Right,' she said, beaming. 'It's official: bench therapy has worked. You're cured. Come here.'

She drew me into her, and we stood holding on to one another. Her breasts were splatted up against my chest, and I broke her embrace the instant I felt a stirring in my groin.

'I'm so proud of you,' she said, tapping the backrest of the bench. 'Not just for this but for everything. You nearly died, Llew. You scared me. It's made me realise just how much you mean to me.'

Before that moment I hadn't thought it possible to experience despair and joy concurrently. Her pride in me, and the value she placed on my friendship, were about to become memories.

I felt sick, so sat on the bench, elbows on knees, drawing in slow lungfuls of air. She joined me, placing a protective arm about my shoulders.

'Are you having a panic attack?'

'No. It's worse than that.'

'Llew, you're crying. What's up? Tell me.'

I sat back, and took a deep breath.

'Look, Thirza, I've got some things to tell you, and they're bad, really bad. So bad, I worry you'll probably never want to see to me again. So before I tell you everything, there's something else I want to say.'

She met my words with silence, and an expressionlessness I took as my cue to continue.

'You said I had to work out who I am, and what I want. Well, I've done that, thanks in no small part to you, and these benches.' I patted the wooden slats as if they were a beloved pet.

'So tell me: who are you, and what is it you want?'

'The who and the what are kind of rolled into one,' I said.

'Go on.'

'What I want is to be someone who tells the truth, someone who's honest with himself and others. Not just when it suits me, either, but all the time. I know that probably sounds mad to you because you're honest all the time anyway.'

I looked to her for encouragement, but got nothing but a poker face.

'My folks raised me to be decent and honest,' I continued regardless, feeling as if I were referring to someone from another age, another world, another universe. 'That's the real me, but somewhere along the way, that version of me got lost – I'm not sure how, or when. But now he's back. The me who's sat in front of you right now, telling you the truth, that's the real me. The one who did a ton of bad stuff, he's dead. Gone.'

She stood. 'A ton of bad stuff? Let's walk, while you talk.'

It took three laps of Southsea Common before I was done telling her everything. She kept her counsel the entire time, her face betraying no emotion. Her silence and inscrutability were unnerving; the calm before the storm, surely. She led me back to the same bench, and we sat.

'You're right,' she said. 'Clearly, I had no idea who you really are, or who Emdel is, for that matter. So you're a criminal, basically, and by the sound of it you should've been jailed three times over – for the altar, for Skinner's porn ...'

She sprang from the bench, and leaned over me, holding a quivering talon inches from my nose.

'... and for that obscene fucking library, you sick twat fuck.'

Fifty yards away, a man walking a black labrador turned in our direction. I thought she might hit me, and I held up both hands for protection.

'I know, I know,' I said. 'I wasn't thinking.'

'So this *new* you' – she made the word sound like it was something to be mocked – 'who's decided all of a sudden to be honest, has he also decided to actually start using his fucking brain?'

'Yes, he has.'

'Fucking good. And you can fucking well walk back to that shitehole B&B on your own. Tell you what, seeing as you're Mr fucking Honest all of a sudden, perhaps you should swing by the police station first, and tell them what you just told me.'

'Maybe I will,' I said with a level of defiance that surprised me.

'Yeah, right.'

She wheeled away and set out across the Common. I watched her shrink into the distance until she disappeared from sight, certain it would be last I'd see of her. In a vacuum of numb hopelessness, I made for the police station.

*

There were just six steps feeding into the station, but it may as well have been the north face of the Eiger. Up I trudged. The ornate brass handle of the door was polished with use, and cold on my palm. I opened the heavy oak door and stepped inside.

'Stop.'

I turned around. Thirza was at the bottom of the steps.

'What the fuck are you doing?' she said. 'Have you lost your fucking mind?'

'But—'

'Don't say a word, not here. Come with me, for fuck's sake.'

*

She sat on my lumpen bed. I stood, leaning against the wall.

'I can't believe you were actually gonna go in there. It was just as well I fucking followed you, wasn't it. What were you thinking? And what the fuck were you gonna tell them? Everything?'

'No, just about the altar.'

'And what d'you think that would've achieved?'

'I just thought ... I thought it would make me measure up, in your eyes.'

'Are you fucking kidding me? Jesus fucking Christ, Llew. Be honest because it's the right thing to do, not because you want to impress someone. That's how it fucking works, you twat.'

'But you were so angry. You stormed off. I thought I'd lost you all over again.'

'And I'm still fucking angry, and for the record, you didn't lose me – you binned me, remember? You said our friendship was dead.'

'Yeah, but—'

'Stop.' She held up a hand, traffic-cop style. 'We're not raking up all that shit again. That's done.'

We allowed silence fill the room for a time.

'I need to know if you can forgive me,' I said, in time. 'For what I did. For all the lies.'

She looked me hard in the eye. 'I'm sat here looking at your ugly fucking face, aren't I.'

I smiled.

'Thank you, Thirza. You've been a real friend. The best.'

She stood, took a few steps towards me, then poked me hard in the bicep.

'Let's get one thing straight. If you ever lie to me again, about anything, I'll fucking well shop you myself. For all of it. Got it?'

With that, she left, not bothering to close the door behind her.

FORTY SIX

MAX IDLY FLUNG A STONE into the waves, as we sat alongside one another, looking out to sea. It was a clean, crisp early March day. The Isle of Wight was a distinct dark band on the horizon, which was otherwise uninterrupted, save for one of the four colossal circular forts that stood sentinel in the Solent.

'Did you know it was Palmerston that had those built,' Max said, pointing at the fort. His voice was no longer a whisper, and there was no need to lean in to catch his words, even against the backdrop of screeching gulls and whooshing waves.

'The forts were meant to protect against invasion by Napoleon the Third,' he continued, 'but by the time they were finished, any threat from the French had long since passed. It's why they're known as Palmerston's Follies.'

'I always wondered what the story was with them,' I said. 'Do I take it you're a history buff?'

He cast a couple of stones into the water.

'I suppose you could say that. I did want to be a history teacher once.'

'But you became a priest instead?'

'I don't think I ever really *became* a priest.'

'What d'you mean?'

'I mean that it was an escape – you know, from the world. From everything.'

'From Skinner, you mean, and what he did to you?'

'Yes, of course. What else.'

I ignored the mild rebuke.

'David came to see me the other day,' I told him. 'At my B&B.'

'Yes, I know. He's very fond of you. Thank you for being his friend.'

'David told me he couldn't remember you being in the least bit religious, back in the day. So why the priesthood?'

'I've always been a spiritual person,' he said, punctuating the sentence with another stone. 'What happened to me and to David left me broken and confused. I thought the clerical life might provide some kind of sanctuary, and maybe some healing. And not just from what Skinner did to me, but my father too.'

Wordlessly, Max began flinging a conveyor belt of pebbles, picking them up with one hand and feeding the other.

'When I was twenty-three, I came out to him and Mum,' he said, a dozen or so throws later. 'He disowned me. All he cared about was protecting his reputation. He was an MP, you know. A Tory. He even banned me from coming to the house. I had to visit Mum in secret, when he was up in London, sitting in Parliament. He was always standoffish with me as a child. I think maybe he suspected something, even before I did so myself. But to be rejected like that.'

I watched his stones fly and plop, fly and plop.

'But the Catholic Church?' I said, trying not to sound overly incredulous. 'Did you not know of its views on homosexuality?'

'Of course I knew,' he retorted. 'I'm not an idiot. I'm the child of Irish Catholics. We were church-goers. I went to Catholic school. I was taught by nuns. But when the whole of society seems to hate you for being gay, including your own father, then it's any port in a storm, isn't it – especially when you're as messed up as me.'

'I'm sorry, I didn't mean to—'

'But you're right. It was naive.'

He ceased lobbing stones and looked out across the foam-flecked water, forearms on knees. I sensed he was sharing this for his benefit, not mine, and so I gave him enough space to field his own question.

'When some moron on the street wants to kick your head in because he thinks you're gay then you can almost forgive him because you know it's down to ignorance and stupidity. Such hatred doesn't make you question yourself – in fact, if anything it makes you stronger. But when you're told that being gay is a sin? A crime against god? That leaves you feeling unworthy. Unclean. Unnatural. It eats away at your sense of who you are.'

He gazed into the mid-distance. We were inching towards the reason he had asked to meet me. What the hell, I thought. I may as well give us a shove in that direction.

'Was there a snapping point?' I asked. 'Was there one particular thing that made you want to, you know, do what you did?'

He turned to face me. He'd aged since I'd last seen him, when Mike had vomited on his already sullied altar. His eyes communicated a deep weariness that I'd not seen before. Or maybe it was just that I'd not been looking. He gave an ironic little laugh.

'You're so ashamed of what you did you can't even bring yourself to say the words, can you? I took a shit on my altar in order to make a stand. But you? You did it for profit.'

I shifted my weight from buttock to buttock, but could not get comfortable. His gaze was again drawn to the sea, and he got lost in its ebb and flow for a while.

'It was this one catechism class,' he said, eventually. 'Someone asked whether it was wrong for men to like men, and do you know what I told them? Do you know what my church obliged me to say? That homosexuality is a 'disorder'.'

'Jesus Christ,' I said. 'Sounds like something from Nazi Germany.'

'Quite, but that wasn't what pushed me over the edge. There was this boy in catechism, Philippe. He was French. Very sweet, and very camp. After class, I had to return to the hall, to fetch my Bible. The hall was empty, but I heard crying coming from behind one of the curtains on the stage, and I went to investigate. It was Philippe. At first he wouldn't talk to me, but I think he sensed that I wasn't a threat; sometimes it takes one to spot one. Anyway, he told me that on the way out of class, a couple of the boys had taunted him in front of the others, calling him all sorts of horrible names. And it was all because of what I had taught them to think, just moments earlier. I wanted so badly to tell him that I was gay and that he should be proud, not ashamed, but I said nothing. I just told him not to listen to name-callers, and that everything would be okay. In that moment I felt more degraded than at any point during those disgusting films Skinner made me do.'

Tears rolled down his cheeks. He magicked a tissue from the sleeve of his coat and dabbed at the dampness.

'So what about you?' he said when he'd composed himself. 'What's your story? Why did you shit on my altar?'

I sighed.

'My story is very simple compared to yours. I shat on your altar because I'm an idiot. A lying, deceitful idiot.'

'Did you do it for the money?'

'No, no,' I said, as if crapping on an altar for money was somehow more base than doing so for any other reason. 'I ... I did it to escape.'

'From what, or who?'

I laid the whole Thirza-Emdel saga on him.

'So you felt betrayed,' he said. 'You blamed them.'

'Yes, but I don't feel that way any more. I'm seeing things more clearly now.'

'And not before time,' he said, with a chortle. 'There was also that mermaid business wasn't there – not to mention Santa's grotto.'

He belly laughed.

'Oh, I thought that was hilaaaarious. Santa on a cross? Absolutely priceless. You went up in my estimation after that, although in truth you couldn't've sunk much lower.'

We considered one another, unblinkingly.

'I really didn't like you at all, truth be told. I found you ill-mannered and uncouth, as well as unprincipled, and that was before you shat on my altar.'

'I'm sorry, Father.'

'This isn't a confessional,' he said, his tone betwixt admonishment and surprise. 'And anyway, I'm no longer a priest; I was defrocked, by the Bishop of Portsmouth, no less, although I'd've quit anyway. Once one has defecated on one's own altar there are credibility issues.'

He wagged a finger at me.

'You know, I disliked you so intensely that I was quite happy to let you carry the can for all of the desecrations, but then you published David's interview, and there was the attempt on your life.'

'Thank you for taking the blame. You saved my career.'

'Oh, don't flatter yourself that I did it all for you, because I didn't. It struck me that coming forward would get the issue of homophobia in the church on the front pages, where it belongs. Community service and court costs seemed to be a small price to pay.'

'Well, you were right. The story ran everywhere.'

'Yes, you and I have a certain notoriety now, don't we. We have that much in common.'

'And David,' I added, feeling the need to counter his disdain.

'Yes, and David. Dear David.'

'If you don't mind me asking, how do you and David feel about the prospect of giving evidence at Skinner's trial?'

'David's all gung ho about it; he can't wait. His need for revenge is burning hot – too hot if you ask me. I think you ignited that in him.'

'And you?'

'I'm apprehensive. I never want to see that man's face ever again, but I know that when I help send him to prison I'll finally be able to move on with my life.'

'Same here.'

'Well, there's something else we have in common,' said Max. 'So how do you feel about giving evidence against Skinner? I mean, the man tried to have you killed.'

'I'm with David. My need for justice and revenge is running hot.'

'And those other men? How will you cope with facing them?'

'I'd rather not think about it, until I have to. Since the attack I've been seeing their faces everywhere. I've been a mess.'

'Oh dear. I'm sorry.'

'But I'm much better now, thanks to Thirza.'

'What a gem that girl is. You're very lucky to have her as a friend.'

'Yes, I am. Very.'

He stood, and tapped his wristwatch. We trudged up across the beach, towards South Parade Pier.

'So, what's next for you?' he said. 'Professionally I mean. I imagine that you're quite in demand.'

'I was, yeah, but not any more. That said, I did have a call from The Insider a few days ago, asking if I'd like to head up a new investigations unit.'

'That rag? You'd work for them?'

'I've already worked for them. The editor's some sort of psychopath, but it's a national paper and it has some clout, so if I do end up hating it then it shouldn't be too difficult finding something else.'

'Sounds like you've already made up your mind.'

'Kind of, yeah.'

'Well, I've got to head,' he said. 'David's cooking lobster tonight.'

'Lobster? I didn't know he could cook.'

'Let's just say he's enthusiastic. I hope Mother keeps an eye on him, or the lobster will be vulcanised.'

'It's nice that you and him are together again,' I said. 'After all those years apart.'

'You've no idea,' he answered, clasping his hands to his chest. He was way more effeminate now that he'd shed the dog collar and the choke chain of the church. No surprise there, really. 'David adores Mother,' he went on, 'and she him. Two or three nights a week we watch musicals together. He has them all you know.'

'Oh, I know. We spent many a long, long night above the Mow watching them together.'

I wondered if my smile completely masked the grimace that lay behind it.

'Yes, I heard,' said Max. 'I tell you what, why don't you pop over and join us for a musicals night – you know, before you leave for that awful rag in London. I know that you and I got off to a bit of a rocky start, but David would love to have you over, and that's good enough for me. What d'you say?'

'T'rrific.'

FORTY SEVEN

Being honest on one's own behalf is fine, but to be honest on someone else's? That's another thing entirely – snitching, essentially, but in my solipsistic quest to rediscover the real me, I had rather lost sight of this fact.

'Come on Emdel, please,' I said. 'I'll get down on my knees and beg if I have to. Please come to my leaving do. Thirza'll think something's off if you don't show, and we can't have things going all weird between us again.'

'Something bloody well *is* off though, isn't it. You told her I was a pornographer. How can I ever look her in the eye again? She hates porn. You know that.'

'Look, she doesn't know that you had a porn problem,' I protested. 'I made sure not to tell her that. She thinks all the porn was Skinner's.'

He threw his arms up, theatrically.

'Oh, that's okay then. So she only knows that I helped run an illegal mail-order porn business and a porn library. I'm in the clear then, aren't I. And for your information, I didn't have a problem. It was a hobby.'

I let that one go.

'Don't make me beg,' I said, casting my gaze around the Mow saloon bar. 'Not in here, in front of Alfred and Blanche. Look,' I added, when Emdel showed no sign of softening, 'I can't say sorry any more than I have already. It just all sort of came out in the wash.'

He leaned forward across the table.

'If you want to wash your dirty laundry in public then that's your business, but you should have left mine the hell alone.'

He sat back, then realised he had put one elbow of his maroon sweater in a puddle of beer that I'd spilt moments earlier. He jumped up, sending his chair crashing to the floor.

'Oh, for fuck's sake,' Emdel cried, before storming off to the gents, tugging at the sopping sleeve.

With knitted brow, Blanche watched him go.

'What's yanked his chain?' she asked, from behind the bar.

'It's nothing,' I said, picking up the chair. 'They're a bit temperamental, these computer types. Highly strung. He'll be fine.'

'Hothead,' Alfred announced to the room, swilling a fresh triple brandy around his glass. 'Liability in battle. Would've got himself killed within five minutes. Or someone else.'

'Yeah, well, he's only going to the bogs, Alfred,' I pointed out. 'He can't kill anyone in there.'

As Emdel returned to his seat, Alfred held aloft a wagging 'mark my words' finger, as if he expected armed conflict to break out in the Mow before closing time, and for Emdel's hotheadedness to cost lives.

'Even Blanche bloody knows,' Emdel said, in a whispered growl as he retook his seat. 'She's looking at me all funny. I bet Thirza's told her everything.'

'Blanche has thrown people out of here for less,' I said. 'That's why she's eyeing you. Just calm down and drink your pint.'

I'd got us another drink when he was in the gents. It was our third pint – the Magical Third, and I was hoping this would tip things in my favour. See, I have a theory about beer consumption. One pint is unlocking the door, while two pints is opening it. Nothing has changed at this stage; you're still where you were when you started. But pint number three? That's the one that ushers you through the door to another place. Subsequent pints take you deeper in – sometimes so deep it can be difficult getting back out – but it's that third pint that has magical qualities. That's the one that transports you someplace else. Not very far away, but just far enough to offer a fresh perspective on things.

'Look,' I said, wiping my chops after downing two-thirds of my ale, in a bid to encourage him to follow suit. 'Everyone's meeting down here in a couple of hours. All you've got to do is stay, and drink.'

I was delighted to see him neck half his pint in a couple of gulps.

'I s'pose the fags'll be coming,' he said, belching.

Emdel's third pint had clearly ushered him through a door into some kind of gay-bashing convention.

'Jesus Christ,' I said, trying to keep my anger low-decibel. 'Blanche is gay. Her brother's gay. Are you trying to get us thrown out?'

'No, I'm just—'

'And in case you've forgotten, Thirza's also gay. I tell you what, if you're gonna be like this then maybe you shouldn't come tonight, unless that is you want Thirza to pin you up against the wall by your throat.'

'Right!' he said, springing up, and again knocking his chair to the floor. 'That's it. I'm definitely not coming now.'

'Liability,' Alfred reminded us, once Emdel had left.

*

'Big Al sends his apologies,' Thirza said, pulling up the same seat Emdel had tipped over. 'His wife's sick. He's got to babysit the kids.'

'Can you babysit your own children?' Max said, greeting me with a handshake. 'Isn't that just parenting?'

'Lleeeew.'

David enveloped me, before planting a peck on both cheeks.

'Did you enjoy our musicals night last week?' he asked.

'It was a joy,' I said. 'I'm still picking bits of lasagna out of my teeth.'

'Yes, I'll admit it was a tad overdone,' David said, blushing. 'I got my Celsius and Fahrenheit mixed up.'

'He was a big hit with Mother,' Max said, pointing at me while addressing Thirza. 'I wasn't expecting that.'

What had he been expecting, I wondered. For me to swipe his mother's photos from off her mantelpiece and run a juicy exposé on how her son's sexuality had torn her family apart?

Blanche glided over and hugged Thirza and David in turn.

'Lovely to see you all. First round's on the house.'

We chorused our thanks.

'Where's Emdel?' Thirza asked me. 'I thought he'd be here with you.'

'He stormed off,' Alfred boomed from his spot by the bar. 'Liability.'

'What's he talking about?' said Thirza, waving and smiling at Alfred.

'Ignore him,' I said. You know what he's like after his tenth triple cognac. Emdel wasn't feeling well, that's all.'

Alfred's keen interest in our group soon waned once Max and David held hands. Had David not been Blanche's brother, it would surely have been just a question of time before Alfred was proclaiming aloud the combat deficiencies of homosexual mariners.

'Oh,' said Thirza, shoulders slumping. 'That's a shame. It'd've been like the old days – you, me and him in the Mow. I was looking forward to it.'

As if his cue to emerge from the wings, Emdel strode into the Mow. He'd changed clothes since I'd last seen him, having swapped his beer-soaked maroon sweater for a dry one.

Thirza leapt from her seat, sending it clattering to the ground.

'Not you as well,' Blanche said.

Thirza saved the biggest hug of the night for Emdel. As I watched them embrace I waited for the pang of jealously, but nothing came. I'm cured, I thought. At last, I'm cured.

'What are you smiling at?' David asked me.

'It's just nice to have everyone all together like this,' I said.

A couple of hours later I was staring agog at David, Max and Emdel. It was as if they had been friends for years.

'How can one man know so much?' Max said, laughing, after Emdel had successfully fielded yet another scientific poser. 'I've got it, I've got it,' Max continued, bouncing up and down in his seat. 'I bet you don't get this one. Why is the sea salty? No one's ever been able to explain that to me.'

Thirza harrumphed. 'It'll have to be tougher than that.'

'Airborne carbon dioxide dissolves into rainwater, making it acidic,' said Emdel failing miserably in his attempt to seem a little bored by all the attention. 'The rain then washes mineral salts from the bedrock, and this separates out into ions, which enter the seas and oceans as run-off water.'

'Told you,' said Thirza.

David planted a kiss on Emdel's cheek. 'You're amazing,' he told him.

I froze, mid-sup, waiting for Emdel's reaction.

'What?' Emdel said. 'No tongues? Call yourself a fag.'

Max and David hooted in unison, leaving Thirza and I to exchange bewildered – but delighted – grins.

'He's priceless,' said Max, patting Emdel's knee. 'Can we take him home?'

'Three's a crowd,' said Emdel, all of a sudden looking more like his old mistrustful self.

'Actually, we've some news,' said Max, taking David's hand.

'You're not pregnant, are you?' Thirza said.

'Warm, but no cigar,' said David, chortling. 'Go on, Maxie, tell them. I can't bear the suspense.'

'We're getting dogs,' Max said, clapping like a seal. 'Emsworth is such a lovely part of the coast, and there are some beautiful walks. We're thinking of getting a couple of poodles. I hear they've a wonderful temperament.'

Emdel choked on a mouthful of beer, half of which ran down his chin.

'I'm not sure that's wise,' he said, mopping his face with a maroon sleeve. 'You might as well walk about in big sandwich boards, saying "We're a couple of pooftas". It's asking for trouble.'

'Oh, d'you think?' Max said.

'Totally. What you two need are a pair of Alsatians – dogs that might actually protect you, and you will need protecting at some point. It's inevitable.'

'Right, that's it,' said Max, standing and then plonking himself in Emdel's lap. 'We're definitely taking this one home, aren't we Davie.'

Emdel carried on drinking his pint as if the twelve-stone gay man perched on his knee was a figment of his imagination.

*

'I'm still in shock,' I said, as Emdel walked me back to Seaview. 'This afternoon you were one of Portsmouth's top homophobes and now you're some kind of gay icon. How does that work? What did you do when you went home – down a magic potion?'

'I just thought about what you said, you know, about how Thirza would think it weird, me not being there.'

'See, I told you she's forgiven us, didn't I. She's moved on. We've all moved on.'

'Yeah. S'good.'

'So what about the rest of it? You know, your new best mates, Davie and Maxie.'

'That just sort of happened.'

'You mean you found yourself actually liking them?'

'Yeah, kind of. They're funny – I mean funny ha ha, not funny queer.'

'Well that's good, because there's no way Thirza would knowingly be friends with anyone who had a problem with gays. You'll probably be seeing quite a lot of those two now.'

'I don't mind that, although I can do without them sitting in my lap.'

'Did you have a hard-on?'

He gave me a lop-sided grin.

'Yeah, how'd you guess?'

It was a cold March night, and some big weather was beginning to sweep in from the Atlantic. Thunderclap waves exploded on the beach, and the wind – briney and damp – had a cut-throat edge. But as I walked alongside my old friend, I was filled with a warmth that reached my marrow, as if I'd been sat in front of a glowing hearth for hours.

FORTY EIGHT

I SAT IN MY VW Golf. Rain thrummed the bodywork, and water dripped steadily in through the perished rubber seal of the sunroof, splish-splashing into a plastic bag I had lain between the seats. The car was a recent purchase, and the leak was a new discovery, the latest malfunction in an ever-growing list of faults. I missed my shit-brown Austin Allegro. There was a lot I missed: Portsmouth, the sea, Big Al and Emdel. But most of all, I missed Thirza.

I unfolded that day's issue of The Insider, for which I'd been working for just over a year. I leaned it up against the steering wheel and studied its front page. I'd been staring at that same page on and off for most of the day. 'Shamed news boss caged for 23 years' ran the headline. The paper had made the most of my heavy involvement in the story, running a side-bar on my career, and trumpeting me as God's gift to journalism. It made me want to puke, given the gutter-sniping crap they'd had me – and just about everyone else – doing since I'd joined.

But at least Skinner was behind bars, which made me feel safer, if not happier. He'd been given fourteen years for blackmail, plus nine for the attempt on my life. Freddie had received a twelve-year tariff, while Herr Porno copped a nine stretch.

Two weeks earlier I had given evidence at their trial at Portsmouth Crown Court. Coming face-to-face again with Freddie and Herr Porno had taken a toll on my nerves; I'd had a panic attack in the court toilets. But I was at least able to draw some comfort from the sight of Freddie sporting a pirate patch and Herr Porno, wearing a pair of spectacles with one lens frosted. They looked like something from an Ealing Studios crime-caper comedy.

On cross-examination, Skinner's QC did a stunning job of characterising me as the most heedless, irresponsible and unprincipled journalist in the history of newspapers, mainly because I'd already done most of the hard work for him. But when he'd most needed his planet-brain – to sniff out my lie (under oath) about how I had come by the blackmail tapes – it failed him.

Skinner hadn't taken his eyes off me the entire time I was on the stand, and I'd felt his hatred even when I wasn't looking at him. Work commitments meant I couldn't stick around for Daphne's evidence, nor that of David or Max, but Thirza told me that all of them performed magnificently, especially David and Max, who were disgracefully misrepresented as a pair of degenerate perverts.

On the day of my final stint on the stand, I'd found Rollo waiting for me at the entrance to Portsmouth and Southsea Railway Station. He had followed me.

'How are you, Sabler?' he'd said. 'Is he going down, Skinner?'

'Yeah, he's going down, all day long.'

'Great. Good riddance to bad rubbish. So, you staying out of trouble, then?'

'Rollo, what do you want? I know you want something.'

'You suspicious bastard. Can't a fella have a catch-up?'

I crossed my arms and tapped my foot.

'Okay,' he said, palms up. 'Listen, my girl fancies getting into papers. You've only gone and inspired her, ain'tcha. D'you think you'd be able to land her some work experience, you know on that rag of yours?'

'What, The Insider? No way, they don't do work experience, and besides, it's horrible there; she'd hate it. No, I'll have a word with Al, my old boss on The Probe. I'm sure he'd be happy to sort something out.'

'Great. Thanks. Hopefully he won't nearly kill her, like you did with your work experience girl.'

Rollo laughed long and loud, dragging a smile from me.

'Listen, Sabler, I don't wanna get all maudlin, but when I first met you I thought you were a total cunt.'

'I'm not sure that's the definition of maudlin,' I said. 'But thanks. I think.'

At that, we'd shaken hands, and I'd headed back to my lonely life in London. As the train had eased from the station, I sighed heavily as Portsmouth slid into the distance.

The rain continued to drum on the car roof of my VW. I refolded the newspaper and tossed it on to the passenger seat, where it landed on top of a pair of soiled celebrity underpants. Sharing a leaking car with skidmark-slicked grundies belonging to a minor TV personality was not what I signed up to when I joined The Insider.

'I want you to head up a new investigations team,' the editor had said, the same editor who believed vituperative personal abuse to be a soft skill, and the same editor I had once banned from nothing in particular.

'I want you to sniff-out the important stories of the day,' he'd added, before going on to offer me a triple-your-salary package, with the promise of my own column 'if things go well'.

But things had not gone well. First, I discovered that the investigations 'team' was in fact, me. As for the 'important stories of the day', these proved to be little more than tawdry celebrity dirt-digging. Cheating celebs. Snorting celebs. Lying celebs. Greedy celebs. Egomaniacal celebs. Warring celebs. Divorcing celebs. Dying celebs. A conveyor belt of 'red-hot leads' landed on my desk, and it was my job to seek confirmation and attribution. As far as I could tell, it was also everyone else's job, such was the volume of near-the-knuckle celebrity content that we ran every day.

'Where the hell are we getting all this stuff?' I asked the news editor a few weeks into the job. 'It's like a never-ending torrent.'

'Don't fucking ask,' was all the news editor had said, and I hadn't, not again.

Instead, I kept my head down and did what was expected of me, which was mainly interviewing the families and close friends of famous people who were in the paper's cross-hairs – actors, singers, entertainers, broadcasters, politicians, prominent businesspeople. Almost inevitably, all of those I spoke to would ask the same question: 'How could you possibly know this? Only my family and closest friends know that.' Few ever denied whatever was being put to them, however outlandish or scandalous. They might decline to comment, but that would be as far as it went. In time, I became deadened to it. It became normal.

But there was nothing normal about having a pair of unlaundered underpants belonging to a hard-drinking and heartbroken children's broadcaster on the passenger seat of my car.

'We've had word his missus has ditched him,' the news editor had told me earlier that day. 'She's had it with his boozing. Go doorstep him,' he'd ordered me.

And so an hour-and-a-half later, I was knocking at the front door of the beleaguered broadcaster's modest semi-detached home in Acton. There was no answer. I took a closer look at the property. The sash windows were peeling and blown, and can't have been opened in years. Ankle-high weeds grew in squares in between patio slabs, and a three-foot buddleia stood proud in the guttering. I took pictures on the office SLR of these signs of decay, knowing that the Picture Desk would send me back if I didn't. A rusty wrought-iron gate guarding the side of the house was ajar, as was the kitchen door. I knocked on it, calling the celebrity's name. No reply.

And then I found myself standing in his kitchen, staring at a mountain of encrusted plates, bowls and pans in the sink, and trying not to breathe-in the fug of old grease and ingrained dirt too deeply. I moved from the kitchen into a narrow utility room. His wicker laundry basket was overflowing, its lid perched jauntily on top of a mound of dirty clothes. I lifted the lid, to be greeted by the underpants. A toilet flushed upstairs, and in a panic – and for no reason I shall ever be able to adequately explain – I grabbed the underpants, and fled.

And now, in my car, I glanced across at those same Y-fronts, just to be sure I wasn't seeing things. But they were very real, so real that they seemed to be mocking me.

'I'm as good as it will ever get,' they said.

Please God, no, I thought. Don't let that be true. But it felt very true indeed.

I was catastrophically single, having recently dumped my fiancée the night before our wedding. I'd met Emma in a pub, just a couple of weeks into the job. She was a window dresser at Selfridges, and gorgeous. When I'd first spotted her I thought she was Thirza, so uncanny was the resemblance. Then one day, in a supermarket, not long after, I proposed to her by mistake, only to later shatter the poor girl's heart into a thousand pieces. Her psychotic farmer-dad wants me dead. I don't really blame him; it wasn't my finest hour. All I can say in my defence is that mentally, I wasn't quite right. Anyway, that's another story.

So now I was back on my own, living in a pokey flat near Tower Bridge. I was also a confirmed teetotaler, because I no longer trusted myself to drink. I made too many bad decisions when drunk or hungover, such as getting engaged. In my free time, what little there was of it, I now wandered around London, exploring, visiting galleries and museums, and going to see films and the occasional play. But I did not belong – not to anyone, anything or any place. I simply *was*.

A week or two ago, these feelings of alienation reached spacewalk levels, and so I'd returned home for a few days, to reconnect with the mothership. The folks' pride in my career had of course gone interstellar.

'You're a media star,' Mum would say.

'I shovel dirt on celebrities. It's nothing to be proud of.'

'People see your name on their stories each morning,' Dad would add.

'Yeah, racists, bigots and curtain twitchers, mainly.'

My attention was drawn away from the wretched underpants by a car that was being parallel-parked on the opposite side of the road. A twenty-something female slid from the vehicle, looking sharp in a navy pinstripe jacket and skirt. Notepad in hand, she strode up to the door, flicking her hair. When there was no answer, she shouted through the letterbox and continued shouting until the door opened, revealing the dishevelled presenter, after which she stood there, scribbling for a few minutes. Then from a shoulder bag, she whipped out a compact camera and fired off some shots in his face. He screamed at her as she returned to her car. I felt sorry for him and wondered if I ought not to return his pants. But I thought better of it, and instead stuffed them into the sunroof, to plug the leak.

The editor would go inter-galactic on my arse for allowing a rival paper to steal a march on us, that much that was a given. I could already see him, waving our rival's scoop in my face, as screamed obscenities tumbled from his spittled lips. But I no longer cared; he could go screw himself. I'd already decided to look for another job. Cleaning municipal toilets, perhaps? The stench could hardly be worse.

'You had a call,' the news editor said, upon my return. 'Some bird or other.'

He handed me a page torn from a notebook, on which was scrawled a Portsmouth-area telephone number, and a name: Daphne.

FORTY NINE

When living in Portsmouth, I had seen the Eastney offices of The Tribune just a few times, when taking a stroll down the Esplanade to the eastern-most point of Portsea Island, just across from Hayling Island. It was an art deco building that looked out across the Solent, and was far too attractive to warrant a spot on Thirza's wall next to the Tricorn Centre. I'd always given the building the finger, and now here I was easing into its car park.

It was raining, and had been all morning, but the celebrity underpants wedged into the sunroof had held firm all the way from London. I had grown accustomed to driving around with six inches of stained gusset dangling down near my left ear.

'I'm here to see Daphne Read,' I told the receptionist, who with her red suit and bold make-up might have been air stewardess. 'My name is Llew Sabler.'

'Oh, I know who you are,' she chirruped, smiling. 'He was an awful man, that Mr Skinner. So rude. Thank you for what you did.'

'You're welcome.'

'A word to the wise,' she added, beckoning me closer and casing reception for prying ears. 'There's still a lot of his people upstairs, and they're not all fans of yours, not like me.'

'Okay, thanks.'

'Anyway, you need the first floor. You can't miss the newsroom. That's where you'll find Miss Read's office. It's a big glass-fronted affair at the far end. Lovely she is, Miss Read. Not like him at all.'

With each successive stair, my guts tightened another notch. The war with Skinner had been long and bitter and fought almost to the death. But I hadn't just been fighting him, I'd been fighting his people – the ones at the barbecue. And I was about to walk straight into their lair.

I pushed through the double-doors leading into the newsroom. It was an open-plan expanse of reporters, sub-editors, artists and photographers. Empty, the room could have accommodated a full-sided football match. It was alive with the din of computer keyboards being clattered as hard as typewriters, and of phones ringing. Overlaying it all was the hum of busy chatter – face to face, and face to phone.

I made for the glass-fronted office, keeping to the perimeter of the room, to draw as little attention as possible. But before I reached the office, the din had died down; I felt eyes on me. I quickened my step, until I was power-walking. When I reached Daphne's door I didn't even knock, but walked right on in. I shut the door behind me and leaned against it.

'I've got to go,' she told whoever was on the other end of the phone.

'Are you okay, Llew?' she said, coming over and giving me an unexpected kiss on the cheek. 'You look a little pale.'

I blew hard. 'It's that lot out there. I think they want to lynch me.'

'It doesn't sound like they want to lynch you,' she said, smiling. 'Not all of them anyway.'

'What d'you mean?'

'Shhh. Listen.'

I did, and heard applause, polite rather than rapturous. I turned to face the newsroom. Half of them were on their feet, clapping. The rest were seated, eyes locked on screens.

I nodded my thanks to them through the glass.

'The ones clapping, they're my people,' said Daphne. 'The others are his. It's a big problem. My biggest. I can't get rid of the bastards.'

She looked me up and down. 'You've lost weight.'

'Yeah, well, I've given up the booze.'

'And I've given up the you-know-what,' she said, tapping her nose.

'You look well,' I said.

And she did. Her face still told of long years spent with Skinner, but her eyes were brighter and her tone lighter, like she had the sun on her back for the first time in an age. She was wearing jeans, and a maroon roll neck sweater that put me in mind of Emdel. She ushered me to some art deco seats that were arranged around a glass table.

'So tell me, how's life on The Insider?' she asked, her back to me as she poured coffee from a cafetiere.

'Y'know, I always had this big dream of working in Fleet Street, about how glamorous and exciting it would be, but I hate every single second of it. It's awful. All I do is hound down celebs, all day long.'

'Well, you wouldn't have to do that here. Have you thought about my offer?'

When I'd spoken to Daphne the day I'd stolen the underpants, she'd revealed that, in divorcing Skinner, she'd been offered half of his estate and had been instructed to take either the house or The Tribune.

'That house was evil,' she'd said down the line. 'I didn't want to profit by it, and so I took the paper, which means you're speaking to the new owner of The Tribune.'

Daphne handed me the coffee.

'Look,' I said, 'I'm desperate to leave The Insider, and I appreciate the offer massively, but I don't think I'm editor material, not yet. Investigations are my thing. That's what I love doing.'

She slumped in her seat and sighed. 'I was pinning my hopes on you saying yes.'

'I'm sorry, really I am.'

She stood, and paced the room, before stopping, with hands on hips. 'Investigations, you say?'

'Yeah.'

'Okay. Name your job. Whatever it is, it's yours.'

'Are you serious?'

'Yep, after everything you did for me, it's the least I can do.'

'Wow. Thanks. Right, er, okay. So, what about, um, investigations editor.'

'You'll need a team. How many?'

'Yeah, course, well, how about, um ... two?'

'Done,' she said, extended a hand with such haste it left me wishing I'd asked for three or four people.

'I doubt I'll be able to match your current salary, but I'll get as close as my budget allows.'

She sunk her head into her hands and gave a muffled cry.

'What's wrong?' I asked.

'Every time I think about money I want to scream.'

'Are things really that bad?'

'Worse. This paper's drowning in debt. Those tossers out there, the ones who weren't clapping you – they're still drawing the salaries *he* gave them, and I can't get shot of them. It's crippling me, and to make matters worse half of them are bloody useless. I've got to get rid of them, and soon, but I don't know where to start. This place is rudderless.'

'So who's the editor?'

'See that big goofy idiot over there,' she said, pointing, 'with the pink shirt?'

I turned and scanned the newsroom. 'Oh him. I met him at the barbecue. Nigel, right?'

'Yeah, well he's editor in name, and salary, but he's not running things. I wouldn't let him run a tap. I've got my own team heading things up. Some were here already, some I hired. They're good people but they need leadership. They'd look up to you, Llew, after everything you did. They'd listen to you. Are you sure you won't take the editorship?'

'Daphne, what you've got out there is a civil war,' I said, aiming a thumb over my shoulder at the newsroom. 'Old versus new. His people versus yours. Corrupt versus clean. You need a Ulysses S. Grant, and I'm not that man.'

'Does it have to be a man?'

'Well, no, but ... hang on a second.'

'What is it?'

'You need someone who can bully Skinner's people out of the door, right? A sergeant-major type?'

'That would be nice.'

'And you also need someone who can lead your team – editorially, I mean. Someone your people will love, and respect. Someone they'll run through brick walls for.'

'Yeah, but that's just a fantasy isn't it. People like that don't grow on trees.'

Daphne sighed and ran her fingers through her hair. She looked to the ceiling and then at me.

'Why are you grinning like a Cheshire cat?' she said, with a shake of the head.

I stood, walked to the window, and looked out across rooftops and crowns of trees, in the direction of Southsea.

'It all depends what tree you look in,' I said, tapping on the glass.

THE END

AUTHOR'S NOTE

Although writing books is a lonely endeavour, it is not possible to succeed at it without the help of friends, family and talented professionals.

So, thank you to fiction editor, Averill Buchanan, for helping me find my writing 'voice'. Without your expertise this book would be vastly inferior. Thanks also to Rebecca and Andrew at designforwriters.com for their stunning cover.

Also of incalculable help were the many people who voluntarily sunk time into highlighting the kind of typos, glitches and inconsistencies that can ruin a reading experience and sully years of hard work. These include: my sister, Frances; Colin Cameron; Chris Dean; Justin Shaw; Simon Jones; and Simon Griffiths. If I have missed anyone out, I do apologise.

Others provided encouragement and support, often at times when the endeavour was weighing heavy, and my spirits sagging. So thank you, Neil Ashcroft, Thierry Allsop-Menist, Ivan Schmidt, Douglas Simmons and Phil Tuck.

But most of all, thanks, and love, to my wife, Naomi. You gave me the time to follow my life-long dream of becoming a novelist. Without you, none of this would have been possible. I am a very lucky man indeed.

Made in the USA
Columbia, SC
31 October 2021

48151035R00159